MW01140316

Published by Nemours Publishing

This book is a work of fiction that was inspired by some true events. Any resemblance to other actual events, locales or persons, living or dead may be coincidental.

What is Normal?
(2nd Edition)
ISBN # 13: 978-1508511793

For more information visit:
www.NemoursMarketing.com

Sue was sucking her thumb. Again. She'd already chewed her cuticles down so far they were bleeding. She couldn't help it. She was thinking about spending the next three days at Uncle Larry's house. Uncle Larry always wanted to play those games in the bedroom with her and her sister Connie. Sue felt funny about it. It seemed naughty, but she sometimes could see her Aunt Janet cooking in the kitchen and smell that familiar rotten-egg odor that came from the well water her aunt had to boil before anyone could drink it. The door was always wide open, so everyone must know about the games. It must be all right for Connie and Sue to be under the covers with Uncle Larry, all three of them naked and touching him like that, right? It made Sue feel a bit tingly and knotted her stomach at the same time. She knew she'd go into the bedroom with him this weekend because it happened every time she went for a visit.

In the meantime, she continued to suck her thumb, chew her cuticles and daydream in class. Sue remembered how the morning had started, just like any other day.

Acknowledgements:

Thank you for believing in me and your intrepid support. Anne Mackenzie, Carrie Anne King, Stephanie Kelsey, Grandpa Jim, Dyan Foster, Erin Brey-Patton, and my precious sons, Stevie and Tommy Medeiros.

A special thanks to my Love and best friend Juan Carlos Castellanos Islas, Who is behind me one hundred percent in "ALL" that I do. Last but not least, Thanks for the unconditional love from Boss, Ripper, Boots and all the other creatures in my world.

In Loving Memory of

Olive Mary Donlin AKA Sue and Mom

Steven Michael Medeiros

Chapter One:
The Johnson Family: Henry's Life

The Johnson family tried to live a normal life. Henry Johnson went to work. May Johnson stayed home, and the two girls went to school. In the evenings and the weekends, most of their time was spent in church. The small Johnson family, as well as the extended Johnson family, was very involved with the Faith Baptist church. It was a strong fundamentalist church, and the family followed its guidelines for living according to their perceptions of it as best they could.

Henry Johnson wasn't the best man, husband or father, but neither was he the worst. As with all normalcy, it depends upon what yardstick you used. For his era, his background and his family history, Henry was a normal man.

A thin, bespectacled man with a bad complexion, Henry Johnson was one of five children of a poorly educated, backwoods family in upstate New York. His overbearing mother ruled his childhood and most of his adulthood as well. She loved weakness and insecurity, and since Henry was the one child she could completely control, she therefore loved him in her fashion.

Henry had survived his childhood by developing a harsh outer shell. His mother was hard pressed to ever say a positive thing about anyone. She considered telling everyone what they should do and how they should do it her natural right. Henry's father, though known as a jovial and kindly man, was more involved with working, drinking and avoiding his wife

4

then childrearing. Henry's brothers, like most brothers everywhere, buffeted and ridiculed Henry whenever the urge came upon them, which was often.

Henry felt each and every unkind comment and criticism in a personal way. He felt as if it had been done to him with the intention of doing him as much harm as possible. The internalizing of his pain created within him a need to withdraw from people, to always assume everyone was out to hurt him in whatever way they could and to feel an intense raging anger at times. He felt that fighting back to protect himself was his natural and inherent right.

Henry was a poor student, always struggling to pass his classes at school. Having been told all his life by either his mother or his brothers that he was stupid and would never amount to anything, Henry had no expectations of ever being successful in any way at all. He had no evidence that he could do anything or be anything special. He knew he was neither smart nor handsome, and knowing this, he knew his options would be limited. He saw proof of this every day of his life by the way he was either picked on by others or completely ignored.

What he really wanted was to just get by. If he could find some way to slide through life without making too many waves or getting too much attention, he thought he'd make it through. As low as those expectations might have been, Henry wasn't sure he could even accomplish those.

When he met May, he was attracted to her passivity and to her intense insecurity because it made him feel strong...at least, stronger than her. May was someone he could rule over. Here was someone who would do what he wanted her to do, when he wanted her to do it. This made him feel like he had some power in the world, some strength as a man. Though he secretly hated his mother's domination of him, he thrived on being the dominant one in his relationship with May.

Henry and May, both just a mere sixteen, had met one week prior to getting on a bus to Maryland and eloping, where it was legal for sixteen-year-olds to marry without parental consent. Both were seeking a better life than the one they had. Henry wanted to assert control over his life by being a married man and having his own home and family. May wanted to escape a life of drudgery with no hope of the future. Their marriage may not have been made in heaven, but for both of them, it was better than how they'd been living.

They had no money, no car, no job and no plan for their future. When they came back to upstate New York, they had nowhere else to go but Henry's parents' home to start their new life. May's angry mother-in-law was not happy to meet her, and even less happy to allow May and Henry to move into the apartment over her garage. It was not an auspicious beginning.

Henry's mother was a bitter and mean-spirited woman, having suffered a life full of cruel disappointments of her expectations, which culminated in not being chosen by the pastor as his bride. The husband she married as second choice was now surviving on an oxygen tank, sick with emphysema, after a lifetime of smoking and alcohol. It was a sad ending for such a lively and fun-loving man.

For Henry's mother, every Sunday reminded her that her life wasn't as she expected it to be, and if it had been, she would have had a wonderful life as the pastor's wife. She was sure of that. There would be people kowtowing to her and praising her piety. She would have been busy every day going around town helping all the sinners change their ways. The inner bitterness and resentment she harbored because life had treated her so unfairly ate away any human kindness she might have had, and not being one to keep her unhappiness to herself, she spread it around wherever and on whomever she could.

Henry had let May know right from the first that he would side with his mother. May never went against his mother after that first time. Henry accepted his mother's rule over him as her right, and because it was so ingrained in him from childhood, he had never questioned it. However, he chose to rule over his own family just as fiercely, as *his* right.

Henry never allowed his wife to wear makeup. He liked May to be on the plump side, making her less attractive to other men and therefore, more likely to be faithful to him. He didn't let his wife drive. Henry's church taught and strongly reinforced that the man was the head of the household. It was the natural order of things, as far as he was concerned.

Henry may have always sided with his mother, but he hated that he and May had to move into the apartment over her garage. He couldn't make it on his own, and now he had May to take care of, too. He didn't know how to be a man yet. He had no means of providing for his wife and himself. It made him frustrated, angry and scared. His rage was boiling up within him. Henry reacted to these feelings just like his mother did, by fueling an obsession to control everything and everyone. Having a sense of control over May made him feel better about himself.

It didn't take long before May was pregnant. Now Henry, just seventeen, living with his mother and watching his young wife's belly get bigger and bigger, was torn between pride for siring a child and fear of the future.

Though his hopes for a boy were disappointed when the baby was a girl, she was still his flesh, a part of him. He felt a kind of happiness at her birth. He knew in time she would also be of use to him in the never-ending fight to survive, once they moved and got their own place.

He finally had landed a job doing janitorial work for the local high school. It wasn't an important job, but it was full time and the pay was steady. He felt relief to have finally gotten work. The thought of not having a job terrified Henry. He was committed to keeping his job and was very careful not to do anything that might jeopardize his security.

After his daughter Connie was born, his older brother Bob reached out and offered him a small, old trailer on his property for Henry and his family to live in. It wasn't a great place to live, but at least it would be their own place. He moved his wife and new baby out of the apartment over his mother's garage in town and into the old trailer on his brother Bob's property.

The trailer was small, but it did have two bedrooms. It had an old musty smell to it that never seemed to go away no matter how well May cleaned everywhere. The tiny kitchen bled into the living room, where there was a sliding glass door that was the front entry to the home. They had so few possessions that it all easily fit into the trailer. Much of their household items such as dishes and pots and pans and linens were either given to them by family members or bought at the local thrift store. It wasn't much, but it was theirs, and for two teenagers with a baby, it seemed as if they were living the life of real grownups.

Like real grownups, Henry had a job, a place for his family to live, and they were getting by. Not with any extras, but it was more of a home than living over his mother's garage. It was his time to make all the rules, just like his parents had made all the rules for him when he was growing up. Henry felt as if he could handle his life, and maybe even make it work for the first time.

And then, May was pregnant again, just three months after Connie was born. How could he take care of another child? They were barely getting by now as it was. What was he going to do with this new baby coming? How could he do the colossal task of taking care of four people? His fear grew. He felt helpless. He became a quiet loner of a man who was often subject to sudden uncontrollable rages.

Henry's mother was angry about the new baby too. When she asked Henry, "Are you sure it's yours?" she didn't care that May was standing right there. In fact, she'd said it specifically within May's hearing, as she wanted to hurt May and shake Henry's insecurity in one blow.

Henry knew his wife too well and knew she'd never cheat on him. She was too insecure and too lost in her own world. As Henry expected, May's reaction was predictable; his mother's words did not faze her. His mother could have just as well said it looks like it's going to rain, the way May responded to it.

May was in her denial daze, which Henry found useful sometimes and annoying at others. This time, Henry gave his wife an ugly look as if to imply she had gone and gotten pregnant on her own, even knowing Henry couldn't afford another child. Henry's mother shook her head, encouraging her son's disapproval of his wife's condition.

Secretly, Henry wished that May would lose the baby. Yes, he wanted a son, which would mean having another worker to help out, but not yet. Not before he had gotten a raise or another job, something that would help financially. He couldn't turn to his mother; that would give her more power over him again. He had no choice. As if he'd ever had a choice. This new baby began to symbolize all the burdens that were too much for him in his life. He resented this pregnancy greatly. The only saving thought he had for this new baby was the hope May would deliver a strapping boy to do some of the harder work at home.

But no, life was not so kind to him. It wasn't a big strapping boy, but a tiny, undersized girl they named Sue, with crooked legs right from birth. The doctor told Henry his new daughter needed casts put on in order for her legs to grow straight. Henry's face turned bright red, and the veins on his neck were pulsating as the doctor brought up the question of payment. Again, he felt helpless. Fortunately, the local Shriners ended up stepping in and paying the bill for the casts.

Henry knew right from the get-go that this new baby was going to be a problem, and of course she always was. He couldn't help himself from resenting this burdensome child. She became his inner symbol of how hard his life was and how helpless he felt to change it. Sue cried all the time. This added to the overall household tension.

The Johnson family was like many other families of their time and place. They struggled to survive with what little they had. For the most part, it was extremely difficult. Each day was spent watching every cent. When a family starts out lacking, everything that isn't a bare and absolute necessity is cast aside without question. Any extra expense becomes a financial crisis. Poverty was normal. Since lack of money ruled the decision-making, figuring out how to survive without cost triumphed over comfort.

Family toothaches were treated with icicles that hung off the old trailer they lived in. When the pain got bad enough, for a flat fee, the local dentist just pulled the tooth. One day while Sue was having her tooth pulled, she could feel the pain of it being pulled and hear the cracking. Sue started to get out of the chair.

The dentist pushed her down hard, back into the chair. "Sit back down, you little brat, I'm not done."

Before she left, he pointed out a back tooth that would have to be removed soon. On the drive home, Sue started pushing back and forth on that tooth as hard as she could. Within a few days, she had removed it herself. She didn't want to go back to that dentist ever again.

Both Henry and May had had all of their teeth removed and wore dentures in their late twenties. Though May had been concerned about being put to sleep and having her teeth removed, since Henry wore dentures, he thought it best that May did too.

There was little food in the house and what there was, Henry controlled—only May was allowed to open the refrigerator. The girls' clothes were hand sewn by their mother, who didn't know how to sew very well. Seams weren't straight, zippers were unfinished and many other sewing mishaps were visible. They rarely had store-bought clothes.

The Johnson family had routines they maintained. There were daily and weekly chores to do around the home. There were church functions on weeknights and Sunday too. The whole family had to participate, including Awanas, Prayer Meetings, and Youth program every week. Sometimes there would be a family birthday party. The family of the birthday person would make a cake and serve soda pop. Every Sunday, Henry took his family to supper at his mother's house. They would spend the afternoon time, between the morning church session and the evening session there.

One Saturday a month, all of the Johnson family spent the afternoon at the church social. May liked being around the other women and socializing. It was one of the few times she got the opportunity to talk to women outside her family. She really liked listening to others share their family concerns and to talk about the second coming of Christ. May looked forward to that wondrous day the Book of Revelations described and hoped it would come very soon.

Henry tolerated the church functions. He was not a social man, having spent most of his work and family life in silence; he was not good at small talk. He didn't feel comfortable in the company of men, even if those men were his brothers. He didn't consider doing anything differently, going to the church social and other events were simply something expected, like work or fixing the fences. Sure, he didn't like it, but he still had to do it, so he did.

Connie and Sue preferred the monthly church social to anything else the church did except the Christmas and Easter gatherings. There was more food on the table than they had ever dreamed of. Though the children had to wait until the adults were served, there was always a fair amount of food left for the kids.

Connie and Sue weren't comfortable with the other children. Many were schoolmates who ridiculed them in school for their poorly made clothes and awkward ways. These same children had to be nicer to Connie and Sue than they would have normally been, because it was a church function. The girls knew it was not genuine.

Nevertheless, the abundance of food made the church socials one of the highlights of the young girls' lives. It almost made up for never being allowed to go to the movies or to go to a dance, as their religion preached that movies and dancing were of the devil.

Very rarely, Sue and Connie would be allowed to spend the night at the pastor's home. The pastor's daughter, BethAnn, was right between the two girls in age, being six months younger than Connie and six months older than Sue. The pastor liked to alternate girls from different families having a sleepover at his house so his only child could have experiences of sharing with siblings.

He was also protective of his only child, because she had been blinded in one eye when someone threw a piece of concrete while playing. In return, BethAnn was the only person who was ever allowed to spend the night at

Sue and Connie's house. Naturally, BethAnn was a quiet and good child who was no trouble when she stayed over at the Johnson's.

As far as their home life was concerned, it was normal for May, as the wife and mother, to stay home. She cleaned, cooked and took care of the family. May didn't know how to drive, but even if she had, Henry wouldn't have allowed it.

Once a week, Henry would drive May and the girls into town to do their grocery shopping. He would wait out in the car. While Henry waited, he read comic books; Beetle Bailey, Archie and Superman, to name a few. He bought them without covers for only five cents apiece. It was his one frivolous habit.

He always gave his wife and girls a strict time limit for the shopping to be done. One time they were late, and he left without them. They weren't late again.

Henry also drove May and Sue, once a week, to the laundromat to do the laundry. Sue liked going to the laundromat. She would search between all the washers and dryers for coins. Then she would check the change returns, hoping someone had left coins behind. Sue was lucky on most laundry days and could buy herself candy from the snack machine. Sue took her time looking at all her choices. Hershey's almond chocolate was her favorite. She would always have a little time for herself before she helped fold the dried clothes with her mother. Again, like the grocery shopping, Henry gave them a strict time limit.

There was no telephone in their home. If they had to use a phone, they would walk the long path to Henry's brother Bob's house. There was, of course, no TV for many years and once the nineteen-inch RCA black and white TV did arrive, Henry controlled what was watched. Henry's choice seemed to be war movies with only male actors. While the TV was on, there was no noise allowed. No distractions or movements. Silence. Stillness. Obedience.

Their home in the back woods was very far from town. The only real neighbors were Henry's brother Bob and his family. Bob let Henry and his family live in the tiny run down trailer he had on his property because he knew Henry couldn't afford anything else. Bob and his wife had discussed using it for another chicken coop, but they decided to let Henry's family use it instead. They were family, after all.

They did have a couple of so-called neighbors. There was a man who had lived in his handmade house down the road a few miles. One winter, it was severely cold and he was low on money, so he started busting off wood from a wall in the back part of his own home to burn as firewood.

Then there was the hermit who lived in a mud cave at the end of the road. It looked like a small mud tunnel. His front yard was an active pigpen. Henry said he came out a little more often when the dandelions were out so he could make dandelion wine. Sue felt badly for him and begged to bring him some food at Thanksgiving one year. Sue and her mother walked the couple miles or so and tried to get his attention. They ended up leaving the food in a place where the pigs couldn't get at it and included a note. The hermit continued to live there for many years. For the most part, only Uncle Bob's family could be truly considered neighbors.

Uncle Bob's property was nearly a thousand acres of mostly worthless land. You could farm it some, but not much. There were trees, but not ones that anybody really wanted to buy. There were a few maples that they tapped for syrup. You could use some of the land for grazing or hunting. Every year they shot a deer for food, and it lasted for most of the winter. They made spiedies, which tasted good because of the marinade. All the other ways they cooked venison made it taste too gamey. Bob and his family did manage to make a living from the land, though his wife drove a school bus to help make ends meet.

Henry would drive his daughters to school in the morning early enough for him to be on time for his job as the janitor at the local high school. He was a hard worker. He may have had to do things he didn't like doing, but he did them anyway. That's what men did, he told himself. They didn't shirk, and they didn't complain.

He cleaned up every mess that came along. He did every job he was asked to do. Sometimes that included working on the weekend, if there was a weekend school function. He would bring Sue and she would have to run around and check every door making sure it was locked. It was a huge responsibility. What if she didn't pull hard enough on a door, and it wasn't locked? She would be in big trouble if her dad lost his job because of her.

If Henry minded that some teachers were more demanding than others, he didn't say so. If he thought the principal talked down to him, he endured it. In general, the teachers were nice to him. They respected that he had an often unpleasant job to do, and they were grateful he did it instead of them.

He organized much of his cleaning jobs by assigning certain days of the week to do certain weekly jobs and maintained a daily schedule also. All the hallways had to be swept daily. All the trash had to be taken out daily. All the bathrooms had to be cleaned daily. Windows, dusting, grounds maintenance all could be done once a week. He was the only janitor, so he had no one to talk to during his workday. There was no one to share his thoughts or ideas with, which made him rather isolated in his work even though people surrounded him. These factors made him more determined to rule over his own household and family, as he felt so overlooked at his job.

Chapter Two:
May Johnson's Non-Life

May Johnson had been raised in the same, very rural, backwoods section of
upstate New York as Henry. In a family of eleven children, May was one of the oldest daughters. She had been trained to be the traditional female. Brought up in a strong Irish Catholic family, May was raised by uneducated parents and lived a life of serious poverty. She was secluded from the mainstream of America. Her world-view was restricted by a complete lack of experience outside the limits of her backwoods reality.

There was no such thing as television when she was growing up. Her family didn't read newspapers. Her only exposure to anything outside of her family was the Catholic Church, which totally supported her parent's view, and school, which echoed it. Born right before WWII began, her early childhood was the wartime world. Already in poverty, the shortages and the rationing were more severely felt than the average American family. There simply wasn't ever enough. The traditional gender roles were unquestionably maintained. Women were in the kitchen. Men were in the world. Hidden in those guidelines for correct gender behavior was the unspoken belief that women were inherently not as valuable as men, and needed to be protected and dominated by men in order to best serve their purpose in life.

May incorporated those unspoken beliefs within herself with a quiet acceptance. She survived her childhood and most of her life by living in a fantasy world of her own making and by completely denying everything else. She didn't see or hear things she didn't want to and she definitely didn't know things she didn't want to know. Kind and submissive, she said yes to just about everything and everyone rather than cause any trouble. She was very shy and awkward in social settings, having a low sense of self-esteem and fearing anything she had to say wouldn't interest anyone. She didn't make waves, speak out or challenge anything; she just did what she was told.

There was such a sense of hopelessness in the draining daily routine of living in the O'Connor family that it was felt as a dark cloud of despair surrounded them. The best way to describe the family's approach to life would be their attitude about Christmas. They didn't believe in Santa Claus, so they didn't anticipate any Christmas presents. They didn't expect good things to be given to them or to happen to them. Naturally, tragedy seemed to follow them. Twice the family home had burned to the ground with all of their possessions inside.

More than anything, May wanted to get away from all she'd known. It just seemed so hard, and so hopeless. She had a soft beauty, not distinct but rather blurry around the edges, which seemed to reflect her personality. Though she certainly was attractive, she'd never had a boyfriend. She married the first boy that showed an interest in her, Henry Johnson.

Life with Henry wasn't easy, but it was definitely better than what she'd grown up with. May liked living in the woods, away from her unhappy mother-in-law and having the little trailer all to themselves. It may not have been much but at least it was theirs.

It was always a struggle. There weren't any extras. Even having the basic necessities of living was difficult to manage sometimes. Now that Sue was born, it was even tougher. May had to watch nearly every mouthful just to try to make sure everyone was fed. She always did her best to stretch the food as far as she could, and to do without as much as possible.

Chapter Three:
And Then There Was Connie

Connie had started out as such a sweet and easy baby, and grew to be a sturdy and athletic child with straight blond hair and pretty blue eyes. Barely a year old, and already she was the elder sister and no longer the beloved only child. Perhaps it started then—when she was so young and unaware—that she began to resent her younger sister and feel that life had treated her unfairly. She secretly wished she was the only child still, and her sister's presence was a constant reminder of how her life wasn't the way she wanted it to be. She was like both her grandmother and her father in that way; always wishing for something that wasn't there and forever feeling powerless.

Like her father, Connie was easily enraged and needed to dominate others in order to feel some kind of power and control in her life. Yet like her mother, when faced with the anger and unhappiness of her father, Connie retreated into feelings of low self-esteem and, finally, a martyred and depressed acceptance of a world she couldn't change. She was not a happy child and a complainer.

Needless to say, because she was a strong and sturdy child, Henry began putting her to work as soon as he could. He liked that she was useful, and as she grew, he taught her many of the things he would have taught a son. She was his workhorse, his helper, and for that reason, he much preferred her to Sue.

For Connie, her young life was spent far more often working and doing chores than playing. Since they lived so far from town, it was hard for Connie to really have any friends, except for the brief hours she was at school. She felt the unfairness of life and became more taciturn and withdrawn. Again, like her father.

Always trying to please her father, one day Connie offered to break one of the wild horses for him. She hoped this would impress him enough to think that she was just as good as having a son. The horse bucked her off and then picked her up with his teeth by her stomach. Connie was hurt very badly, and yet was not taken anywhere for care. Another instance in which she was not treated with the love and attention she felt she deserved.

She knew her sister Sue wanted to work outside, but was not strong enough to be useful. This in itself made the hard outdoor work preferable, as it showed off Connie's value and Sue's flaw. Connie liked being preferred by her father, even if it was only because she was better than her weak baby sister. Connie always made the most of the fact that she was stronger than Sue, often by taking out her anger on Sue as her father had taken out his anger on Connie. In Connie's mind, Sue deserved it for messing up her life and for not being able to ease Connie's burden of work.

Being her father's so-called favorite didn't keep Connie safe from his anger or his criticism. Connie couldn't seem to help herself from questioning his authority, even knowing the consequences would usually involve a spanking.

It was almost as if somebody else rose up inside of her and made her say those foolish things to her father. That somebody else inside of her was so angry and felt that she was treated so unjustly that she just couldn't stop herself from lashing out and saying things to try and stand up for herself. It never helped her situation. She always ended up making the problem worse.

Yet, being punished didn't stop her uncontrollable outbursts of rage. She was often filled with feelings of anger, frustration and a deep helplessness about her life, even when she was a young child. Her only way of expressing or releasing these feelings was her outbursts.

The truth was, Connie had good reasons for her anger and unhappiness. Her uncle Larry began molesting her from the time she was four. When her younger sister Sue turned four, he began to molest both of them together. Connie didn't like it. She didn't want to be naked in bed with her uncle and her sister or have to touch his privates. She felt guilty, ashamed and embarrassed.

Even though she complained about everything, she didn't dare mention that. No, she never told her mother or anyone else. Her uncle had told her that if she said anything, her dad would know she was the one that wanted it and he'd punish her, not him. Connie knew her dad's temper, and was convinced her uncle was right about this. She endured it and would never tell. It became another source of powerlessness and rage within her.

Connie did the best she could. She had her mother's need to please others, and so she did all the chores she was told to do. She fed the horses, fixed the fence, cleaned the stalls, and helped her father build, repair and maintain the trailer home they all lived in. This made her favored by her father, but that favoritism didn't ease her load at all. It mainly meant her dad liked her better than he did Sue.

That made sense to Connie, as she didn't like her either. Sue didn't help outside, because she was such a weakling. Connie was always told to do the harder jobs. Sue washed dishes and did housework that a baby could do, Connie thought.

It enraged Connie that Sue was smarter than Connie and didn't have to work as hard, so Connie justified the anger she took out on Sue as something that would toughen her up and balance things out in Connie's mind.

When Connie went to school, she had wanted to be liked. She wanted to fit in and not make any waves. She adapted to school. It was very different than her home life, but she adapted. She did what the teachers asked of her, and was an average student. She probably could have done better, but doing well in school wasn't required of her. If her father could have kept her home working all day, he would have. Her dad said work at home was more important than going to school.

Like any school kid, being accepted and popular would have been great, but Connie was happy to blend in. She had one friend who was new to the area and very shy, so Connie felt she had the upper hand and some sort of control over her friend. The two of them got along well. Connie was happy to go to school and not be doing men's work back at home. She dreaded being off for holidays and those unexpected snow days. Her father had work for her most of the time. Having one friend was nice, too.

Connie almost trusted her friend enough to tell her about the secret touching games with her uncle, almost, but not quite. Her life had already taught her quite well that trusting others to help her or to be nice to her or to understand her wasn't a safe thing to do. It usually made things worse.

Chapter Four:
Second Grade for the Second Time

Sue was sucking her thumb. Again. She'd already chewed her cuticles down so far they were bleeding. She couldn't help it. She was thinking about spending the next three days at Uncle Larry's house. Uncle Larry always wanted to play those games in the bedroom with her and her sister Connie. Sue felt funny about it. It seemed naughty, but she sometimes could see her Aunt Janet cooking in the kitchen and smell that familiar rotten-egg odor that came from the well water her aunt had to boil before anyone could drink it. The door was always wide open, so everyone must know about the games. It must be all right for Connie and Sue to be under the covers with Uncle Larry, all three of them naked and touching him like that, right? It made Sue feel a bit tingly and knotted her stomach at the same time. She knew she'd go into the bedroom with him this weekend because it happened every time she went for a visit.

In the meantime, she continued to suck her thumb, chew her cuticles and daydream in class. Sue remembered how the morning had started, just like any other day.

"Mom, can I have some butter on my toast? Please? It's so dry. Please, Mom?" Sue kept thinking, *Dad's not here right now, he'll never know. You can give me the butter, Mom, and he'll never know.*

"Now, Sue, you know your Dad said we have to watch every bit this week," came the gentle response.

"But Mom, I want some butter this morning. I'm sure I won't need so much next week. Please, just this once, Mom?" Sue knew her mother never said no to anyone, unless Dad was in the room, and then she rarely said much of anything at all.

Her mother relented and taking the piece of toast, spread a bit of butter on the bread and handed it back to Sue. She reached over and did the same with Connie's piece of toast.

"Thank you so much, Mom! It's just how I like it!" Sue swooped up the toast and happily ate her breakfast as if it was the greatest piece of toast she'd ever had.

Sue was so hungry for that butter. She seemed to always be hungry for something, hungry for, well, *more* of everything. This hunger, this wanting, this desire to reach out beyond herself to get what she wanted was something new. At seven years old, she felt there was a whole world outside her home and church life that was calling her.

Last year and all the years before, Sue had been too overwhelmed with the many difficulties of her life. She reacted to everything by putting her thumb in her mouth and trying to hide, if she could. But this year was different. This year, she asked for things when she thought she could ask without being punished just for asking. She began to think of ways she could somehow get the things she desired. It was still a new way of thinking for her. She knew she had to figure out the best way to get what she wanted, but her strong will and determination would surely find a way.

As usual, Sue got up early enough to feed the horses and check on the sheep, and maybe give them a kiss or two, before she could finally come in from the cold for the usual breakfast of toast. Thankfully, their drafty old trailer was warmer than the shed. Her Dad was still getting ready for work, so Sue and her older sister Connie could sit on the heater in the kitchen a while, warming up their mittens and snow boots before it was time to leave for school.

Finally, everyone had eaten breakfast, and Dad was ready. Sue and Connie gathered their schoolbooks and the lunch their mother made them. Sue hoped it was going to be a butter, sugar and cinnamon sandwich and not bologna again.

They went outside and got in the truck, which was so old that Sue had to place her feet very carefully so they wouldn't go through the rusted-out holes in the floorboard. She liked watching the road through the rusted hole. It was hypnotizing, and scary too. As always, it was a long silent drive. Dad didn't talk and didn't want to listen to anything either, so neither girl dared say a word.

Dad stopped the truck right out front of the school to let the girls off, and then he drove on to the local high school, where he was the janitor. The girls got out and went their separate ways without saying a word to each other. They weren't close, even though they were only a year apart in age.

Slipping into the classroom, Sue looked around to see if Mrs. Gow was there yet.

For the past two years, Sue had been in the same class. Mrs. Gow was absent only five times in those two years. Sue was so anxious on those days. She made herself sick and spent the entire day in the nurse's office lying on a fold-out cot, waiting for her dad to pick her up at the usual time, as there wasn't anyone else to come and get her. One time on her the way to the nurse's office, Sue took a bead she found and put it up her nose. Panic set in when it would not come out. She had to think of a lie. *Okay,* she thought, *my necklace broke, and the bead bounced on the hallway floor and back up into my nose. Yes,* she thought with great relief, *that would do.* Just then, the bead dropped out.

Sue had been held back last year because the school administration had wondered if repeating this grade would help her to catch up to her classmates. Sue was very relieved to find out she was staying back a grade with Mrs. Gow. Sue wanted her for all of her grades forever.

Mrs. Gow looked right into her eyes when she spoke to her. Mrs. Gow didn't say, "Take that thumb out of your mouth, young lady!" like the kindergarten and first grade teachers did. She understood Sue. She was very kind.

Looking around to see if anyone would notice, Sue slid out behind the old wooden desk that was connected to her chair. She went up to her teacher. Leaning close, Sue spoke very softly and said, "Mrs. Gow, I don't feel very good."

"Why, Sue, what's wrong?" asked Mrs. Gow, concerned.

"My stomach hurts, Mrs. Gow. I think the beans we had for supper last night, they must have been ten years old, and I think they poisoned me." Sue wasn't really lying because she was sick of eating beans every night. She wouldn't be surprised if they were poisoning her.

"Sue, I don't think the beans poisoned you, and besides, probably what you had for breakfast is what's bothering you now."

"Oh, Mrs. Gow, I didn't have any breakfast," Sue said, her head bent down pitifully. *If I hold my head in just this way, she'll think I'm sad and then she'll be very nice to me.*

"Oh my word, you poor child! Here, I just happen to have some Ritz crackers. Why don't you take a few of these to keep you until lunch, all right?"

"Thank you, Mrs. Gow! Thank you so much!" Sue joyfully took the crackers as if they were a special treat, and for Sue, they were. She walked away thinking, *Wow, Ritz crackers! We never have crackers like these at home! We only have plain white saltines sometimes.*

Sue was learning how to lie just right to Mrs. Gow. Lying was a wonderful skill she had just learned and was still in the process of perfecting. It simply amazed her that people believed her lies. She had no idea it could be so easy. She felt a sense of power and control. It was one of the most useful things she had learned in her life so far.

Sue wanted Mrs. Gow to love her. Telling lies to her was an effective way for Sue to get the attention and sympathy from her kind-hearted teacher that she craved. It wasn't a big lie. Dad said there was no money for food this week, so Mom was feeding the family with what little they had in the house. Most of Sue's lies did have some truth in them; they were just twisted to put her in a more sympathetic light. Sometimes she just lied because it felt good being able to control things. Sue did think sometimes it would be nice to tell Mrs. Gow the truth about the secret games, but she knew she couldn't tell anyone so lying had to be okay too.

Back at her desk, she ate the Ritz crackers. *These are delicious! Mrs. Gow is the best teacher in the world!* Finishing the crackers, she then put her thumb back in her mouth.

When Sue started kindergarten, she hid under the piano in the back of the room, most of the time. She was always sucking her thumb. She seemed like a scared little bird that just crashed into the window, not sure what had happened to it until it came to inside a dark cardboard box. She often had that feeling of being scared inside a dark box at school.

Sue needed all the soothing things she could find. Being left at a school full of strangers scared the four-year-old. Because her birthday was in November, she started school younger than most, and that did not help her situation at all. The teacher had tried to talk to Sue, but she had other students and she couldn't spare the time to acclimate her. Sue didn't know how to handle strangers or the school environment, so she slipped into a feeling of detachment and observed everything, just like the way she did when her uncle first started the touching game.

First grade was pretty awful too. The other kids made fun of her scrawny body and her badly sewn, handmade clothes. Sue tried to ignore them and to stay away from the other kids as much as possible, even at recess. She didn't make any friends. She didn't learn anything. She didn't fit in, nor did she try to. Sue innately had an inner strength she had created from living in her own world.

There were a few things Sue had found that were nice about being in school. She loved the sweet smell of ditto paper, which had pictures to color or maybe a dot-to-dot activity on them. She would make a mistake on purpose sometimes just so she could get another piece. Sue would often smell the paper and chew on it.

Sticking her finger in the big tub of white paste and licking it was what Sue liked best. It smelled almost of wintergreen, and it would last a long time in her mouth before she swallowed it. Sue really liked the white liquid Elmer's glue too. She would sneak a bottle of it and keep it in her desk and then, whenever she got a chance, she would coat her hand with the glue and let it dry. Then slowly, surely and for a really long time, she would peel it, trying to get the whole hand in one solid sheet. She was fascinated by all the lines in her hands that showed up on this glue sheet. These were the fun things about going to school, and of course, Mrs. Gow.

Mrs. Gow was a kind woman who felt a calling to teach. She felt all children could learn and she wanted to help as many as she could. When she first saw Sue in her classroom, she was appalled at her tiny, scrawny appearance, the sucking of her thumb and her lack of social skills in the classroom. But she wasn't repulsed. Quite the contrary, Sue became her pet project, and so Mrs. Gow focused her considerable, compassionate heart on reaching this child and bringing her into the fold of learning.

Patiently, kindly, gently, she lured Sue into her trust. It took nearly a year before Sue started coming out of her shell. It was a pleasant surprise to find that Sue was actually quite intelligent instead of the slightly delayed child Mrs. Gow feared she might be. Her kindness and gentle persistence paid off. Sue was now a student in the class.

Second grade for the second time was the opening of a door for Sue. From the safety of Mrs. Gow's kindness, Sue began to step out of her self-imposed exile from school and into a functioning relationship to the world around her. Sue began to see that there were things out in the world that she wanted for herself, and she applied her considerable determination and will into the process of getting them.

One of the things she wanted was Mrs. Gow's attention. Sue soaked up kindness as a flower soaks up sunlight. Sue's mother had a kindness within her, but she rarely let it out, as her behavior was so restricted by the rules of her husband. But Mrs. Gow was Sue's first experience with someone who was kind without restrictions, and Sue loved her for it. Young Sue was beginning to see the world around her and learning how to manipulate that world to her best advantage, when possible.

Being raised in a Baptist fundamentalist church, lying was considered a terrible sin, and Sue had never tried it before. Now she was testing it out. She found if she told Mrs. Gow a sad story about her home life, Mrs. Gow would get that kind, caring look on her face and would try to help Sue feel better. Sue loved that.

What surprised Sue was that Mrs. Gow never accused her of lying, or doubted what Sue said. She was almost ready to try out a lie at church to see what would happen there. She was considering the possibilities of lying at home, for if it worked there, her life could really change.

It was recess again. Sue stayed close to Mrs. Gow then and any other time that she could. Mrs. Gow would talk really nice to her. Sometimes, Sue just stood by her and felt her warmth. Sue wished she could be Mrs. Gow's little girl and go home with her every day. Sue would daydream about how they would talk about everything they saw out of the window on the way home to a real house. Sue was sure Mrs. Gow only used real butter and the kind of Italian bread Sue loved. Sue imagined how jealous the other kids would be, and how they would have to be nice to her, or Mrs. Gow would give them bad grades.

At the end of the day, Sue stood by Mrs. Gow's desk again. "Um, Mrs. Gow. Would you like to have one of these pretty kitties I found yesterday? Somebody had left them out in the field by our house and I'm finding homes for them. I'm sure they'll be good at catching rats and stuff. They're really nice kitties. Do you want one for your house?" Sue pleaded. *And maybe you'll want me to come home with you and live with you forever.*

"Oh, thank you, Sue, but I already have two cats and wouldn't dare bring any more home. It's good of you to try to find homes for them. Honey, don't you need lots of cats at your house?"

She loved when her teacher called her 'honey'. "I would keep all of them, but we've got lots of cats at home. People keep dropping off litters of kittens or puppies in the field near the road where I live. I always find homes for all of them, or they'll die. Once, when I was much smaller, I couldn't find homes fast enough for a batch of kittens and a boy put them in a paper bag and threw them over the bridge into the creek. I was so sad I never stopped crying for a whole year. That was when I knew it was up to me to find them all homes."

Hearing Mrs. Gow's gasp, Sue continued, "Please, Mrs. Gow, these are the best kitties in the world and I know one of them should be with you, the best teacher in the world." Sue silently added, *I know you'll take one, Mrs. Gow, because you must have one of my kitties, something from me that will be with you at home. Maybe I can come see the kitty at your house and live with you forever!*

"Oh, Sue, I really shouldn't, but I can see you care so much for them and want to make sure they get good homes. I'm glad you think that I will provide a good home for one of your kitties. Why don't you pick one out and bring it in tomorrow for show and tell? That will be the one I take home with me." Mrs. Gow gathered up her things. "I have to go now and get home to make supper for my husband. See you tomorrow!"

Sue grinned from ear to ear and skipped out of the classroom. She always found takers for her strays. She often walked the five miles to town, holding a box of kittens or puppies, and then stood out in front of the local market until they all had homes. Sue was smart and already had an understanding of the basics of selling. Sue knew that the best way to give away her animals was to offer the stray to a child with an adult in tow, and the child would then beg their parent until the answer was 'yes'. It worked almost every time.

Her sister Connie was waiting out in front of the school and Sue walked over and stood next to her. Without saying much, they both waited for their father. It seemed natural that Sue wasn't close to her sister. They each lived in their own little made-up worlds. They each had their jobs to do and their separate lives to live, all within the same household. Each member of this particular household, including the parents, seemed to live alone, in a strange isolated world of their own individual making.

The lack of closeness between the family members made it easier for the molestations to happen and for nothing to be said. It also made it confusing for the girls.

Sue didn't understand. She knew it was somehow naughty, but it also felt exciting and she really wanted to know about bodies and how they worked. It was really more like what children call 'playing doctor', except with an adult instead of a child. Sometimes, Uncle Larry would be in his robe in the kitchen and would allow Sue to see his privates, then quickly close the robe when his wife or another family member came in. It was a naughty game the two of them played.

Grandma Johnson saw what was going on. She gave Sue threatening looks when she would witness the 'sneak a peek' game. Of course, this only confirmed in Sue's mind that she would be the one that got in trouble, not her uncle Larry, if she would ever dare tell. It also proved to Sue that the game wasn't really secret, because even her grandmother knew about it.

Sue felt, after being molested once, she couldn't say no when it happened the next time. At first she would fall for her uncle saying, "Come here, I have something special for you." Sometimes he would say, "Let's go to the store and I will buy you a bag of penny candy. You can pick out whatever you like."

She loved candy. There were so many that were her favorites like the fire balls, red waxed lips, salt water taffy, those little wax soda bottles with the sweet fluid in them, pixie sticks and those fake little ice cream cones made out of marshmallow. She loved them all. Uncle Larry knew how to get her in the position of owing him. Sue wanted candy that badly.

Though Sue didn't feel terrible about the molestation, she did feel fearful and anxious about it. She wanted it to stop, yet sometimes she didn't want it to stop, and that made her feel very guilty and scared. This anxiety, as well as the fear of punishment from her father, made Sue feel fearful all of the time.

She chewed on her cuticles until they bled. She became addicted to the adrenalin of the fear of being caught. She would act out by putting things up her nose or sticking her fingers or toes in tight dangerous places, just to feel the rush. She lied, stole and lived in a fantasy world where she was special and everyone wanted to know her. And perhaps one day everyone would know that Sue was special, but for now, all she could do was to try and get through one day to the next.

All these thoughts passed through Sue's mind as she and Connie stood silently together, waiting patiently for their father to pick them up after school. Finally, the old truck rolled up to the curb and both girls got in. As usual, the drive home was silent.

When they got back to the small trailer they called home, Sue's mom was at the stove cooking another pot of beans. Yesterday, her dad had announced that he needed to buy a part for the truck. He said the only way he could afford it was for the family to live on beans for another week. No one complained or said anything. Everyone just ate the beans in silence.

Her father would occasionally buy what he thought was a real treat for the family, Banquet Turkey TV dinners. At Sue's house, if her father liked it, then he assumed that everyone else did too. The stuffing, which came in one section of the aluminum tray, made Sue nauseous. Sometimes, when Sue didn't like what they had for supper, she would chew up the food and sneak it into her paper towel and then go to the bathroom and flush it down the toilet.

Food was too scarce to waste, so even if Sue didn't like it, she had to appear to eat it or she would be severely punished. Sue had to eat everything on her plate or she wasn't allowed to leave the table. Sometimes, she was at the table for several hours trying to finish her meal. She knew three trips to the bathroom with her chewed-up food in her paper towel was the limit before her father might catch on. This trick was a proven way to help Sue get rid of any disgusting food, and Sue was wise enough to never pass her limit.

It was Wednesday, and Sue had on her Wednesday underpants. Every Christmas, both girls got one new package of underpants with each day of the week on them. Those underpants reminded her of what day it was, too. On Saturday nights, Sue took a bath with her sister. Wednesday meant it was prayer meeting night. After supper, Sue did the dishes and Connie did some chores in the shed with Dad. Once all the chores had been done, everyone got into the truck and they drove to the Faith Baptist church in town.

Sue was angry with God. She didn't want to go to church all the time, and she didn't know why God wasn't helping her more. There was no doubt in her mind God was real, and she thought He was not doing a very good job of taking care of her or her family. It didn't seem right. It didn't seem fair that Sue had to go to church all the time to worship Him and He didn't give them enough clothes to wear or food to eat. They were often cold in their own home too. Why should Sue sing songs of praise to Him? What had He done for her?

Why, Sue could be home right now, taking care of the kittens in the shed, feeding them with the doll's bottle she stole from her sister to keep them alive. Sue had already taken a box of powdered milk from her Grandma Johnson's cupboard and hid it in her coat. She knew exactly how much water to add and filled the bottle. It wasn't very often that an animal in her care died, but when one did, Sue would make a cross out of sticks and bury them in her pet cemetery, deep in the woods.

Ever since Sue was a tiny girl, she felt connected to animals. She knew it was her job to care for as many animals as she could. She loved all of them.

Growing up on her uncle's property gave Sue lots of access to many different kinds of animals. She loved all the cats, dogs, sheep, chickens and horses on the farm. She loved any of the wild animals she saw or could get close to. The animals seemed to know how much Sue loved them, as they all loved her right back.

Every morning before going to school, Sue would always make time to go out to the shed where the sheep were and to spend some quality time with them. She'd lie down with them and hug and kiss them. She'd talk to them and tell them about her day. If she had gum, she'd share some right out of her mouth with them. She loved the sheep. At night, whenever she could get away with it, Sue would sneak in a cat or two to sleep with her. She was sure having one of the cats or dogs with her would keep the nightmares away. Most of the time it seemed to work, so it was always worth a try to bring them in.

The horses were so big, but they would let little Sue hang on their legs just to be with them. She'd feed them apples from the trees. Sue would pet them and talk to them and, like all the animals she knew and loved, she'd kiss them and revel in the sense of love and caring they gave her. She did seem to have a perpetual case of pinworms from her animal friends, but they were well worth the trouble. She felt it was a small price to pay for the love and affection she got from the animals. She would just take those little purple pills.

She would rather be out in the pen, talking to the sheep and cuddling with them, instead of here in this stuffy old church building, listening to the preacher spout off about giving the church money and calling people back sliders if they didn't attend every week! Sometimes, she just hated God, and yet sometimes she daydreamed about marrying his son Jesus.

God didn't keep Uncle Larry from touching her or making her touch him on his privates, causing her to feel anxious and funny inside. God didn't keep Dad from getting angry with her when she tracked mud in the house or smuggled a kitten into her bed. God didn't make Grandma Johnson like her or stop being so mean. What good was God if He wasn't helping? And why didn't He just make money for the church? Why did He need to ask us for it?

So Sue hated going to church most of the time, which was Sunday morning and back again in the evening, and every Tuesday, Wednesday and Friday evenings, not to mention the socials and the family readings of The Daily Bread every night. They had to look up all the bible verses that went with the readings too. It was long and boring, she thought.

Finally, the evening church service was over. Sue and her family got back into the truck and drove home to the woods. There were always more chores to do, until at last, they could go to bed. Sue tried to sneak one of the kittens in the house with her. This time she was able to get the kitten in without anyone seeing her. Putting the kitten under the covers, Sue stoked its soft fur and listened to its soothing purr. Maybe the kitten would bring a good dream like the inventions Sue had dreams about.

In Mrs. Gow's class, Sue learned about Eli Whitney inventing the Cotton Gin, who was a blacksmith and had never worked with cotton. Sue knew his invention came from God, and she wanted an invention too. When she did get a kitty to sleep with, she rarely had one of her frequent nightmares.

It was just another normal day for Sue....

Chapter Five:
Digging for Treasure

Sue awoke sweating. At least, she thought she was awake. This was a familiar state but almost in a different dimension; maybe she was still asleep and in the nightmare, and this was part of it. It was so hard to know, to orient herself to what was real and what wasn't. The nightmares were always of witches and evil energies after her, and she could feel the cold air where her covers were pulled away from her body, leaving her vulnerable and paralyzed.

She would often tell herself to wake up. As soon as she went back to sleep, ten or fifteen minutes later she was right back in the same nightmare. The fear of falling back to sleep was almost as frightening as the nightmare itself. When she did finally wake up, she felt so shaken and unsure of what was real, and she felt guilty and scared, as if she'd done something terrible, like murdering someone or something.

As she would finally awaken, she had the familiar knot in her stomach of anxiety from not knowing if the touching and the nakedness games she played with her uncle were really okay or not. Maybe it was. From an early age, Sue had guilt as a constant companion. Yet, she felt scared and excited, both at the same time, whenever she thought about those hidden games. It was all so curious to her. She wanted to know more, to experience more. It had to be okay, because didn't Aunt Janet at least know what was going on? The bedroom door was always open and she must have been able to see inside, so if she didn't mind what they did in the bedroom, it must be because it was okay, right?

Maybe it wasn't. Maybe there was something wrong about doing it. If only Sue could tell someone, talk to someone about all this, but Uncle Larry had told Sue to never tell anyone. He said if she ever told anyone, he would tell them that she started it, that she wanted it, and they'd believe him. They'd think she was lying if she tried to blame it on a grownup. They would blame her, and not Uncle Larry.

That made sense to her, because she knew she was often blamed by adults for things she hadn't done. The guilt, fear, shame and anxiety were just tearing her up. There had been too many nights of endless nightmares. Too many times she had awakened, not sure she was awake or asleep, or what was real anymore. It was too much for her body and mind to bear. Sue suddenly decided to pray and to ask God whether what she was doing was a good thing or a bad thing, because she just couldn't bear not knowing anymore. She asked Him to give her a sign.

Getting up at last, Sue went into the kitchen to have some breakfast. Sue did not feel like she had a full night's sleep. She woke up with an emotional hangover. Nowadays, breakfast was cereal, which was much better than just toast. However, Sue, and all of the family members, must eat without making any noise whatsoever. Quiet. No lip smacking. No crunching. Heaven forbid anyone got caught eating with their mouth open! They'd get a whack for sure. So Sue sat at the kitchen table and carefully put the cereal box right in front of her face so no one would see if her mouth was open and hopefully any noise would be muffled.

It was Saturday, and Sue was going to a new school starting on Monday. Her family had moved to town and into the apartment over her grandmother's garage because the old trailer they'd lived in was falling apart so badly, they could no longer afford to keep fixing it. It was very different living in town. The family could walk to all the places they needed to go. Even the laundromat was right across the street.

Of course, the bad part was that they were now living very close to her grandmother, and they had to leave some of the larger animals behind. She still had her cats and a couple of dogs. It was a good thing the animals served a purpose. The cats were needed for keeping rodents away, and the dogs guarded the place.

Sue decided to walk to the school and see what it was like. She didn't want to be surprised by it all when she went for her first day on Monday. Sue was in the third grade now, and would soon turn eight. She knew this year would be very different than any other, and she was somewhat excited by that thought. Sue naturally expected good things to happen to her. Sue was always looking forward to the mail delivery, as she had this feeling something was on its way to her, and that thought kept Sue motivated in her life. She had no idea what it was, but she knew something wonderful was on its way. The overall feeling she had every day was that this could be the day.

Arriving at the school, Sue walked around the outside of the building and peeked into a few of the classroom windows, but for the most part, the school looked like her other school, only bigger. She then walked over to the playground. As she entered, Sue saw some older kids. There was a group of boys, maybe twelve or thirteen-year-olds, hanging around the swings, though they weren't swinging on them. They just seemed to be talking and laughing, but Sue couldn't really hear them.

There also was an older man, maybe eighteen or twenty years old, who was sitting on a bench. He saw Sue and motioned for her to come over to him. As Sue got closer, she saw that he had his peepee out of his pants! Sue knew what his peepee was because she had seen her uncle's, but she was shocked that this man, a stranger, would have his out in public. Sue came a bit closer just to make sure of this puzzling situation, when the man said to her, "Hey, little girl. This is my baby bottle. Do you wanna come over and suck on it?"

Sue shook her head and began to back away from him. She turned around and ran over towards the direction of boys hanging out around the swings. Her instincts were to get out of there fast. She didn't try to join the group of boys or to talk to them, but at first it was the safest place for Sue to go at the time. After a few minutes spent regaining her composure, Sue became curious, wanting to know what the boys were doing over there.

The boys were talking about something and they kept laughing and hitting each other on the shoulder, often saying things like "You're lying! You didn't really do it!" in a playful way. One of the boys spit on the ground. *Ewew, that was gross*, Sue thought. They seemed to be talking about something secretive, but Sue could never quite hear what they were saying until suddenly one word was said very loudly that Sue had never heard before. One boy practically shouted, "Fuck!"

Sue's thoughts stilled. She said the word 'fuck' in her mind, and couldn't find any frame of reference for it. She'd never heard anyone say that word before and she was really, really curious about it. What could it mean? Why did the boy practically shout it the way he did? Why did all the other boys laugh very loudly after the boy had said it? It must mean something, and Sue really, really wanted to know what it meant.

All the way home as Sue walked she said the word over and over again inside her head. Fuck, fuck, fuck. She wanted to remember it so she could ask her mother what it meant. As she walked, she'd say again and again, fuck, fuck, fuck.

Finally, she was home and Sue gratefully found her mother alone in the kitchen. Before even saying any kind of greeting to her mother, Sue blurted out, "Mom, what does fuck mean?"

Sue's mother reacted with shock, embarrassment, shame and guilt all at the same time. She immediately told Sue to never, never, never say that word again, and especially to never say it around her father. Sue's mother didn't explain the word or why she shouldn't say it, she simply told Sue to never say it again, and her reaction told Sue even more.

Sue knew that whatever that word meant, it was really bad. She also knew it was something disgraceful that people did, and suddenly, Sue knew that what she'd been doing with her uncle had to be somehow associated with this word. She understood now that the secret games Sue did with her uncle was like that word, something people didn't talk about because it was exceptionally bad. She wasn't sure how but she just knew it. Finally, she had her answer. God had given her the answer through others, as she had often heard about in Church. Along with the answer came this incredible strength to make the decision, right then and there, that she would never play those secret games again. Never!

It felt like she was lighter and finally free of a heavy load. The colors were more vivid and brighter; was she starting to wake up? Moving into town, starting a new school and finally figuring out about these games with her uncle made Sue very hopeful, even if they did have to live so near Grandma Johnson. In the back of her mind, she knew she could withstand Grandma as long as she had to.

Sue wandered into her new backyard. There was the huge acre garden, some pear trees and the creek that ran along her Grandma's property. She picked up a stick and continued her wandering until she was drawn to one spot in the backyard. She didn't know why, but this one spot seemed different or something.

Getting closer, she looked but she couldn't really see anything, so she took the stick and began to dig with it into the dirt. The stick didn't work too well, so Sue got up and went back up into the house and began to look around the kitchen for something she could use to dig. In the utensil drawer she found a large serving spoon, which looked rather old and beat up, so she took it and went back into the yard.

Once again, Sue sat down and began to dig in the dirt in that one spot. She didn't really notice how long she dug, but surprisingly, she found something! She found an old broken cup, with a bottle cap, a button and a coin inside it. This was great! It was like finding buried treasure. She was thrilled that her digging had found something of value, and brushing off the coin, she saw it was a nickel with an Indian on it. Wow! A whole nickel! Sue could buy some candy with that nickel. The other parts of the treasure were not so wonderful, but fun just the same because they were part of her first buried treasure.

Sue took the other items inside to show her mother. Her mother said to save that nickel, that it was very old and worth more than a nickel. This made Sue even more inspired to make this a daily routine. Sue had already carefully hidden the spoon where no one would find it in the backyard, so it would be there for her on her next day of treasure hunting.

Being Saturday, it was laundry day, so after Sue showed her mother her 'treasures', Sue began to help her mother gather up all the dirty clothes that needed to be washed. Now that they were in town, they could walk across the street to do the laundry, instead of having Dad drive them.

Sue and her mother carried the laundry across the street, taking only two trips, and began to sort the clothes according to colored, dark or white and put them into piles.

Once the clothes were in the wash, Sue's mother would sit in one of the chairs there and read a Watchtower magazine left by the local Nazarene church. Sue, on the other hand, would begin her search for coins. Maybe God would give her lots of coins today!

First she would check behind and under all the washers and then the dryers. Often, she found a coin that had slipped between the machines and was too hard for adults to reach, but easy for smaller hands like Sue's. She also checked the change machine in case someone hadn't gotten all of their change out of the scooped opening. Sue would be quite diligent. She took her time and really, really looked, and most of the time, she found at least one coin and sometimes more. Today, she found a dime, which was just enough to buy two candy bars from the vending machine. God always seemed to provide for her in mysterious and wonderful ways.

Sue loved candy. She just never seemed to get enough. She always found ways to give herself a treat. It was just such a happy, happy feeling to buy herself something she wanted, no matter how small. Sue looked for every opportunity, every single day, to be able to get herself what she wanted. She knew without a doubt it was up to her, no one else was going to do for her. She had a very strong knowledge that she could have anything she wanted by making it happen herself.

Sue waited, very patiently, until her mother had to use the bathroom, and as soon as she was gone, Sue used her found dime and bought two Hershey's Almond bars. Once her mother returned, Sue told her mother she was going to get a drink of water at home, and slipped out to eat her candy. It was a better idea to not let her mother know what she was doing. Sue had found that her mother seemed to not really want to know what Sue or Connie were doing, so Sue figured it was easier to not tell her in the first place, plus she might say Sue would have to wait until after supper and then share it with her sister.

When the washing machines were done, Sue and her mother took the wet clothes and carried them back home to hang them outside to dry. Sue wasn't strong, but she was determined, and she helped as best she could. She would hand her mother the next piece of clothing to hang and then hand her the wooden one-piece clothespins. It was a tried and true method they had long ago worked out between them. Sue loved the smell of her sheets and clothes after they had been hanging outside all day.

After the clothes were hung, Sue decided to start her search around town for empty soda bottles that could be returned to the local Reliable Market for cash. Sue walked around the streets of the small town of West Corners, looking in allies, trashcans and any other likely place for bottles to be left or hidden. She usually found a few, and today was no exception. Carrying them the best she could, she brought them into the Reliable Market and then back to the butcher section, where she knew she could return them.

Once at the butcher section, the butcher would count up the bottles and figure out how much was owed Sue and write the amount down on a piece of white butcher paper, using a black wax pencil. Sue would then take the slip of paper up to the front cashier and they would give her the money out of the cash register. She knew all about returning bottles from the times she'd visited her Grandma's in the past. Her Grandma would say, "Here, Sue, take these bottles to the store and bring the money back so I can afford to feed your family supper."

Goody! It was fifty cents today! Just enough to go to the ice cream store and buy a hot fudge sundae. Sue loved hot fudge sundaes. She wanted to have one every day, if she could. Taking her bottle return money, Sue happily went into the ice cream store, ordered her sundae and thoroughly enjoyed every bit of it. It was turning out to be a very good day!

When Sue got home, it was afternoon and her dad wanted to go fishing as usual. He asked if Sue was going with him; Sue evaded by saying she had to weed the garden for Grandma. It was a true and good ploy. She did weed the garden several times a week, but Sue also knew that her dad would always let his mother's needs override his own, so he let her go.

Sue didn't like to go fishing with her dad, mainly because she had to spend almost all of the time sitting still and being quiet. Sue liked to eat fish, but she didn't like to go fishing. She had been taught how to gut, scale and clean the fish her father brought home and that didn't bother her that much, but she did feel badly about catching them. She also didn't like watching her dad pinch the worms in half and put the hook through their bodies.

Sue felt so close to all creatures, even fish, that she always felt badly when she had to eat them. She even felt badly when she ate chocolate bunnies at Easter! She would imagine that every time she ate a chocolate bunny, it was okay because the bunny was joining the other chocolate bunnies, and at least they'd all be together.

Sue went out to pull weeds in the garden. There were still green beans, peas, tomatoes, potatoes, yellow squash, beets, horseradish root, cucumbers, green onions, lettuce and some regular corn on the cob, but not many now. Sue would sometimes take some of the brown corn silk on the end of the ear, roll it up in a piece of brown paper bag, light it and then smoke it like a cigarette. It tasted strangely harsh, but it was fun to do.

Grandma Johnson made homemade pickles. Sue didn't like the taste of them, nor that big piece of dill floating around in the jar. Once a week, May and Sue would spend hours downstairs at Grandma Johnson's canning green beans, corn, peas, carrots or making horseradish out of the roots. The garden also had popping corn. It grew hard on the cob and had to be removed for popping. Sue loved eating fresh tomatoes off of the vine, peas out of the pods, fresh corn on the cob and making and eating blueberry jam. Grandma always had a big garden, but now that Sue's family was living with them, they really needed it.

Sue was grateful it wasn't Sunday. She liked church a bit better now that she had an understanding of how God worked in her life. Sue had come to the realization that God really was looking out for her and so she often asked Him for favors and for help in understanding some of the feelings she had. Sue had to admit that God had been pretty consistent with His answers and with granting her desires if, of course, it was in His perfect alignment for her to have it.

She understood that she wouldn't always get what she asked for, but she felt that God knew best. She understood that if she didn't get something, maybe it was not good for her or might get her in trouble. She began to feel as if God was her parent, her guardian, as she felt more comfortable asking Him about things than she did asking anyone else. All in all, she didn't mind going to church these days and she refused to feel guilty about not wanting to go sometimes. She wasn't convinced that it was God's idea to be at church all the time. She knew God entrusted her with many homeless animals, and it took time to find them homes.

Sue was also grateful it wasn't Sunday because it meant she didn't have to have supper at Grandma's and didn't have to sit in the car for hours on the usual Sunday drive. She did know if she went for a drive, they most likely would stop on the way home for an A&W root beer in a frosty mug; nothing tasted better than that! Saturdays were really the only day of the week that Sue had lots of time on her own. Any day she didn't have to eat with her grandmother was definitely a good day.

Wherever Sue was or whatever she was doing, it all had to stop at dusk because she had to be home when the streetlights came on. Sue didn't have a watch but she had learned long ago to pay attention to the fading sunlight and any clocks she could find because being late meant a spanking and no supper. Her father made her pick the switch off of the tree and then stung her bare legs with it all the way home. One experience of that was enough.

After supper, there were still chores to do, dishes to wash, clothes to fold, things to be cleaned. If there was still daylight, they were free to roam. On Saturday nights, Sue and Connie took a bath together; it saved time and hot water. Connie would use the plastic bottle cap from the Suave shampoo to pretend to shave her legs. Sue would go under the water and come back up in an imaginary underwater cave. This was an adventure she played over and over. Sue liked to feel nice and clean, then put on a clean nightgown for the week and get into clean sheets, all on the same day.

Finally, it was time for bed. Naturally, Sue and Connie shared a room. Sue had the top bunk. Because it had been such a good day today, Sue really hoped she wouldn't have the nightmares again tonight. She hated waking up in the morning not sure whether it was morning or whether she was awake or not. It frightened her to be so disoriented and confused when she first woke up and tried to start her day. She couldn't have one of the kitties with her now, but she did have her stuffed Bugs Bunny to sleep with. Hopefully, Bugs would keep her safe…

Henry really didn't want to move back to his mother's house. He hated the idea of it, but every which way he tried, he couldn't figure out any other way of taking care of himself and his family. The old beat-up trailer was falling apart every time he turned around. He didn't have the money to fix it, and wasn't sure it could be fixed anyway. He had to move, but where? There was nowhere else he could afford to live except with his mother.

May didn't want to move either. She found her mother-in-law to be difficult at best, and the thought of living within a stone's throw of her, as she had the first year of her marriage, was depressing. Henry had control of the money and he said they had to move, so they had to move.

May liked and didn't like living in town. She really liked the convenience of being able to go to the store and to the laundromat all by herself, without having to bother her husband. She also had less work to do in the smaller apartment and now that she didn't have the outside chores living in the woods required. However, her mother-in-law's close proximity was like being in the presence of a very draining negative force. May would be doing her chores and taking care of her home when suddenly, it was like a black cloud just came over her. May didn't complain. Henry wouldn't allow her to say anything about his mother and they had nowhere else to go, so May tried to endure the daily rants of her mother-in-law while Henry was at work.

May had learned when she was very young to turn her mind away from unpleasant things and to allow herself to live in a kind of waking fantasy state. She was very good at it by this time in her life so she functioned quite well in her role in this world, but her mind was actually far away, in a much happier place than where the rest of her lived. It was the only way she had endured for so long without falling into a very deep depression and ending up in a mental hospital somewhere.

Now the whole family had to get ready for moving out of their home and moving into a smaller apartment with limited storage in the garage below. Even though they were poor, somehow they still had lots of stuff, which now had to be sorted and packed or thrown out. Most of this job fell to May, but Henry too had the shed and the outside areas to deal with. Of course, the girls had to help. Finally, the house was packed up and they were ready to move. It took several trips in the truck and Uncle Bob had to help unload, but they were moved at last.

It was quite an adjustment for the family. They all were so used to living out in the woods on so much land, with both domesticated animals and non-domesticated animals to deal with and now they had a backyard. There were houses nearby and they were within walking distance to the stores. They also were now under the manipulative eye of Grandma Johnson, who seemed to make it her business to know everything everyone was doing, or as much as she could find out. It was definitely an adjustment.

The girls had to go to another school district now. Connie turned nine and was in the fourth grade, and Sue was eight and in the third grade. Henry still worked at the high school, so his drive to work was much shorter and he didn't have to take the girls to school every day. May no longer needed Henry to drive her to the grocery store or the laundromat, as she could easily walk to all the stores in the tiny town of West Corners. This move to town did give most of the family members a certain amount of freedom they hadn't had before.

Though they had lived in a small trailer before, the apartment over the garage at Henry's mother's house was even smaller. It had probably been a one-bedroom with a kitchen, living room and bathroom, but the living room had been converted into another bedroom, so the only communal living space was now the kitchen. The rooms were small and the family felt rather cramped and closed-in compared to the trailer and the open space of the woods. The solution seemed to be that most of the family didn't spend time in the apartment unless it was too cold outside. In the winter, upstate New York got down in the teens and sometimes below zero. Sue's lungs would hurt sometimes because the air was so cold.

Henry went fishing nearly every day in the creek behind the house. It was an activity he enjoyed and it actually put food on the table, so he happily killed two birds with one stone and no one could complain that he was goofing off. He would take one of the girls with him sometimes, but they often had chores or other things they needed to do, so he mostly went by himself.

Connie had a friend or two, and she had a boyfriend. Yes, a real, live, kissing and hugging boyfriend whom she had been going steady with since she was eight. She needed someone to want her. She needed someone who gave her attention, who was focused on her and she was willing to pay the price. She spent every free minute she had with her boyfriend and if not him, then with one of her two friends.

Sue was on a road of discovery. She clearly wanted to somehow, someway get money every day to fulfill her desires for the food she wanted to eat like donuts, Jax, Wise Potato Chips, fresh Italian bread with real butter, Trix, Fruit Loops and cereal with good prizes inside. Sue wanted a box of cereal with one of the 45 records on the back that you cut out with scissors and really could play on the record player. There were so many things she wanted to buy for herself.

So everyday Sue would check the laundromat for any coins left or lost there. Every day she would go around town, looking in all the places empty soda bottles might be that she could return and get money for. And every day she would dig in her backyard for buried treasure. It was amazing how successful she was at all three of these occupations, because she always found/got money for her needs. She truly enjoyed her daily hot fudge sundae she had at the tiny ice cream shop in town. She loved being able to buy candy for herself. Most of all, she loved having the power and the choices money brought her.

May stayed home. It may have been a small apartment, but most of the time, it was all hers. She lived her life contained within the four walls of the kitchen as she cooked and cleaned. She would do daily walks to the grocery store to do a bit of shopping for dinner. She would spend some time in the garden and if something were ripe enough, she would pick some vegetables for supper that night. She kept herself occupied with the chores of her life, which kept her from ever thinking too much about anything. She felt more peaceful that way.

Grandma Johnson was not happy with her son's family moving into the apartment over her garage, but then, she wasn't happy about anything. She was sure Sue would be noisy and disturb her peace and quiet. She was certain that May would need something from her, whether it was an ingredient for cooking or a ride somewhere, though May had never asked for anything before. She was also positive that Henry would never make enough money for his family to live anywhere else and would have to live off her generosity for the rest of their lives. And even if none of these things ever came true, she wouldn't change her mind one bit about any of it.

Sue wasn't afraid of her new school. She was older, smarter and had learned to adapt to being in school, thanks to Mrs. Gow. Now that she was eight, she seemed to have more awareness of the other people around her and she noticed the differences between herself and them. She could see that her clothes weren't store bought like the other kids.

She often thought if she was going to have to wear homemade clothes, she wished her grandmother, who had been a seamstress at Sears, made the clothes instead of her mother. Every Easter and Christmas Grandma Johnson did make the girls matching outfits, right down to the hats and coats. They were beautiful. Mostly, she wished she had store-bought clothes.

Sue would look around and see the things that other kids had, and she wanted them. She also wanted them to want what she had, if she only had something of value. This wanting seemed to become the focus for her considerable determination.

One of the really good things about the third grade and living in town was that Sue made a friend, Tawny. Tawny lived down the street, so it was easy for the two girls to spend time together. One of the things that both of them loved to do together was to dig for treasure. Now Sue had someone to dig with her almost every day.

The two girls were best friends and they made a pact about their diggings. They agreed that no matter whose yard they were digging in, whatever they found would be shared fifty/fifty. The two girls spent as much time as they could together, though Tawny never let Sue into her house. Sue would stand on the porch and could look in the doorway while Tawny went in to get something, but Sue wasn't allowed in. It was some kind of rule at Tawny's house.

Sue would stand there at the doorway, look in and see stacks and stacks of newspapers, magazines, mail, clothes, dishes and lots of cats and cat poop too. Tawny's mom always had her nightgown on and wore her hair in a very high twist. As Sue looked in, she thought a person would have to walk through these very narrow aisles in order to get from one room to the other. Sue had never seen anything like that before, but she supposed that Tawny's parents just had lots of things they wanted to keep and were too tired to clean up. Tawny felt Sue accepted her. Everyone else got mad that they couldn't come into Tawny's house, but Sue didn't. She didn't say anything about it at all. Sue felt Tawny accepted her too.

In Tawny's front yard, were two juniper trees; one was male and one was female. The female had yummy little berries. Tawny said the tree had the little berries because the female tree loved the male tree.

Sue only had one friend at a time. She was fiercely loyal, but she also expected an equal loyalty in return. Her friend couldn't be anyone else's friend beside Sue's. If a friend of hers wanted to be friends with Sue's sister, Sue would stop being their friend immediately. Loyalty was really important to Sue. She valued it above all other things. Trusting one person at a time was all Sue could do.

Tawny was a loyal friend. She had no other friends, just Sue. There were a couple days that Sue's sister Connie had no one around and started to play with Tawny. Sue just got up and walked away. Tawny got the hint.

Sue's daily routine began to expand. One day it occurred to her that she might go around the back of the Reliable Market and just pick up the empty returned bottles stored out there. She had noticed them last week when she used the bathroom out back. She would bring them back around the front into the market and cash them in. Again. *Why not?*

She went around the back, checked to see if there was anyone around or watching her, and when there wasn't, she picked up as many bottles as she could and boldly walked back around to the front of the store. No one noticed. No one said a thing. Sue was able to return their own bottles and get the money for them without having to spend the hour or so she usually spent searching for a bottle or two. Wow. This was great! Sue was amazed at how easy it was and was determined to do this whenever there were a lot of bottles back there and no one would notice.

It made Sue happy to know that she could have her daily hot fudge sundae without having to scrounge around for bottles every time! Now she would have more time to look for money in other ways. This opened up lots of possibilities for her, as getting more and more money became one of her daily goals.

When Sue got home, her mother asked her to go across the way to her grandmother's and call the school to see if Henry had left yet. Sue smelled the roses and other flowers that adorned her grandmother's house as she dutifully walked over and knocked on the door.

Standing there, her thinning, strawberry blonde hair put up in an artificial roll she'd made of her own falling hair, was Sue's grandmother, the bane of her existence. She smelled of her musty old house and of the soup she was cooking on the stove. Seeing who had knocked on her door, Grandma Johnson glared down at Sue and said, "What do you want? You know you're not really my granddaughter. Your mother was cheating on my son with the heater repairman and you're really his child."

Sue didn't say anything. She just stood there, held her ground and stared hard at her grandmother. She's heard all this before. She knew it was best to ignore it. Sue couldn't quite ignore the only animal that didn't like her, her grandmother's vicious black and white bulldog. Even when Sue was in the house, with her grandmother looking on, the bulldog would try to bite Sue's ankles. Sue usually turned her back on him, knowing it was not his fault, that he was just obeying his owner. Her grandmother watched and did nothing.

"What are you standing there for? Come in, and don't let any of the flies in," said Grandma Johnson as she turned away and walked further into the kitchen.

"Mom wants me to call the school to see if Dad is still there. May I use your phone, please?" Sue asked calmly.

"Sure, go ahead. My phone is just another thing your whole family thinks they can use whenever they want to." She turned, going back to the pot of soup she had cooking on the stove.

Sue went to the phone and dialed the number she'd memorized long ago. The phone rang and rang, but no one answered. Finally, Sue hung up and tried again. Again the phone rang and rang, and no one answered. Not knowing what else to do, Sue hung up the phone, told her grandmother that no one answered and when her grandmother only shrugged, turned and went back to her home. Sue was able to sneak one buttermint candy from the bowl her grandmother always kept full. Sue hated the red and white peppermint candies that were in that dish too. They were so strong they made her head ache.

That evening, when her father came home, his mother came out to meet him as he drove into the driveway. As he got out of the truck, his mother started in.

"Do you know what that misbegotten child did today?" After he shook his head in surprise at her sudden attack, she continued. "Well, she came over here and demanded to use my phone and after I kindly let her use it, when the line was busy, that little brat threw herself a complete hissy fit, right on my kitchen floor! I don't know how you let May raise her to be so disrespectful to her grandmother, but I've never seen the like of it!" She turned on her heels and nearly marched back into her house.

"Sue!" Henry shouted. "Where the hell are you? Get over here right now!"

Sue, who was in the backyard playing with a kitten, heard her dad yelling and came at a terrified run to the front of the garage.

"Yes, Dad. Here I am. What's the matter?" She asked, hoping she could somehow deflect him.

As soon as she was in reach, he grabbed her and began to spank her, saying, "Who do you think you are, disrespecting your grandmother that way? I don't want to ever hear that you have thrown some kind of tantrum again, and never, never, never do anything like that again to your grandmother. Do you hear me?"

Sue, of course, couldn't really answer him as she was crying so hard. Turning away from her and going up the stairs into the apartment, he said, "You'd better not do anything like that again, little girl, or I'll really give you a whipping!"

Sue lay crumpled on the ground, crying. She could see into her grandmother's kitchen window as she lay there and she clearly saw the smile on her grandmother's face. Her grandmother even knew that Sue could see her gratified smile and with a satisfied nod, she turned away from the window.

Sue learned a valuable lesson that day. Adults lie and they get away with it. If Sue had ever had any doubts about her own lying, she didn't now. She also resolved to work really hard to never put herself in a position in which her grandmother could tell a lie to get her in trouble again. That woman hated her, and she didn't understand why.

Of course, Sue had a nightmare that night. She must have been making noises in her sleep because she awoke to hear her father yelling at her to shut up or he'd put her outside with the dogs. Sue didn't want to go back to sleep for fear of being in another nightmare and waking her dad again, but, of course, her tiredness overcame her and she did fall back to sleep. The night seemed to be filled with evil witches chasing her and demons holding her down. Morning took forever to come.

No one spoke to Sue at breakfast and so she gladly hid behind the cereal box so she wouldn't have to speak to anyone either. Sue was saving cereal box tops and daydreaming about winning the five hundred dollars given away to five lucky winners.

Every Tuesday and Thursday after school all the children went to the Faith Baptist church for an hour of lessons. These lessons usually consisted of the pastor's wife talking about Jesus for about fifteen minutes and then the kids spent the rest of the hour making arts and crafts projects. Sue really liked to make the macaroni plates, yarn necklaces and other fun crafts. They also served Kool-Aid and Ritz crackers, which were Sue's favorites.

After the church lesson, Sue did her usual route, making her first stop at the laundromat to look for coins. Then she went to the Reliant Market. After Sue scouted out the area and picked up the empty bottles from the back of the store, she carried them to the butcher's section. By now the butcher was used to her and expected her daily empty bottle returns. It was becoming ridiculously easy. At last, Sue went to the ice cream shop for her daily hot fudge sundae.

She couldn't help but ponder the events of yesterday in her mind. It surprised her that her grandmother, who always acted as if she was the most religious person in the room, would tell such an out and out lie, especially to make trouble for her granddaughter, which seemed to be an unchristian thing to do. Yet, that's exactly what she did.

Sue thought this must be a sign from God that it was okay for her to lie to get what she wanted and needed, since her lies were at least to help her instead of hurting someone else. She quickly said a little prayer and asked God to somehow let her know if it was okay for her to lie or not, just to be sure.

After her sundae, Sue went over to Tawny's house to see if she wanted to dig for buried treasure with her. Tawny said sure, and the two girls went into Tawny's backyard to do some digging. They each had their own way of deciding where to dig. For Sue, it was as if the area lit up or looked kind of different than any other part of the yard. For Tawny, it was more methodical. She had mentally formed a grid work in her backyard and was daily choosing the next square in the row she was working on.

Some days neither girl found anything and just had a companionable time digging up the backyard. Other days one or both of them found something but it wasn't of any value. On the best days, they both found money or something special like a piece of jewelry. Today, Sue found a few coins just under the surface of the dirt. She found a dime, a nickel and three pennies. Since it wasn't an even amount, Sue and Tawny went to the store together and decided to buy some candy and split it, that way each of them got an even share. Both girls went home happy.

Sue no longer had Mrs. Gow as her teacher. Though she missed her, Sue had gained confidence in herself and was able to handle school much better now. She did average work, though she was much smarter than the grades she made. She just didn't want to stand out or even to participate if she could avoid it. She didn't see any real advantage to getting good grades, as it made the teachers expect more of someone and gained the resentment of the other kids. Sue wanted the other kids to like her and see her as special, but in a good way.

When Sue arrived home, she was still eating the candy she and Tawny had bought.

"Sue, where did you get that candy?" Her mother asked, looking a bit confused.

"Tawny and I bought some at the store, Mom," Sue answered truthfully.

"But where did you or Tawny get the money to buy the candy?" her mother asked tentatively, as if she was trying very hard to figure out this mystery.

"Oh, I found it, Mom, in the cracks of the sidewalk," Sue said somewhat fearfully, unsure of her mother's reaction.

"Well, that explains it, then. How nice for you. I'm glad you could get yourself some candy." May turned back to the stove and continued making dinner.

Sue, on the other hand, was shocked. She had just lied to her mother, and her mother had completely and unquestionably believed her. Not only that, she didn't have to lie today, as she had actually found it in Tawny's yard. This particular lie was a pre-planned lie Sue had made up just in case she ever got caught with any stolen stuff. Sue suddenly realized that this was a sign, the answer to her earlier prayer to God, asking for Him to let her know if it was okay to lie or not. Obviously, it must be okay. Sue was incredibly happy. If her mother believed her and God said it was okay, Sue knew she could do whatever she needed to do to take care of herself and get whatever she wanted. This was great news!

That night, Sue slept well, without nightmares for once. In fact, she had another invention dream. Sue really liked it when she dreamed of inventing something that could be useful in real life. She didn't get these dreams too often, so she always liked it when she remembered them. She had dreamt that she invented some glasses that helped people see without going to the doctor. In her dream, someone in class was already wearing them. In Sue's mind, this was proof her idea was useful. She knew that someday one of her dreams would be turned into a great invention, and knowing this was a great inspiration to her!

Sue's sister Connie really liked living in town, because she was closer to her boyfriend, Mike. She had met him one Sunday in town when she was visiting Grandma Johnson. She had seen him every chance she could get after that, which wasn't often, but now that she lived in town, she could see him all the time. Grandma Johnson wasn't sure she liked Connie having a Catholic boyfriend. Catholics and Baptists don't mix. They had been going steady now for over a year. He was two years older than Connie, and all the other girls at school were so jealous that she had a boyfriend, especially one who was in the seventh grade.

Connie had accidentally learned when they went camping last year that the older boys liked to play the games her uncle played, but this time, she had the power. They came to her and wanted her to play spin the bottle and Truth or Dare. Right from the get-go, Connie liked to spend her time with the older kids.

The summer when Connie was eight, she learned that boys would pay lots of attention to her if she let them touch her or if she touched them. She already had budding breasts that were bigger than most of the seventh graders. She really liked being wanted by the older boys. It made her feel special. She got to tell them what they could do to her and what they couldn't. Until then, Connie had had no idea that those awful games with her uncle could be anything but yucky. Now she was glad she'd learned how to play them, because it gave her some control and power over boys, and having that power made Connie feel really great.

Once Connie was playing spin the bottle while camping, and it landed on a girl. The boys started taunting them, "Come on, fair is fair!" and Connie and the girl kissed. Connie wasn't sure, but she thought it might have been more fun than kissing a boy. The next day at the campgrounds, Connie asked the girl if she wanted to play house. Connie would be the wife, the other girl would be the husband and therefore, they would have an excuse for kissing each other. This is what they called playing house, and they played it for the rest of the three-day weekend.

That camping trip was just one of many the Johnson family took over the years. They didn't have much money, so having a trip in an airplane was out of the question, but they could afford to drive down to the Adirondacks and spend a few days there in the summer. They had a tent and brought all the food they needed, so it didn't cost them much except for gas. They usually stayed at a campground where there were other families, so the girls would spend the few days there playing with the other children.

During the camping trips, Sue would try to find someone who was close to her own age and see if they could play together or maybe even look for interesting things on the trails. One time she found a nest and on the last day of the camping trip, Sue took one of the eggs home. When Sue got home she used a light bulb for heat and put the egg carefully in a box. When the egg hatched, the sad reality hit. The baby bird had no mother. The Science teacher at school took it and assured her he knew how to take care of this hairless baby. Sue never did that again.

Henry and May didn't keep track of where the girls went or whom they went with. They only required that the girls be back in time for supper.

Sue noticed that these camping trips were especially hard on her mother. While everyone else in the family got a vacation with time to spend enjoying the outdoors and the change in their daily life, May only had more work than her usual life contained. Cooking outdoors was a much more demanding chore than it was at home. Washing dishes was cumbersome and the water was cold, so it was harder to get them clean. Often May would walk the long trail to the washhouse, only to return to a mess the raccoons had made. She was just grateful it wasn't a bear. Everything took more time and effort for May, so she was always relieved when she could finally get home to her own kitchen.

The summer Sue was eight, after one of their camping trips, Sue had one of her invention dreams and it was such a good idea that she could not stop thinking about it. Sue had seen postcards for sale at the campgrounds with people in them and the words "Wish you were here!", but the people in the postcards were strangers. Sue wrote a letter to the Polaroid company and suggested that they sell a postcard kit with their film, so that when people took Polaroid pictures of themselves on vacation, they could use an adhesive postcard and stick their picture on it and send it as a postcard to their friends and family.

Sue found an envelope for her letter, but had no stamp. She remembered how her mother had gotten upset when a bill had come back in the mail because she didn't put a stamp on the envelope. This gave Sue an idea. She knew about addressing an envelope because everyone in her second grade class wrote a letter to the President as a class exercise. She used her address as the recipient and Polaroid Company as the return address. She dropped the envelope made out to her, with no stamp on it, in the mailbox and waited. The letter didn't come back. Her post card idea was so good that Polaroid actually did something very similar to what she suggested thirty years later.

During the summer vacation from school, the girls had much more free time. Once they got whatever chores they had to do done, they were free to go and to do whatever they liked until suppertime. They could come and go as they pleased without having to ask permission or tell anyone where they were going. They only had to be home in time for supper. Both girls took advantage of this freedom, and were usually out and about.

Now that they were living in town, both girls really wished they could have a bike to ride around on in town. Of course, there wasn't any money to buy one, but one day, Henry found an old abandoned bicycle in a field by the high school. He put it in the back of the truck and brought it home to the girls. He fixed it up a bit, the girls painted it, and now they had a bike to share.

Having more time in the summer and a bike to get around on, Connie was spending most of her time with her two girlfriends or with her boyfriend. She practically lived at her girlfriend Linda's house, so much so, that Linda's mother jokingly said she had two daughters instead of one. Connie and Linda would spend most of the day in Linda's room or would spend hours just wandering around the small town. Secretly pretending they were husband and wife, it was like 'playing house', and they both liked playing this game.

Connie also spent many hours with her boyfriend Mike. He was older and had more chores to do to help out at his home, but he managed to see her almost every day. Connie was nearly ten and had blossomed into quite a buxom young girl. She had started her period at nine. She had the body of a woman. Her uncle had noticed that also. She was in many ways a sexual object with the mind and maturity of a child.

The ten-year old Connie's sense of sexuality was caused by her life experiences. She had touched and been touched inappropriately since she was four and she had no sense of liking or not liking it. Except with Linda, physical touching was, for Connie, either something that was done to her, demanded of her or hurt her like the spankings her father gave her did. In truth, she was mainly unfeeling about her body; as if her body was just a tool she used to get what she wanted.

That summer, her boyfriend Mike was slowly escalating the touching. He was now thirteen and he wanted more. Connie wasn't sure about that. She was still technically a virgin, and since it was still her choice, she didn't want anything inside her. She didn't desire sex, so she wasn't at all crazy about doing anything more than what she was already doing. Mike thought about going all the way all the time and was trying to talk her into it. Perhaps Connie sensed she would lose her power over Mike if she gave in too much, so she continued to hold out.

Sue loved summer vacation. Having more free time gave her more time to hunt for treasure, whether by digging in her back yard or by finding change. Wherever she could, she was always on the lookout for treasure. While digging, it occurred to her that she could get worms and sell them to the guys who went fishing at the creek. Of course she priced them less than the store price. She sold them in a paper cup with dirt included—fifty earthworms for twenty-five cents. *Heck, she was already digging in the dirt; she might as well make some money at it!* Sue thought.

One thing that Sue began to notice was how easy it was for her to do whatever she wanted without being questioned or restricted. Her parents didn't know where she was and they didn't care what she did, just as long as her chores were done.

Sue also realized that most other adults didn't seem to notice her or care what she was doing, if she didn't look like she was doing anything she shouldn't. So she could go to the laundromat and look everywhere for fallen coins and even if someone was there, they didn't tell her she couldn't do it or try to stop her. They basically just ignored her. Wow! This was great! Sue felt kind of invisible. She could go almost anywhere and do almost anything and nobody said no, as long as she didn't draw any attention to herself.

That summer of discovery for both Sue and Connie would continue into the school year when it started in September. Sue was now in the fourth grade and Connie was in the fifth. They still lived over the garage at Grandma Johnson's. During the summer, Henry had converted a portion of the garage into a living area, so the family actually had a room to be in besides the kitchen and their bedrooms.

The canning was done. The garden was turned under. The weather began getting colder as the season turned from fall to winter. School was in. Henry went every day to the high school and worked hard as the janitor. May continued to do her daily household chores of cooking and cleaning and still lived in her dream-like world of denial. Connie was becoming better and better friends with Linda; spending more time with Linda than with her boyfriend Mike. Sue had a hot fudge sundae every day, thanks to her efforts of finding treasure, selling worms or returning bottles. Both girls got to go ice-skating almost every day once the creek froze over.

During that winter, one cold day, Sue was playing 45 records on the record player and dancing around her room while listening to The Everly Brothers and Elvis Presley. Without thinking, she left a few records on the radiator instead of putting them away in their sleeves. After dinner, when she came back to her room, she found the records she'd left on the radiator had warped! These were her dad's records, and Sue knew she was in trouble. She was petrified, knowing the kind of punishment she would get. She was telling God she hated him for letting this happen to her. She put the records back into their sleeves and quietly put the records back in her father's room, hoping he wouldn't notice or when he did find out, there would be enough time for him not to remember she'd borrowed them.

But no, that escape was not going to happen for Sue. Unfortunately, Henry chose that night to listen to music in his room. Going through his stack of 45s, he found the warped ones immediately. With a roar of anger, he yelled, "Sue! What the hell did you do to my records! They're ruined! Get in here right this minute!"

More than anything, Sue didn't want to go into that room, but she knew if she didn't go now, it would be worse when he found her, and he always would. With the reluctance and terror of a prisoner going to their death, Sue went into her father's room.

He spanked her long and hard this time. Sue tried not to cry, but it really hurt. Afterwards, as she tried to calm herself down, she thought how unfair it was that she was punished for something that was really an accident; she hadn't meant to harm the records.

She felt so sad for herself and that one afternoon shortly afterwards, Sue's eye happened to fall on the row of photo albums in the living room. Picking one out, she sat down on the couch and started to look through it. Inside were pictures of all of her family, which naturally included pictures of herself from babyhood to her present age. Maybe it was because she was feeling sad or maybe it was because she was feeling angry, but Sue noticed that in all of her pictures, she wasn't smiling. Since Sue wasn't very happy at that moment, she decided she didn't like any of those pictures, so she got the scissors and cut up every unsmiling picture of herself that she could find.

Unfortunately, that was almost all of her childhood pictures and when her parents found out later, they were very unhappy with Sue, to say the least.

Feeling a bit better the next week, Sue was back doing her usual rounds at the laundromat and Reliant Market. While at the market, Sue had to go to the bathroom, so she asked the clerk for the key to go around back. The clerk said, "The public bathroom is broken. Please use the employee's restroom in the store." The clerk directed Sue to the back, through the swinging doors where she would see a door marked employees. Sue found it, used the bathroom, and when she came out of the stall, she noticed the coats hanging on the wall.

A new idea occurred to Sue. Walking forward, she began going through all the pockets to see what treasures she could find, and treasures were exactly what she did find. She found a number of coins and a few packets of cigarettes. Sue didn't smoke, of course, but she knew some kids that hung out around the ice cream store that did, and Sue wondered if she could sell these cigarettes to them. What a great idea! Sue carefully stashed the cigarettes in one pocket and the coins in the other pocket.

As she walked back through the swinging doors, she saw the butcher counter ahead of her, but she didn't see the butcher anywhere. Walking to the butcher counter, Sue carefully looked around for the butcher or even a clerk. No one was in sight. Then another new idea occurred to Sue. What if she took a piece of the butcher paper and wrote on it an amount with the black wax pencil, just like the butcher did, and then took it up to the front counter. How would they know up at the counter that she had written it and not the butcher?

Glancing around one more time, Sue took the paper, wrote the amount on it, tore it off and went up to the front where the cashiers were. Handing the cashier the piece of paper, Sue watched her carefully and hoped she didn't reveal any of her fears to the young woman. Apparently, Sue's fears went unnoticed, as the cashier simply opened up the cash drawer and gave Sue the money. With amazement and an intense happiness, Sue walked out of the market.

She immediately went to the ice cream store. Seeing the older boys out front as usual, Sue cautiously approached them.

"Hey guys, um, where do you get your cigarettes?" Sue asked timidly.

"Why do you want to know, little girl, you thinking' of taking up smoking?" One boy said and then laughed with all of his friends.

"No, but well, I have some cigarettes that I found and I thought maybe you guys would like to buy them," Sue said, cutting to the chase.

"Oh yeah? Let me see those cigarettes," the same boy asked with interest.

Sue took the cigarettes out of her pocket and showed them. She had only two partial packs, but she sold them to the boys for twenty-five cents each. What a haul! Sue had really made lots of money today and she had lots of ideas of what she could do to make even more money tomorrow! With pride and joy, Sue went into the ice cream shop and thoroughly relished her hot fudge sundae.

When she got home, her mom said, "There is a letter for you." Sue was elated! It was from Polaroid. The letter said, "Thank you for your great idea. We are not interested at this time. Please understand that if this idea or something similar is used in the future, the letter you sent may have been one of many with the same type of idea." Sue was on cloud nine. She had gotten a letter from Polaroid! They said it was a great idea! That was enough for now. That night she prayed to God thanking Him for all that He was bringing into her life.

That Sunday, the whole family went over to Uncle Larry's for breakfast. Sue feared what would happen, as did Connie, though neither girl said anything to one another, or even made eye contact with the other. Because the girls were older now, Uncle Larry was using different techniques to get them alone.

Acting as if he wanted to give the girls a treat, Uncle Larry said, "Connie! Sue! Why don't you girls come in here, I have something special to give you," giving them a big smile.

Connie come forward and went to her Uncle Larry with a quiet acceptance.

Sue calmly said, "Sorry, Uncle Larry, but I'm going to stay with my mom."

"But Sue, I have something special for you," Uncle Larry said pleadingly.

"No thanks, Uncle Larry, I just need to be with my mom right now," Sue said with a look on her face that even Uncle Larry could see she wasn't going to change her mind.

With a shrug, Uncle Larry put his arm around Connie and went into the bedroom.

Never again was Sue molested by her uncle. She made sure she was never alone with him. She would often just stay wherever her mother was or even with her aunt, but she never allowed herself to be caught by him again.

Unfortunately, Connie didn't learn that lesson.

Chapter Six:
The Art of Selling

Maybe it was because Sue was now ten years old, but she felt older. She was too old now to dig for treasure. She had stopped digging with Tawny after they found a beautiful hunk of topaz or something. Tawny went in the house to show her parents and came back out and said, "My dad said this is their yard, and they're keeping it." Sue wasn't really friends with Tawny after that.

Sue knew she was smart. She might not be book smart, but she was smart. She was only ten years old, but she had more spending money than the sixteen-year-olds and she was always planning on ways to add to her treasures. She knew how to steal and she knew how to sell. She was pretty good at lying too. These tools had gotten her loads of money and tons of things that she'd never imagined she could have. Most of all, she enjoyed the thrill and the payoff.

She watched people. She observed what they did and noticed why they did it. The last couple of years of her life, she'd been learning many things about how she could have the freedom to do what she wanted without getting in trouble and how to sell things. Somehow, all by herself, she'd figured out that the best thing to sell was whatever people wanted. The trick was to figure out what people wanted and then how to make it or get it herself, so she could sell it cheaper.

She'd already learned about selling worms. There were a lot of fishermen in the area, so it was easy to just dig up the worms and sell them at a lower cost than the local bait and tackle shop. She'd noticed lately at school that everyone was chewing on cinnamon toothpicks. Those toothpicks were really popular, especially because the kids could chew on them in class and the teachers didn't mind. Sue guessed it was because it wasn't gum and it wasn't against the rules, so the kids didn't get in trouble for them, but for whatever reason, those toothpicks were the biggest thing in school.

Those toothpicks would be a really good thing to sell, thought Sue. *I wonder how I could make them?*

When Sue put her mind to something, she got it done, so Sue decided to go to the pharmacy to talk to somebody there, hoping they would know how to help her. At the back counter, Sue saw Mr. Woods in his white coat. Sue knew him; he was a very nice man. She would get her allergy medicine from him. He and his wife worked at West Corners Pharmacy and store. The only men she'd ever seen in white coats like the one he wore were doctors, so Sue figured he must be a doctor.

Sue stepped up to the counter and said, "Excuse me, Mr. Woods, I would like to make my own cinnamon toothpicks, like the ones you sell."

Mr. Woods said, "Sure, I can help you with that, but I will have to order the oil. The oil is called Cinnamon Extract. It is *very* strong, so you will not need much." Then he said, "That will be two dollars and fifty cents for the oil in advance."

Sue said, "Great, please order it for me," took the money out of her pocket and paid for the oil. Sue checked back every day until it had come in. Finally, it arrived.

Mr. Woods reached under the counter and handed Sue the small bottle of cinnamon extract that she had ordered and suggested she smell it. Unscrewing the cap, Sue leaned in, took a deep whiff and thought, *whew! This is strong!* as she jerked back her head to get away from the pungent odor. Turning to Mr. Woods, Sue said, "This could burn someone's mouth!"

Mr. Woods chuckled softly and said, "That's true if you used lots of it, but a tiny bit goes a long way. In very small amounts it's safe. Use a flat dish and put a thin layer over the toothpicks; the toothpicks, being porous, will soak it up pretty fast. Why, this little bottle will flavor many packs of toothpicks! Be careful not to leave them soaking too long. Turn them over, try one and you will know after a couple of tries what's the right amount of oil and time to soak them until they're the way you'll need them to be."

Sue's face lit up like a candle. "Really?" She asked excitedly.

"Really," he answered kindly.

Sue knew that the cinnamon toothpicks the kids bought cost twenty-five cents a pack for twenty toothpicks. Sue bought two boxes of the plain flat kind of toothpicks that the kids in school liked for fifty cents for a box of two hundred.

The pharmacist took her money, bagged her purchases and watched her walk sprightly out the door. In the weeks to come, he would become even more familiar with his young enterprising customer. Sue came often. And she bought more cinnamon oil and lots of toothpicks.

Sue went home immediately to make her new product, cinnamon toothpicks. Taking a small flat plate, Sue spread out a pile of toothpicks in a single depth on the plate. Then taking the bottle of cinnamon oil, she barely poured any of the oil on the toothpicks, yet all of it was quickly absorbed into the wood. She carefully turned them over. Then she let them dry. It really was pretty easy to do, she just had to be careful with the oil and be sure and let the toothpicks dry before putting them all together in small wax paper bags of twenty each. Mr. Woods gave her the bags for free. Sue could see that the little bottle of oil would go a long way and so her main cost was going to be the toothpicks. Sue knew that the store sold the cinnamon toothpicks for twenty-five cents for twenty toothpicks, so Sue would sell hers for a penny each, five cents less than at the store.

Sue was really hoping she could make lots of money from selling the toothpicks. She had plans for the money. She'd been reading the ads in the back of the comic books her dad had and she saw the most amazing things to buy there. She wanted to buy the special x-ray glasses and the spy camera, the trick gum pack and the fake bullet holes you could put on your window, and she especially wanted both the soap that turned your hands black and the fuzzy wuzzy bear soap that grew hair when it got wet and had a prize in the middle.

Sue longed to have these special items from the back of her dad's comic books as well as many other things she'd seen in magazines or even on the backs of cereal boxes. She'd seen these special boxes of cereal that had a real 45 record attached to the back that you had to cut out with scissors, and Sue was just dying to buy one and see if they really would play on the record player.

Sue found that she could make about a thousand toothpicks with one bottle of cinnamon oil for two dollars and fifty cents, plus the cost of toothpicks of five boxes for two dollars and fifty cents, making a total cost of five dollars. That gave her a profit of five dollars for every batch. Her toothpicks were a hit at school because the flavor lasted longer than the store-bought ones, and it was more convenient for the kids, as Sue always had them for sale at school and the kids knew it. After her first batch went over so well, she charged the same price as the store and got it because hers were better quality. All of the proceeds from her sales would come in handy as the fair was coming to town this weekend.

Finally it was Saturday, and the local fair was in town. Sue was really excited about going because Dad was going to give Connie and her five whole dollars each to spend. With the twenty Sue had of her own, that was twenty-five dollars! There was always so much to see and do at the fair, and Sue couldn't wait until it was time to go.

At last, Dad and Mom were ready and they all got in the truck and drove to the outskirts of town to the field where the carnival-fair had been set up. Just like last year, Dad gave the girls their five dollars and then he and Mom went off by themselves while Connie and Sue went their separate ways.

Sue watched for a minute to see her parents strolling together, looking at the booths, stopping here and there to watch what was happening or to listen to one of the barkers. Sometimes, her dad would stop and maybe try his luck at winning a prize in one of the game booths. He enjoyed playing at the shooting gallery, and was trying to impress May.

Sue then noticed her sister Connie already on a ride. Sue knew that Connie's money would go to paying for rides, because Connie always told everyone all about the rides she'd been on after they got home. Sue did none of those things at the fair. Sue had motion sickness and even going on one ride would make her ill for the rest of the day, so she went right to where the game booths were set up and just hung around, watching. Sue paid close attention to how the games were played, noticed how the game was won, and focused on what the carnie workers did when demonstrating how to win to the passersby. Sue saw some interesting things.

For instance, in the Duck Pond game, there were about fifty ducks moving around in a circle in the water. According to the carnie barkers, all of the ducks were supposed to be possible winners, but really, only one had the winning number twenty-five on the bottom. Sue looked very closely at the winning duck. She saw that the winning duck had a small, red painted dot on its forehead. It was a minor flaw on its yellow rubber ducky face. All of the other ducks when picked and turned over only had low numbers and no prizes were given. After observing for a while, Sue was ready to pay and play herself. She carefully chose the only duck with a small red dot on its forehead. It was of course the winning duck, which came as no surprise to Sue.

Sue knew exactly what prize she wanted from the top shelf. She chose one of the special yellow stuffed creatures that looked almost like a Pac-man or something, but had a funny face on it. Once it was in her arms, Sue noticed it had a wonderful smell. Taking a deep breath in, Sue smelled the stuffed animal and loved it at once.

Sue spent her day at the fair winning prizes. Sometimes she won because she'd watched long enough to figure out how to win. Sometimes she won just because she was inherently lucky. She came home with her yellow furry creature, a furry, lime green rug in the shape of a footprint and a big stuffed tiger. What a haul!

That evening when the family arrived home, tired but happy after spending the whole day at the fair, they gathered in the downstairs living room and watched TV. A while back, Dad had come home with a black and white, nineteen-inch RCA TV he'd gotten at a sale somewhere. Of course, everybody could only watch what he wanted to watch which was mainly war movies with male actors only, but Dad really liked Sonny on the Sonny and Cher Show, so they watched that when it was on.

The whole family would sit around the TV and watch without saying a word or moving an inch. Dad didn't allow any noise at all when the TV was on so everyone was very careful. Normally Mom would only sit for a bit and then remember something she had to do and leave the room, but not when Sonny and Cher was on. Then she was glued to the TV. Sue liked the show too, but Mom seemed captivated.

All in all, it had been a rather wonderful day for Sue. After her bath, she headed for bed. She slept that night with her new yellow stuffed creature and smelled it while she slept. She didn't have any nightmares all night.

[Ginny Scales-Medeiros]

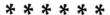

Sue was learning more and more about how to make money and how to win. There were contests at school and every contest had a prize to be won, but also recognition was given to the winner. Sue wanted both.

There was a contest at school called the Bookworm Reading contest. Every student was given a colorful bookworm sheet with lots of lines on it to put the titles of all the books the student had read. The students also had to write a short paragraph on what the book was about. The student who read the most books would win a special stuffed bookworm and the winner would be announced in front of the whole school. Naturally, Sue wanted to win the contest, but she didn't think she would have time to read enough books to win it, not with her chores and all of her moneymaking activities.

Sue thought about it and tried to figure out how she could possibly win. Holding one of the library books she'd checked out to read for the contest, she noticed that the back of the book had lots of writing on it. Looking closer and reading what was there, she realized that most of the story was detailed right there on the back of the book. *Well, heck, I could just write a paragraph from what was already written right here on the back of the book!* So taking a piece of notebook paper out, Sue read and wrote only from what was written on the back of the book with a few changes to make it her own. Sue put the title of the book at the top of the paper and with a satisfied sigh, put the book down and started looking around for other books with the book details on the back.

Sue started spending a little of her after-school time in the library, scouring for books that had the book description on the back that she needed for the bookworm contest. She found quite a few and she turned in a paper for each and every one of them. It was no surprise to Sue that she won the Bookworm contest. She really wanted that bookworm stuffed animal, and it felt great to hear all the teachers tell her how well she'd done to have read so many books to win the contest!

There were magazine-selling contests at school too, which Sue entered and, of course, won at least third prize, but more often, she won first or second. Every Halloween the school would give the students boxes to collect money for Unicef while they were trick or treating. Sue loved those Unicef drives, because for every two dollars she collected, she always kept one.

Sue had noticed, besides the wonderful tricks she wanted to buy in the back of the comic books, there was an ad about selling boxes of greeting cards. Sue read the ad and thought about it. It seemed pretty straightforward and only required that you be sixteen years of age and no money up front was required. Sue decided to do it, so she sent away to the greeting card company, saying that, yes, she was sixteen years of age, and gave them her name and address as requested. Sue was only eleven.

When that big box of greeting cards arrived at her home with Sue's name on it, Sue was over the moon. Sue was just so excited to receive such a big box in the mail; she almost didn't care what was in it. Once she opened it, she found twelve boxes of assorted greeting cards with adorable babies doing different things on them. The enclosed instructions said that she was to sell each of the boxes for three dollars each and then send only a dollar fifty for each box sold back to the greeting card company. Sue would get a dollar fifty for each box she sold! Wow! This was great!

Sue went out the very next day and began to go door-to-door selling her greeting cards. It wasn't the least bit surprising that she sold them like hot cakes. It didn't take her long to sell all of the boxes of greeting cards. Sue then sent the twelve dollars back to the greeting company and requested more. She received a new box of greeting cards about two weeks later. From then on, Sue paid for the greeting cards in advance and then kept whatever she made for herself.

This method allowed her to begin to negotiate the deal. She found that some people wouldn't buy the cards at three dollars, because they only had two-fifty. While other people would buy the cards at three-fifty and sometimes even four dollars, so Sue was learning how to tell whether she had to lower or could raise the price, depending upon the person. She was not only becoming a salesperson, she was becoming a great salesperson and learning the value of negotiation. Some profit was better than none, and it all added up.

Another product to sell that she found on the back of the comic books was the scratch-off card game. Sue would buy the kit for three dollars, which included the scratch-off card and a stuffed animal. Sue would sell the opportunity to scratch off one space for twenty-five cents for the chance to win the stuffed animal. If all or nearly all of the spaces got scratched off, Sue could make almost fifteen dollars on one card! Of course, if someone scratched off the winning spot pretty early in the game, then Sue might not even break even. It was a gamble, but Sue usually did pretty well, and enjoyed the thrill of seeing how much she could make before someone scratched off the right spot.

But the most important contest for Sue was the Bible Camp contest at church. Sue had never spent time away from home. She'd heard from the other kids all about the food, fun games, sleeping in huts with other kids, arts and crafts, hiking in the woods, and swimming that she would get to do if she could go to Bible Camp. She wanted to go so badly. She knew her family couldn't afford to send her and it was more money than Sue had. This contest was very important to her.

The young people at the Faith Baptist Church were divided into two groups, the red group and the blue group. Sue was in the blue group. The contest was to see which group could memorize the most Bible verses before a certain deadline. The winning team got to go to Bible camp for free. The church had a big scale, the kind with the two plates, one on each side, which had to have the same weight on each side in order to balance. Every time a child memorized a verse, one penny was added to their group's side of the scale. Sue memorized fifty percent of all the verses for her group, more than any other child in either of the groups, but much to Sue's deep disappointment, the blue group lost. After feeling like she just got kicked in the stomach, she got a rush of even more determination to start working on something else she could win.

Thankfully, Sue's cinnamon toothpick sales were through the roof. She rarely sold worms anymore, unless someone asked her for them. The greeting cards were great, but it took people a while to use all the cards. She was starting to hear, "We still have plenty, thank you."

While Sue was focused on selling, Connie was focused on trying to figure out more about sex.

Connie was now twelve going on thirteen, but her body and her sexuality was much older than her maturity. Boys noticed her wherever she went. She liked to be noticed. She liked the attention having blonde hair, big blue eyes and large breasts brought her. She liked having bigger breasts than any other girl in school. It made her feel that she was older, better, more popular than the other girls and that made Connie feel special.

Yet, she didn't feel special at home at all. Every day, she had to do the hard chores still because, even though Sue wasn't so small anymore, Connie was still the strong one. Connie didn't think it was fair that her dad wanted her to do more than what was her fair share of work. Sometimes, just out of pure frustration and because she just couldn't help herself, and she would say something to her dad about how unfair it was, and, as always, she would suffer the consequences. The one good thing about moving into town onto her grandma's property was that there wasn't as much work to do as when they lived in the old trailer out in the woods.

Yet, there was talk at home about moving back out to the woods. Connie thought, *Well, if we move back to the woods, I wouldn't run into Mike any more.* She'd gotten tired of him pressuring her to have sex and also hearing her grandma nag her about him all the time. Grandma Johnson thought this relationship was lasting too long to be just a passing fling and she knew Mike and his family were Catholic, not Baptists like the Johnson family was. She wanted to put a stop to it, so she offered to give Connie a beautiful porcelain doll if she'd break up with Mike. Connie didn't have to think twice. She happily took the doll and stopped seeing Mike.

More and more, Connie liked to be with Linda. The boys were okay, but Linda really cared about Connie, really liked her for who she was, and Connie was beginning to crave or need that special someone that loved her for who she really was. She and Linda had begun touching too, that funny kind of touching, like she did with the boys and with her uncle. Connie was starting to really like kissing Linda, maybe even more than she liked kissing boys. She didn't really know why that was.

She still hadn't 'gone all the way' yet. She knew what that was now. She'd learned all about sex from the special health class everybody had to take at school. Connie had talked with Linda about sex and boys and lots of stuff. Linda, who was two years older, seemed to know lots more about it than Connie.

Linda said she'd talked to this friend of her mother's who was a counselor. Connie wasn't sure what kind of a counselor she was, but Linda liked this woman and said she really helped her a lot. Anyway, the counselor explained some of the things Linda didn't understand about sex, and maybe that was why Linda knew so much.

There was no one else to talk to about all the feelings Connie had inside. She couldn't talk to her mother, certainly not her sister, and she didn't know anyone else, other than Linda, to talk to about all the different emotions and thoughts she kept having, so she talked to Linda about almost everything.

Henry, never one to bottle up his feelings for long, was feeling more and more frustrated living at his mother's. He wanted the quiet of the woods around him. He wanted the freedom of his own home and his own rules. He wanted to not have to see his mother every day.

He did like going fishing every day and having less work to do. A creek full of fish, so close at hand, was a luxury that he'd gotten used to. Unfortunately, Sue had broken his good fishing rod by shutting the truck door on it. He whooped her a good one for that, but he still had to get another one. His old pole worked for now. He had had it since he lived here as a boy.

Henry was also concerned about all the freedom May had now that she was home alone and could walk to town. She seemed to be changing. But Henry feared that he was doomed to struggling all his life and would need his mother always.

May did live her life in a daze, but it was a daze of her own making, and perhaps, she was the happiest in her family. She didn't need much, and there was a freedom in that. She loved walking to town and having the house to herself all day. When she walked to the Reliant Market, she always went through the same checkout line in the store, knowing that the cute man, Peter, would flirt with her and make her day. She would never do anything to lead him on, but it inspired her to look her best, and that in itself made her feel better.

She had learned to make do with whatever came her way. When Henry came home with fish, she'd add it to what she'd already prepared or if she could keep what she made for the next night, all the better. When Mother Johnson came over to rain over her head about all that wasn't right in the world, May would make do by focusing on the chores she needed to while murmuring some soothing sounds to her mother-in-law. Whenever there wasn't enough of something, May would make do with something else.

One recent visit from Grandma Johnson put May in quite a pickle. She didn't quite know what to do about Sue's spelling word that caused such an uproar with Henry's mother. It's not that she didn't understand her mother-in-law's position, queer was a word that shouldn't be used in a fifth grader's spelling test. Yes, she knew it also meant 'odd or strange', but everyone knew what else it meant, and fifth graders shouldn't be exposed to that word. Grandma Johnson had been adamant. She went to Sue's school and challenged their right to teach that word to her granddaughter. Boy, Henry was mad. May wasn't sure who he was maddest at; the school, his mother or Sue.

Sue, on the other hand, knew whom her dad had been angriest with, her. He lit into her, shouting and cursing and red in the face. Sue was so overwhelmed; she'd wished she'd never asked her mother to help her study for her spelling test in the first place. Spelling would always be a problem for Sue from then on.

Schoolwork wasn't very important in Sue's life. She didn't give it the full focus of her attention as she did the other aspects of her life. She was doing very well at selling all kinds of things now. Some of the kids at the ice cream store were starting to ask her to get specific kinds of cigarettes and other things for them. Since Sue now knew that as long as she didn't look like she was doing anything she shouldn't, people wouldn't notice her, she had begun a kind of slight of hand stealing at Woolworth's.

Last Christmas, her mother had asked her what she wanted for a gift and she told her that what she really wanted was a poncho to keep herself warm in the winter. But what she really wanted that poncho for was so she could be standing at the checkout counter, with her mother standing right beside her, and could easily steal any number of things, like cigarettes and candy, that were on the shelf while keeping her hands unseen under her poncho. That poncho was put to lots of use, no matter what the weather. The fact that it was red, very warm and comfy too, only added to its usefulness.

It always amazed Sue how thoroughly her mother could refuse to see what was right in front of her. Not only was Sue stealing with her mother by her side, but also when Sue went clothes shopping with her mother, Sue would change the tags on the clothes so they always paid much, much less. One time when Sue's mother was at the checkout stand, paying for a coat Sue had changed the prices on; the clerk told Sue's mother that the price wasn't right. The clerk wanted to imply that Sue's mother had purposely changed the tags, but Sue's mother was so shocked, stunned and innocent, the clerk decided it had to have been an honest mistake. Sue knew it wasn't, but she also knew that the budgeted amount she was given as a limit for a new coat was not enough to buy the coat she picked out. So, once again, she had to take matters into her own hands.

Another time Sue came home wearing a brand new coat she'd stolen from the store. For once, her mother looked at her oddly and said, "Sue, where did you get that coat? I've never seen it before."

For once, Sue decided to tell the truth and with a sincere and straight face, Sue said, "I stole it, Mom."

Sue's mother turned her head with a slight smile and said, "Oh, Sue," as if Sue had told her a funny joke.

Sue really did like to steal. It was exciting. She loved the thrill when she felt that rush of fear, not knowing whether she'd get caught or not. She did get caught once with a friend stealing Popsicles at the store.

Her heart was pounding really fast, worried about what her dad would do when he found out. The store manager called Grandma Johnson's house and asked her to get Sue's mom. He then tried calling Sue's friend's mother. The friend's mother was not around, so the store manager asked May to make sure the friend's mother knew what her daughter had done. May walked the girls home, planning to go back when the friend's mother was home to let her know about the stealing. But Sue told her mother that her friend was the one who stole the Popsicles, not Sue, and that her friend's dad would beat her if he found out. May didn't want to be responsible for a beating, so that was the end of it. Sue was off the hook too.

Sue loved having all the wonderful things she stole or bought with all the money she'd earned. She bought those x-ray glasses, the spy camera, the trick gum pack, the soap that made your hands black, the fuzzy wuzzy bear soap and even the cereal that had the 45 record on the back! She stole more and more of her clothes so that she no longer wore the handmade clothes her mother made for her. She was becoming a well-dressed young lady. Her parents knew she sold the toothpicks and cards. They didn't question where she got her extra money anymore. Connie saw the things Sue had and she wanted extra money too, so she started to babysit. Sue thought babysitting was way too much work for very little money.

Connie would invite Linda to babysit with her and they would put the kids to bed and then have the place to themselves.

That school year when Sue turned twelve and Connie turned thirteen was an eventful year for them both. Both girls were changing in many ways, growing up and filling out and wanting more of life. When Sue came back to school in September, she quickly began to notice how the other girls at school seemed to be talking about her, whispering about her when they thought she wasn't looking. Finally a friend told her that all the other girls thought she stuffed her bra because her breasts were so large, while last year she'd been pretty undeveloped.

Sue was puzzled why the girls were being so secretive and so mean about this whole thing, so she decided to put a stop to the rumors if she could. One day in gym class, Sue gathered several of the girls around her and lifted up her blouse and showed them that yes, she was big, but it was all Sue. She didn't stuff anything, because she didn't need to. The funny thing about it was it didn't seem to help Sue's situation. The girls still didn't like her and talked about her, but now the rumors were implying she was a slut, especially because Sue was wearing such nice clothes and makeup.

Sue was better dressed than a lot of the other girls. She also was pretty, with a healthy white smile. She had one tooth that grew over the top of her other teeth. That actually gave her a cute smile, yet she knew someday she would have the money and wanted to fix it. Sue took great care of her teeth, brushing after every meal. She had thick, long, chestnut colored hair, parted in the middle with big brown eyes and freckles. Sue was a little over five-foot-three, weighed only one hundred pounds and was very well proportioned.

There were also rumors starting to go around about Connie, too. Somebody had seen Connie kissing Linda out in the playing field one day and so everyone was saying she was a queer now. Sue knew what that meant and she really didn't care whether Connie was one or not, but it didn't help Sue's popularity at school at all to now be called a slut with a queer for a sister.

But Sue was becoming really popular with the kids who hung out at the ice cream store. She was now taking orders for the brands of cigarettes they liked and whatever else they wanted. There were some older girls who hung out there too, and they seemed to admire Sue's abilities. One girl was named Brenda, the other Peggy, and one day they started talking to Sue about how she always got away with all this great stuff. Brenda asked, "Hey Sue, how do you get out of the store with all the different brands of cigarettes you get for everyone? How come they don't see you?"

Sue was taking cartons now when she could, right from the delivery truck.

Sue, feeling important that she was being asked about her abilities, said, "Mostly I use my poncho. It works really good to hide what my hands are doing," Sue added with a smile.

"Wow, that's cool, Sue. How do you do it with clothes?" Peggy chimed in.

"With clothes it's easy. You just wear something a little bigger when you come into the store and then in the dressing room, you put on whatever you want and then put your clothes over it. They never notice the difference," Sue said, bragging a little. "The main thing, and the fun of it is, that you look and act like normal!" Then she added, "Hey, you wanna come with me next time I do some stealing?"

Both girls quickly said yes and were excited about going shoplifting with Sue. Over the next few months, Sue, Brenda and Peggy were kept well supplied with lipstick and blue eye shadow, incense and black light posters, and all the clothes they could fit under the clothes they came in with. Though Sue was younger, both Brenda and Peggy liked hanging out with her and all of them loved the adrenalin rush of fear when they went shoplifting together. The fear seemed to be more intense when they shared it. They had a couple close calls.

The girls would meet up mostly on Thursdays at the Faith Baptist church after-school class and then spend an hour making macaroni decorated paper plates and hearing stories about Jesus. Afterwards, they'd go out to steal different things for themselves and for Sue's customers. It worked out really well for all three of them.

Connie, on the other hand, was not working well with her father, as they were getting into more and more arguments and fights. She was thirteen now and she didn't see why she had to do what he said all the time, especially because lots of the time he was wrong. Mostly, their arguments ended with a spanking from Connie's dad, but Connie was getting stronger and bigger and wasn't so hurt by the spankings anymore. She was five-foot-seven and about a hundred and forty pounds, quite busty with long, dirty blonde hair and blue eyes.

Sue would often hide in her closet while the fighting was going on. She hated hearing it or being around it. Sometimes the fights would go on for a half an hour or so, and Sue one time wished her Mr. Potato Head would become mashed potatoes so he could slip under the closet door and she could play with him while she waited for the fight to be over.

May was becoming concerned. Since she usually lived in a bit of a daze, something had to be noticeable enough for her to even see it, but she didn't like what she was seeing with Connie and Linda. It just struck her as odd behavior. Whenever Linda would come over, the two girls would go straight to the bedroom and they would stay in there for hours. May could hear the muffle of them talking, but sometimes they were very quiet too. The long silences were disturbing.

It also didn't feel right the way Connie acted whenever Linda had to leave to go home. Connie would be nearly heartbroken, like a girl would act when her boyfriend was leaving. This had May worried.

Then there was the 'incident'. One day May opened the door to tell Connie something and saw Connie and Linda, lying on the bed, very close. May quickly closed the door without saying a word, but seeing that shocked May. She really didn't know what to do about it. She dared not tell Henry, but she needed to talk to someone, so she naturally turned to Sue.

"Sue, come here for a minute." May waved Sue over to the kitchen table.

With a puzzled look on her face, Sue came over, sat down and said, "What's the matter, Mom?"

"Nothing's the matter, well, I hope nothing's the matter but I don't know quite what to do about your sister," May began to explain.

"What did Connie do?" asked Sue with a bit of complaint in her voice.

"Well, the other day, I had to ask Connie something, so I opened her door and I saw Connie and Linda lying on the bed very close together like they may have been hugging or something. I must say I was pretty shocked. I really want to talk to Connie about all this, but I don't know how to bring it up with her." May turned to look at Sue somewhat expectantly. "What do you think I ought to do?"

Of course Sue had an answer. "Well, Mom, why don't you tell Connie that you heard her talking in her sleep? Maybe she said something like, 'I love you Linda. I want to be with you,' and you heard it and you want to know what she means by that."

"Hmm, that's a good idea. I feel funny talking to her about it, but I guess I have to do it. Thanks for helping me out, Sue," said May kindly.

May did have a talk with Connie a day or so later. She was concerned about the nature of Connie's relationship with Linda and didn't think it was right. Connie was pretty defensive. She loved Linda and didn't want to give her up. May wanted her to start acting like Linda was just her friend again. Connie denied having any relationship with Linda other than just a friend, and said, "I am going to tell Dad if you accuse me of being queer again." This shocked May, and she decided not to mention it again. Connie and Linda were more careful, but knew something would have to change if they were going to be together.

Finally, summer came and school was out. There would be many changes in each of the lives of the Johnson family in the coming months, starting with the move back to the woods and Uncle Bob's property. Bob had gotten himself a newer trailer and offered Henry and his family the one Bob's family used to live in for a modest rent. Bob's old trailer was newer and bigger than the one Henry's family had lived in before. In fact, that old trailer was now the chicken coop.

Chapter Seven:
The Winds of Change

It was a hot summer day. Sue really didn't want to walk eight miles to go see her Aunt Joanie. Mom talked her into it. Aunt Joanie's husband had died a little while ago and as a consequence, Aunt Joanie had moved from Rhode Island to be closer to her family. Mom wanted to go visit her sister whenever she could. Dad didn't like Aunt Joanie. He wouldn't drive Mom the eight miles to get there, but he hadn't forbidden Mom to go, so Mom went. The only way to get there was to walk the eight miles there and back.

Mom promised that if they found any abandoned kittens or puppies along the way, she would allow Sue to get them and go to the market in Glen Aubrey, the little town where Aunt Joanie lived, and find homes for the animals. Sue would never have come if Mom hadn't promised that. It was a very long walk. It took nearly four hours to walk it each way.

At least the trailer that Aunt Joanie bought was a nice one that had air conditioning, unlike the one Sue's family lived in. Aunt Joanie would have something cool for Sue to drink, which would be welcome after this long, humid walk.

Sue and her mom walked the entire eight miles, talking sometimes or walking in companionable silence, but they didn't find any stray kittens or puppies that day. Finally, they arrived at the Glen Aubrey Trailer Park where Aunt Joanie lived. Gratefully stepping inside, Sue sat at the kitchen table and drank her Kool-Aid while she cooled off.

As she sat there, Sue couldn't help but listen to her mother and aunt talking. They seemed so happy just to see each other. Sue had never seen her mother so talkative or so outgoing. Sue's mom was happy. She was enjoying herself. She sounded comfortable and safe and was glad to have someone who wanted to hear what she had to say. Her behavior really surprised Sue, but, after a while, she got bored and wanted to do something else. While they were still talking, Sue let herself out the front door and decided to wander around the trailer park to see what it was like.

Sue was slowly walking around the park, taking her time, noticing the different trailers and all the flowers and plants each of them had. Out of the corner of her eye, she noticed a boy who seemed to be following her. He was a trailer or so behind her, but did seem to be going wherever she was going. Deciding to test it out, she turned suddenly to the right and went into a little park area, where there were benches and a picnic table.

Yup, he was following her, because less than a minute later, there he was in the park too. Sue looked at him and noticed that he was really, really cute, so she smiled. He certainly was looking at her as he continued walking, and he smiled too. As he got close enough to talk, he simply said, "Hi."

Sue said hi back.

"My name's Rob. What's yours?"

"Sue," she answered with a smile.

"Did you just move in here or are you visiting?"

"I'm visiting. My aunt just moved here. I live about eight miles away."

"Oh. I live here. Do you visit here often?"

"Well, my mom wants to come visit about once a week, and I said I would come with her," Sue replied.

"You could come visit me too," Rob said with a big smile. Then, thinking about it, he added, "Do you have a boyfriend?"

Smiling up at him herself, Sue said, "No."

With a bigger smile, Rob said, "It's my lucky day!"

Sue laughed, thinking it was hers too.

Sue and Rob naturally moved over to the picnic table and sat down.

They started talking all about themselves and their lives and their families. He told her he was fourteen, going on fifteen, two years older than Sue. He explained how he'd lost his pinky finger when he was three years old because he got it stuck behind a washing machine at the laundromat while he was looking for coins. They found the part of his finger, but they couldn't put it back. Both of them felt comfortable with the other, and it was easy for them to talk and talk.

In what was probably a couple of hours but only seemed like twenty minutes, Sue heard her mother shout for her, "Sue! Where are you?"

Shouting back, Sue said, "I'm coming, Mom!"

Turning to Rob, Sue knew she had to say goodbye, but Rob asked, "Can I come see you at your house?"

"I think so. It would have to be in the afternoon when my dad's not home, but I think it would be all right. It's a long walk, though," Sue added as a fearful afterthought.

"That's okay. I walk a lot. Would it be okay if I come over tomorrow, do you think?"

"Sure!" said Sue and then she quickly gave him the address and directions of where to meet up at a location close to her home.

Taking her hand briefly, Rob looked deeply into Sue's eyes. "I'll see you tomorrow around noon, okay?"

Smiling in a silly way, Sue said, "Okay, Rob," and then dragging herself away, she went back to her aunt's trailer.

Seeing her mother, Sue waved. As Sue came to the trailer, her mother said, "Your Aunt Joanie would like you to give her a little trim and pierce her ears, like you did for your cousin."

Sue asked, "Do you have a potato, ice, rubbing alcohol and a needle?"

"I'll get what we need and you can do it next time," Aunt Joanie said.

Sue suggested, "Don't forget to get some good sterling silver little hoop earrings too."

They gave each other one last hug. Aunt Joanie said goodbye to them both again and Sue and her mother started the long walk home.

Aunt Joanie yelled, "Soon I'll have a car and can drive you!" She was waiting for more money from her deceased husband's estate.

Sue was really happy. She really liked Rob. He was so cute! He had long brown hair and beautiful teeth. She wasn't sure whether to tell her mom or not, and decided not to for now. All the way home, Sue couldn't help smiling and smiling at nothing at all but her thoughts.

Her dad met them at the door of the trailer.

"So you went out to see that no-good sister of yours again?" he demanded.

"You didn't say I couldn't go, Henry, and she is my sister. She just lost her husband, and she doesn't really know anyone else around here except us," Mom answered apologetically.

"Well, you keep this up and you may end up in the same place she is, with no husband. Then where will you be?" argued Henry.

He turned and went into the trailer, with May and Sue trailing behind.

Supper was a quiet meal that night. Not that the family was ever very talkative, but that night, it was quieter than usual. Sue figured it was because Dad was still mad at Mom, and nobody wanted to give him a chance to direct his anger at them.

Sue didn't mind. She was lost in a daydream about Rob. Would he really come tomorrow? Wasn't he the cutest boy she'd ever seen? Sue wanted to pinch herself for being so lucky that he wanted to see her again.

That night, Sue had a hard time falling asleep. She kept thinking of Rob, and what she would do if he came tomorrow. She decided they would take a walk in the woods, away from the family and prying eyes. Sue went to sleep, dreaming about the two things she wanted most in the world that day: to see Rob again, and to have her very own monkey!

The next day, Sue was so excited. She tried to hurry through all her daily chores of making the beds, sweeping, dusting, clearing off the table and doing the dishes. Today, she had to clean out the fridge. It had been left in the trailer from before they moved in. She had to let the freezer defrost and there was an exploded bottle of homemade root beer in there that made it a mess. The yeast in the root beer made for quite an explosion.

Sue was working as fast as she could, knowing it was going to take about twenty minutes to reach the meeting place she and Rob had agreed upon. When she finally got there, he was waiting. The next couple of hours were the most wonderful in Sue's life so far. Rob asked what her favorite color was, her favorite food, he wanted to know everything about her and he was so cute to look at. Wow, this must be love!

The Johnson family now had some difference of opinion. Some of the family was happy to move back to the woods. Henry in particular was much happier. He liked having his own home where his rules were the only ones that mattered and his mother was a once-a-week visit, instead of every day.

He did go fishing after work often in the creek behind his mother's house, but he could avoid seeing her when he went down to the creek the side way. He had to drive May to and from the laundromat and the grocery store again, but he didn't mind that as much now as he had in the past. He had control again. He'd just chew on a cube of yeast to help his complexion, and read his comic books while he waited. For Henry, the move back to the woods felt like he had come home and that gave him a measure of peace.

For May, the move back was both good and bad. It was good to be away from the daily visits with her mother-in-law and good to have her own home again. May was also happier to move back because she was now closer to her sister, Joanie, who had recently moved to the nearby town of Glen Aubrey. Being able to talk with Joanie and having a friend of her own gave May such a feeling of joy that she had rarely experienced in her life. She felt as if she'd been set free from some kind of invisible chains she didn't know she'd been bound with.

The bad part was she had to always go into town with Henry and the freedom of movement she'd gotten used to having was now gone. And again, she was isolated living away from everything. There was no one around for her to talk to or even to pass the time chatting about the weather with. Living in the woods also meant more work for May to do as there were now outside chores as well as inside chores that had to be done, such as shoveling mounds of snow in the winter. The driveway to the old road was almost a half a mile long, and it had to be cleared nearly every day during the winter in order for Henry to reach the road.

Connie hated coming back to the woods. She now was completely cut off from her couple of friends unless they could somehow come out to see her or she could tag along on a visit to town with her father. Linda was older and would drive out once in a while but after the talk with her mother, Connie had to be very careful how she acted around Linda. One time, the counselor friend of Linda's mother, Ms. Kerry, drove Linda out and stayed to visit.

This situation wasn't satisfying to either Linda or Connie, but it was better than not seeing each other at all. She had broken up with Mike, which didn't bother her, as he had become a nuisance. Connie did miss the attention of boys. She always liked to be noticed. It was impossible to be noticed by anything except maybe the sheep out here in the boonies.

Then there was all the extra work Connie had to do now. She had to muck out the horses' stalls and feed them and groom them too. She had to help her dad with all the repair work and any other heavy and hard job he could think of, while Sue still got easier jobs.

Sue felt mixed about the move back to the woods. She was very happy to be back with the animals. She'd missed the sheep and the horses and having lots of dogs and cats around. Animals were always her favorite companions. Having been raised in the country, Sue loved nature and could happily take long walks among the trees for hours.

Yet, she missed the adrenalin rush of possibly getting caught when she was stealing, and she missed the money. She missed her daily hot fudge sundaes and her customers. Sue was thinking of asking her dad if she could go into town with him sometimes so she could do all of her usual moneymaking methods while he was at work. She wasn't sure whether he'd let her, but she thought she might be able to ask him without getting in trouble. She would have to think of a good reason.

Sue was also walking to Glen Aubrey one day a week with her mother. Her mother would visit with her aunt, and Sue would meet up with Rob and spend time with him. A couple of times a week, Rob would walk to her house in the woods and they would sneak off together into the forest and walk hand in hand. She really liked Rob. He seemed to really like her. She wasn't thinking about marriage just yet, but she was considering it.

One day, after about a month of knowing Rob, they were walking in the woods, talking or sharing the silence, when Rob suddenly stopped where he was and looked Sue right in the eyes. Then slowly and very carefully, he leaned down and kissed her, right on the lips. It was her first kiss, and it wasn't a very good one. He missed her lips a bit and tried to correct it, and Sue was a bit surprised so her mouth wasn't quite right. Both of them knew it hadn't worked out the way each of them had been dreaming a first kiss would be, but at least and at last, it was done. They tried again a minute or so later, and that one was much better. Sue actually loved that one!

They smiled at each other, and started walking again. They knew they'd crossed some kind of milestone in their relationship and were now boyfriend and girlfriend. It was a big moment for them. For the rest of the afternoon, they would stop their walking and give each other a quick peck on the lips, laugh a minute and then go on walking.

May was doing a lot of walking too, but she was walking to her sister Joanie's place. Both May and Joanie were excited about Joanie's newly pierced ears. Sue had put ice on her Aunt's ears and then lit a match to sterilize the needle. Sue held a potato to the back of Joanie's ear. One time, the needle got stuck and Sue had to tug a little on it to pull it back out. It did hurt, but it was worth it. Joanie's ears healed after two weeks of alcohol every day, and she could now wear earrings of her choice. Sue gave her aunt a haircut too. The older girls in town had taught Sue about the ear piercing and about giving each other haircuts.

Henry would never allow May to have her ears pierced. Being with her sister Joanie, away from home and away from Henry, seemed like a breath of freedom. The two women were able to talk about anything. One time, May brought up the topic of Cher, of Sonny and Cher, whom May was fascinated with from seeing her on television.

May had never seen a female act so bold or wear such beautiful clothes as Cher. May loved the way Cher sang, but most of all, she loved the way she talked to her husband Sonny. May was completely taken with the funny things Cher said to Sonny, always showing off how smart she was and how dumb he was. And Sonny never seemed to get mad! May was shocked that Cher got away with saying all of those things and she didn't get hit, and he didn't leave her. Every time May watched that show, she soaked in all the possibilities, the glamour, the comedy and Cher's sass.

Henry didn't like sass. In fact, his wife didn't ever sass him. The only one who did — and he certainly smacked her for it — was Connie. But something was changing inside May.

She wasn't as quiet now when they drove to town. She didn't always have her head down when she went into the market. In fact, she had her head up, like she was looking for someone or something when she went into the market. Henry stayed right there in the parking lot, so he knew she wasn't doing any hanky panky, but still, he worried.

Sue was now very happy to be living in the country again because three days a week, she would get to see her boyfriend Rob. They would always slip away into the forest and touch and kiss and make out. Sue loved it. They were talking a lot less now than they did at first, but they spent a lot more time trying to find a comfortable place to lie down so they could be close to each other.

Rob had already touched Sue's breasts on the outside of her clothing. Now he wanted to see them; he wanted her to take her clothes off and touch her all over. Sue kind of wanted to do it, but she was scared. She was still a virgin, and she knew she would only give her virginity to the man she was going to marry. She wasn't sure that man would be Rob.

One day when they'd been out walking in the woods, Connie showed up. She said, looking him up and down, "Who's your boyfriend, Sue?"

"Connie, this is my boyfriend Rob. He lives in Glen Aubrey," Sue explained.

"So that's why you keep walking to Glen Aubrey with Mom. You've really been going to see your boyfriend all this time!" Connie said, almost as an accusation.

"Yeah, that's why I've been going to Glen Aubrey, and that's why Rob walks here to see me. We're going steady," Sue added, just to make it official.

"Well, hi, Rob. It's nice to meet you. I'm Sue's *older* sister," Connie said flirtatiously.

"Hi, Connie. It's nice to meet you," Rob replied politely. He, too, gave Connie a thorough look, seeing her blonde hair, blue eyes and big breasts as well as the open invitation in her manner.

"Come on, Rob, let's go finish our walk. See you at supper!" Sue said with a flurry and turning Rob away from Connie, walked quickly away, firmly holding Rob's hand.

Connie watched them leave, but she didn't seem bothered by Sue's action. If anything, she looked thoughtful as she saw them walk away together.

If Sue felt insecure about Rob, it didn't show. In fact, the next day she saw a special science program on television that demonstrated how a person could give themselves a tattoo in their own home. All you had to do was wrap thread around the end of a needle, leaving the sharp tip exposed, soak it in India ink and then prick your skin in the design that you wanted. It sounded so easy, Sue decided to try it.

Getting all the necessary parts together, Sue wrapped the needle with thread, soaked it in ink and then began to prick out the letters R, O, B on the inside of her calf. It was a bit painful, but not too bad. The pricks didn't really make a line but stayed more like dots. When it was done, it didn't look that great, but it spelled ROB. Sue decided to wash it off, so she went into the bathroom and ran water over it. It didn't come off, not even a little bit! Now Sue had a permanent tattoo on her leg, and what was she going to tell her dad or her mom if they ever saw it? Terrified, Sue found one of those tiny rectangular Band-Aids in the medicine cabinet and carefully placed it over the tattoo. *Whew! It covered it!* thought Sue. From then on, Sue would steal those tiny rectangular Band-Aids from just about every house she was ever in so she would always have a supply to cover her tattoo.

Summer was passing far too quickly for Sue. She spent time enjoying the horses, sheep, dogs, cats and any stray animal she could find. She rode one of the horses several times a week. Her father had insisted that she never let anyone else ride one of their horses because, if anything happened, they could be sued, so Sue never did. Except just once when a girl Sue wanted as a friend asked if she could.

Sue saddled the horse and boosted her up into the saddle and the horse and rider trotted down the road a bit. Until the saddle slid and Sue's friend fell off! Sue had forgotten to wait for the horse to release its breath before synching the saddle, so it was too loose, causing the saddle to slide. Sue rushed to the girl to see if she was all right. Fortunately, she was, as they hadn't been going very fast or very far, but Sue was terrified that her friend's parents would soon come knocking at her door and tell her father they were going to be sued. Sue waited for several weeks before she could fully relax that they weren't going to sue her family about the fall.

Maybe it was because Connie was bored or maybe she had other ideas in mind, but several times now when Sue and Rob were out walking, Connie would suddenly appear. She didn't stay long, but she always seemed to be talking more to Rob than Sue. He seemed to stare at Connie a little longer than Sue liked.

Rob was starting to pressure Sue to have sex with him. He really wanted to go all the way with her. She really didn't want to go all the way until she was older and ready for marriage. She was scared of getting pregnant. More and more, there was tension on their walks together in the woods rather than talking and having fun together as they used to.

Soon school would be starting, and Sue was now in another district. Once again, she would be the new girl in school, which she hated in the past. Now she was going into the ninth grade, and would finally be in high school. The past years in town had changed her for the better. She was sure high school would be much different than the lower grades, even if she didn't get to go to dances or any of the fun things high school kids got to do, because it was against their religion. Sue began to concentrate on shoplifting more stylish clothes for her entrance into her new school when she made it to town.

Connie was looking forward to going back to school too. She wanted to be around people her own age and to get away from the backwoods and finally have some kind of a social life. She was so bored here in the country!

A week before school started, Sue had had enough. She told Rob she wasn't going to go all the way with him. She was tired of him pressuring her, and she'd made up her mind about waiting until she was older. He just didn't want to take no for an answer. Rob was a bit angry and frustrated with Sue, especially after having walked eight miles just to see her, but he finally stomped off to go back home.

What Sue didn't know was that Connie had seen the fight happen and followed Rob until he was far enough away that she wouldn't be able to hear. Connie approached Rob, and though she could see his irritation, she wanted him. He was a really a cute boy, cuter than the boys she could get, and he'd been Sue's boyfriend, so she really wanted him.

"I couldn't help but overhear what Sue said to you back there. I'm sorry she's such a prissy girl. Why, if you were my boyfriend, I would do anything to make you happy," Connie said invitingly.

Rob, who had been irritated at first because of Sue and now being bothered by her sister, listened to what Connie said with surprise.

"Oh yeah? You'd do *anything* to make me happy?" Rob asked.

"Sure, I'd do anything for you, Rob. Just ask me," cajoled Connie, leaning into him.

"You'll go all the way with me? Now? Or are you just teasing me because you want to make your sister jealous?" Rob taunted.

"No, I'm not teasing. I'll do it with you. Right now, if you want to," Connie pleaded. She was sick and tired of her life, of not having anybody want her and being a virgin didn't matter to her anymore. It had to go sometime, why not now?

"Okay then, let's go to this quiet place Sue and I found and do it." Rob grabbed Connie's arm and led her away.

It was the first time for both of them, and it wasn't a good experience for either. Having sex in the woods was awkward and uncomfortable. Neither wanted to take all of their clothes off, so they only took off as much as they had to. Rob got excited seeing Connie's breasts and was far too ready, far too soon. He entered Connie without much preparation, so it was painful and difficult for her.

Fortunately for her, it was over quite soon. Unfortunately for him, it was over quite soon, leaving Rob feeling barely satisfied physically and almost disgusted emotionally. He felt as if he'd wasted his first time, which could have been so special, leaving him with a feeling of being dirty with shame. He couldn't wait to get out of there and away from Connie.

As they were hurriedly dressing, Connie, though still physically uncomfortable, couldn't help but ask, "Rob, when are we going to see each other again? Do you want to come over tomorrow?"

"No, uh, I can't. I've got work I have to do," Rob said.

"But, Rob, when are you going to see me again?" insisted Connie.

"Listen, Connie, I don't know when I can get back here again," said Rob harshly.

"Well, maybe I can walk to your place. How about I come over day after tomorrow?"

Finally, Rob, who just wanted to run away from the whole experience as fast as he could, nearly shouted at Connie, "You just don't get it, do you? I'm never coming over. I got what I wanted and I don't want to see you or your sister ever again!"

Rob, finally dressed, nearly ran from the forest.

Connie, hurt, alone, abandoned and betrayed, turned her face into her hands and cried.

Chapter Eight:
Freedom

Mom and Sue were walking to Aunt Joanie's house again. It wasn't so bad these days, as Aunt Joanie now had a car and could at least drive the two of them home. It was an Indian summer, still warm in late September. School had started earlier that month, and Sue was glad to be back in school and to finally be a freshman. With all her great clothes, she had hoped the kids would be amazed by her transformation and treat her better than before, but they seemed to not even remember her. *Oh well,* she thought, *that may work out better.*

As Sue and her mother walked, they talked about all the changes that Aunt Joanie had gone through this past year, from her move to upstate New York, her new hairstyle and whole new look, and to actually be going out on the town and meeting men! Sue, full of pride, took credit for doing such a good job with Aunt Joanie's hair and ear piercing, but the changes were more than that. Aunt Joanie was no longer the grieving, fearful widow, but had bought herself some new clothes and a new car and was dating. Sue's mother couldn't wait to hear all about Aunt Joanie's new adventures, her dancing dates and all the excitement of her sister's new life.

Sue was interested in dating too. She'd been checking out all the guys at her new school to see who was popular and what girls were interested in which ones. She'd been interested in one or two herself, but hadn't decided. The principal had told her mother that Sue was one of the nicest dressed girls at the school, so Sue was pretty sure she could get any guy she wanted. Sue had really racked up quite a wardrobe stealing on her visits to town. She had told her father she was selling stuff in town to pay for school clothes and would even get Connie a couple items. Her dad had taken her into town with him a few times over the summer vacation.

As Sue was thinking about boys, and she and her mother had just been talking about Aunt Joanie's dates, Sue wondered about her mother's youth. Looking at her mother in a puzzled way, she asked, "Mom, were you popular in school? Did you date a lot of guys before you married Dad?"

"Oh my, Sue! What a question! As a matter of fact, no, I didn't date a lot of guys. I didn't date anyone at all. Your dad was the first guy to ask me out and I married him a week after we met!" said Mom, with a bit of embarrassment.

"But Mom, you're so pretty! Why didn't you have lots of boys after you?" asked a surprised Sue.

"Well, I guess it was because we were so poor and I had nothing nice to wear. And I'm not pretty, Sue, you just think so because I'm your mom," she said softly.

"But Mom, you could get nice clothes and fix yourself up and you'd be really pretty. I'll bet if you did, you'd have tons of guys after you! You're much prettier than Aunt Joanie, and she has lots of guys after her," protested Sue.

"Now, I don't know about that, but it doesn't matter anyway because I'm a married woman, and I don't want anybody chasing after me," her mother replied rather primly.

"I know you're married to Dad, but you don't have to be, Mom. Dad is mean to all of us. He's never nice and he always blames you for everything. He won't let you do anything or go anywhere. He treats you just like a slave. I've thought about this a lot, Mom, and I think I'm old enough to get a job and I could help take care of us. Don't laugh! I could! I've been making lots of money on my own and I could make lots more if I needed to. Just think about it, okay?" pleaded Sue earnestly.

Her mother didn't say anything but gave Sue a speculative look, as if assessing whether Sue could actually be the main breadwinner in the family. Then she turned away, and they continued the walk in silence.

As they walked up to Aunt Joanie's trailer, they found Rob sitting on Aunt Joanie's steps. Sue was surprised to see him, but told her mother she would only be a minute, as she had to talk to him, and her Mom went on in without her.

"What do you want, Rob?" She remembered all the cruel taunts her sister had been giving her for the past few weeks. Connie would smile snidely and ask, "When is Rob coming back to see you?" That had told Sue all she needed to know about Rob...and Connie.

"I want to see you. I miss you. I miss seeing you, being with you," Rob said with his head somewhat bent down as if he couldn't quite look her in the eyes.

"Well, I don't miss you. I told you we were through and I meant it," she stated very clearly.

"But Sue," Rob looked at her pleadingly, "we were special! We had something important between us."

"I liked you, Rob, I did, but not anymore. So please don't bother me anymore when I'm visiting my aunt. I have to go in now before my mother wonders about me. Goodbye," Sue said with finality, turned away and went into the trailer.

Rob sadly got up and walked slowly home and out of Sue's life.

When Sue got inside the trailer, there was a man she'd never met before waiting in the living room.

"Oh, Sue! I'd like you to meet my new boyfriend Eugene. Eugene, this is my niece, Sue," exclaimed Aunt Joanie.

"How do you do, Sue?" Eugene asked kindly.

"I'm fine. Nice to meet you, Eugene," replied Sue.

Sue got a good look at Eugene and wasn't particularly impressed. He seemed like a nice man with a kindly, though homely face. He was on the chubby side and wore false teeth. Sue could always tell when someone didn't have their own teeth. He looked old to Sue, definitely older than her aunt and mother, but all in all, a nice man.

Sue got herself a glass of Kool-Aid from the fridge and sat down to listen to the adults talking. Apparently, Eugene had taken Aunt Joanie out drinking and dancing at a bar that had live Country and Western music, and they'd had a great time. Sue watched her mother's face light up at the talk about dancing and a live band. Sue knew her mother loved music.

Then Eugene suggested that the two couples, Aunt Joanie and Eugene and Dad and Mom, meet up and all go out for drinks and dancing one night. He seemed to think that was a really good idea, but Sue could see that her mother knew she'd never go out dancing with Dad anywhere. Dad didn't dance and Dad didn't go out, and he thought only sinners did. So that meant Mom would never be able to, either. Sue felt sorry for her mother.

Eugene then said he had to go to work. He leaned down and gave Aunt Joanie a quick kiss, said what a pleasure it was to meet the lovely May and her daughter Sue, and left.

As soon as he was gone, Aunt Joanie and Mom started to practically jabber at each other. The two of them couldn't stop talking about Eugene and what a nice man he was, how he'd taken Aunt Joanie to such nice places and how lucky she was to have caught him. Aunt Joanie was saying that Eugene was a hard worker and had his own home. It still surprised Sue how animated her mother could get when she talked with her sister. Mom was never like that at home.

Finally, it was time to leave, and all three of them left the trailer and got into the car. The drive back was so much shorter than the long walk to get there that the two women barely had time to finish what they'd been saying about the wonderful Eugene, who was the manager of the Giant Market, had worked there for twenty years and even had a retirement fund. What a catch!

Arriving home, both Sue and her mother jumped out of the car and barely said goodbye so that Aunt Joanie could leave before Dad saw her. Dad was always mad whenever he saw Aunt Joanie, so they just tried to avoid making trouble if they could.

Connie saw them when she came out of the shed after mucking out the stalls. She had a mad look on her face, but Sue didn't care. Connie was always mad these days. She liked being back in school and Sue knew she'd been seeing her friend Linda again. Connie didn't seem to care who knew she was seeing Linda, almost as if she wanted to pick a fight. All Sue knew was it was better to stay away from Connie, because she was just impossible to be around.

Mom got supper on the table and everyone ate without saying much. After supper, the family went in to watch television together. It was a Sonny and Cher night, and Mom was glued to the TV.

Sue remembered being at the pastor's daughter's house a few years back and seeing a show called *Bewitched*. Sue was mesmerized by Darrin Stevens, Samantha's husband, and wanted to do what he did when she grew up. Sue thought of all kinds of ways to sell the product Darrin had been given to come up with a marketing plan for. Now that was a show Sue could watch every day!

After chores and the Saturday night bath, Sue turned in to her own bedroom to sleep. She often had a hard time going to sleep at first. She worried about whether they'd have enough money to buy food for next week. She worried about how unhappy her mother was. She worried about having a nightmare again. She didn't worry about her sister Connie, but she did worry about some of her animals. Finally, Sue fell asleep.

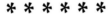

The police car drove up the driveway and parked in front of the trailer. Connie, Ms. Kerry, Linda's counselor friend, and a policeman all got out of the car. May came out of the trailer and hollered for Henry who was in the shed. Henry came around the trailer to find everyone in his front yard area and had no idea what was going on.

Ms. Kerry turned to Connie and told her to go into the house and get her things. Connie looked at Ms. Kerry, asking with her eyes if she was safe to go, and Ms. Kerry nodded her head. As Connie walked into the trailer, Ms. Kerry, with the police officer slightly behind her, approached Henry and

May.

"Hello, Mr. and Mrs. Johnson. I don't know whether you remember me, but my name is Ms. Kerry, and I am a school counselor. I have been aware of the abusive living environment Connie is in for a while now. I contacted Child Protection Services and we have agreed that Connie needs to be removed from your home for her protection. I have arranged for her to stay with a nice foster care family where she will be safe and can attend the same school. Please do not hinder us in any way, or this officer will have to stop you." All of this was said very officially and with complete authority.

Both May and Henry were too shocked to do anything, even if they knew what to do. They certainly were law-abiding citizens and it wouldn't have crossed their minds to question or resist in any way with a police officer.

They quietly stood and watched as their daughter came back out with some bags of belongings and barely looking at them, got into the police car.

Ms. Kerry turned to the Johnsons and said, "Thank you for your cooperation. I will let the Child Protective Services know that the removal went well." Ms. Kerry turned and got into the police car with Connie. The policeman also got in and drove the three of them away.

Connie was gone.

No one knew what to do or say. May, crying quietly, walked back into the kitchen, her only sanctuary. Henry was shocked, angry and somewhat frightened by the whole thing. He never dreamed that anyone could come into his home and take what was his away from him and there was nothing he could do about it. Not knowing what else to do, Henry went back into the shed.

Sue was stunned. She never thought something like this could happen, or that Connie would ever do such a thing. She knew Connie had been unhappy, but Connie was always unhappy. She couldn't imagine what had caused Connie to go to the counselor and tell them what she told them. Truthfully, she felt a little guilty because she had wished her sister gone so many times.

Sue didn't know what this would mean to her family and home life. It was unsettling and reveling to witness how powerless her parents really were. Sue had thought it was God and then her parents that were ultimately in charge. Now she knew better.

Who was going to do all of Connie's chores? What would the kids at school think? These were the thoughts that ran through Sue's mind. It was a major shakeup in her family.

Sue went to get a couple of the new puppies she had found in the field and took them into her room. This time, no one said anything to her about it.

Though Connie and Sue went to the same school, they weren't in the same grade so they didn't see each other much. The next day, school seemed to be pretty much the same for Sue, though she did hear rumors.

Finally, a girl whose older sister knew Connie took Sue aside and told her what had happened. "Your sister Connie is in love with her friend Linda, a girl. Linda's counselor friend, Ms. Kerry, is also queer. Ms. Kerry knew of a foster family that lived near Linda and who would look the other way about Connie and Linda's relationship. So between the three of them, they cooked up this scheme for Connie to be taken out of your home and put in foster care so the two girls could continue seeing each other without being bothered." The girl smirked, turned and walked away.

Sue was both surprised and not surprised. She knew Connie was pretty cowardly about the way she did things, and she knew Connie liked girls as well as boys. Sue was surprised that Connie had gotten away with it, but truthfully, Sue didn't really care. They had never been close as sisters; in fact, they were more like enemies than friends. Sue thought things might be better for her at home now, because her dad would be afraid they would take her away too. Sue didn't miss her sister.

Oddly enough, no one at home talked about Connie or what had happened. Henry and May and even Sue all acted as if nothing had happened. Life went on, though each family member felt more isolated than before. They each lived in their own separate worlds and only crossed paths at meals. Everything seemed to have calmed down, but it was weird. It was as if they had to learn how to operate all over again because of a missing part.

It couldn't have been more than a month later, when Sue came home late from school because she had stayed after and had taken a later bus. She found her mother pacing, white as a sheet, on the front steps with a look on her face that Sue had never seen before. With a shaky voice, May said, "Sue, I want you to go in the house and pack up as much as you can fit in one drawer. You can't take any more than that; we don't have room or time for it, so only bring what clothes you need and your necessities. Joanie will be here in a minute or two and we've got to go. Just get in the house and pack, Sue."

Sue had never heard her mother speak to her so strongly before so she didn't ask any questions, just went into the house to pack.

Looking around her room, Sue saw all of her trophies and ribbons and certificates of success that she'd won at school. Then she looked at all her clothes and knew that one drawer-full wasn't going to be very much for her to get by on. With sadness and loss, Sue began to pack as many clothes and toiletries as she could fit in the one drawer she was allowed, hoping in the back of her mind, she would be able to get the rest later.

When she was finished, she carried the full drawer to the front steps. Her aunt was already there with the car. Her dad was nowhere in sight. May had already put her things in the car and taking Sue's things from her, put them in the open trunk and closed it. Quickly all three got in the car. Joanie started it up, and they drove away.

On the drive to her home, Joanie began questioning May. "What happened, May? What did he do?"

May gave a quick look st Sue in the back seat and then looked at Joanie, as if to say she couldn't say all she'd like to say with Sue within earshot, but replied, "I saw him as I walked into the shed. I'd only gone there to tell him supper would be ready soon and I knew he was feeding the horses. I couldn't believe it at first, but then when I saw what he was doing," and at that point, May deliberately stopped and raised her eyebrows at Joanie. "Henry said 'It's not what you think' and got in his truck and took off. I didn't know what else to do or where to go, so I went to Bob's and called you. I'm so glad you were home!"

"Me too! Oh, May! What are you going to do? Are you going to divorce him?"

"Well, I guess I'll have to. I mean, I can't stay with him. I just can't!" said May, bursting into tears. "I'm so glad we got out of there fast, before he came back because I just can't face him right now."

"Don't worry, May, it'll be all right. We'll figure out what to do and you and Sue can stay with me as long as you need to. Don't worry. We've got each other now," Joanie consoled her sister with what words she could.

Sue sat in the back, stunned. She didn't really understand what had happened in the shed that so upset her mother, but she wasn't unhappy with the outcome. She wasn't sorry to leave her dad, but she was sorry to leave her things. She had to leave behind all the many prizes she had won in contests and at the Fair, her blankets and all her animals. She knew her dad would never miss a day of work, no matter what, and she thought she could come back for the kittens and puppies while he was away. The house would be locked, but the baby animals were in the shed, which was always open.

She did feel some guilt, because she had wished that her mom would leave her dad so it would be just the two of them. She also began to worry if she would really be able to take care of the both of them, as she had told her mother she would. Was it really best for her mom to not have her dad? She knew her mother, knew that she was a submissive person who needed someone to take care of her. Sue would have to be the one to take care of both of them from now on. The reality of this situation was invigorating and frightening too. Finally, Sue decided that it was all going to be for the best and felt an inner strength and a peaceful sense that all was well.

They arrived at Joanie's trailer and carried their things into the bedroom May and Sue would share. Joanie had made one of her sons give up his room and move in with his brother. Setting their things down, Joanie took May with her into the kitchen while she made supper for the larger family that was now joined together. While she cooked, the two women talked.

Joanie, who had had more experience with legalities and government agencies, began to explain to May what she needed to do and how she could get the government to help her. May hadn't known about any of this, so she listened intently to what her sister had to say.

"I think first of all, you're going to have to file for divorce. You might be able to get alimony or something from Henry, and child support too. We can go down to the courthouse and get all the information we need tomorrow. Then we need to go to the welfare office and find out what they can do to help you find a place to live and maybe even a job...and food stamps, of course."

May listened to Joanie with a deer-in-the- headlights look on her face. When Joanie saw it, she rushed in to say, "Oh! I'll help you! We'll go together. It won't be as hard as it sounds now, we'll figure it out. Don't worry, May! You're here with me, safe and sound, and one way or another we'll find a way for everything to be okay, don't worry!"

May was a bit shell-shocked from all the events of this day. She had left her husband of over sixteen years. She had no place to live, no money, she couldn't drive, she had never had a job and she didn't know how to do or get any of those things, and somehow, she was going to have to do all of them. It was an overwhelming moment for May, but with tears in her eyes, she looked at her sister Joanie and hoped with all her might that what Joanie said was true. Hoped that she would be able to find a way for everything to be okay. She just didn't know how she could do it in that moment.

The next day, Joanie drove May and Sue to the local high school and enrolled Sue in school. This was now the second school Sue had been in this school year. Sue hated being the new girl. She didn't know anyone, except Rob, and he didn't count.

Joanie and May left Sue at her new school and went into town to begin the process of filing for divorce and getting government assistance for all the things May would need to start her new life. The two women felt stronger being together, as if the pair of them could do anything together, but apart, each of them were helpless. Their sisterly bond became a tangible energy between them.

Henry drove up four days later. The two sisters came out of the trailer to talk to him before he could even come up the steps to knock. Henry's face was clouded over with anger. "All right, May, enough's enough. You and Sue are coming home with me right this minute, so go get your things. And as for you, Joanie, I've had enough of your meddling. This is between me and May, so you just stay out of it!"

"She's not going back with you, Henry. She's filing for divorce. So you just get on out of here and leave us alone," Joanie said, standing her ground. It was easier for her to do it than her sister.

"Divorce! You're not getting a divorce! I won't let you! You are my wife and I am telling you right now to get Sue and get in the truck!" Henry shouted.

"No, Henry. They are not getting in the truck. You have gone too far this time, and it's over. We never want to see you again!" Joanie said firmly.

For a few moments, the spouses stared at each other as those words hung in the air. May's stare didn't waver. She didn't look down; she didn't try to get Henry's approval, she just stared at him. Henry tried to stare her down. He tried to force his will upon her as he always had done successfully before, but this time, even he could see she wasn't backing down. Finally, with a great huff, Henry turned away and stomped back to the truck, yelling, "I'm burning all of your stuff that you left behind!" slamming the truck door as he got in, he drove off in a flurry of gravel.

May and Joanie turned and hugged each other, comforting themselves for facing him down and surviving. Both knew it was a close call. Henry could have gotten violent, and what could two women do against him? But they both knew they would have fought back to protect each other, and in the end, they would have won. Some part of Henry must have known that too, which is why he backed down and left.

Sue's heart sank. She had been so sure she would get the things she left behind at some point, and now she knew she would never see her bookworm, her stuffed tiger, or her bible covered with white leather that zipped up and had her full name, Sue Anne Johnson, in gold letters on the front. It was given to her when she was baptized. And what about all her clothes?

In the next two weeks, Henry would come four or five more times to try to make May come back with him, but each time the two women faced him down and he left.

He didn't try again. He ended up moving back to his mother's and living in a bedroom in her house. He had given everything away, even his TV. Greatly depressed, he refused to watch television because the family shows reminded him of all he'd lost and he couldn't bear seeing it. He didn't want anything that reminded him of them. He was a broken man.

His mother, Grandma Johnson, wasn't sure what to think. Yes, she didn't like May or Sue, but this was an embarrassment to her. Her son's whole family had left him. Henry was a deacon in her church, and it is a well-known rule that divorced people can't serve in the church, so everyone that mattered to her would know of Henry's fall from grace.

May, on the other hand, was starting a whole new life. She and Joanie began going out together to all the bars and dancing places they could find. May loved to dance and move around to the live bands' music. It gave her the chills. It was invigorating. May was attractive and with a little mascara, blush and lipgloss, she was pretty. May was five-foot-three and had lost some weight with all the stress of leaving Henry. She was down to a hundred and thirty-five pounds and felt great.

May wasn't much of a drinker. She'd only had alcohol in small amounts very rarely in her life, so half of one drink was more than enough to loosen her up. Her neck would turn bright red whenever she drank; an allergic reaction, she said. Having never experienced dating or being admired as a young woman, May was thoroughly enjoying all the attention she was getting now.

The dating scene had changed dramatically since she was a young girl. When May was a teenager, a boy would come pick the girl up at her home and meet her parents first. He would take her to supper and a walk and wouldn't assume he was even going to get a kiss goodnight for his time and trouble. Now, people went out to bars and picked someone up and took them home. They barely knew each other's names!

May was not going home with anyone yet, but she was following Cher's example of being her own person. She felt like she was living the life of a free single woman, and she loved it. She had her eye on a couple of guys that were at the local Country Western bar she and Joanie liked. Sometimes Eugene would meet them there too.

Sue wanted to have fun too. One night, some friends invited her to a party, and since Sue's mother and aunt were going out, Sue felt free to go out herself. Arriving at the party, there were lots of kids there with loud rock and roll music playing; Jimi Hendrix, Steppenwolf, Janis Joplin, and lots of people were dancing.

Sue found a friend to hang out with, and that friend took her to the kitchen and gave her a glass of wine from some bottles they'd stolen from the parent's basement. Sue had never tasted wine before and she didn't like it, but almost within seconds of taking a drink, she began to feel the effects of it. She felt it burn a bit as it went down, and probably because she had an empty stomach, she instantly felt a warm sensation all through her body.

The feeling was comforting and freeing in a sense. It was fantastic. She drank more of the horrible tasting wine because she loved the effect it was having on her. She didn't feel guilty. She didn't feel ashamed. She didn't feel badly about herself at all. In fact, she felt great about herself. She could now see how funny she was, how pretty she was, how smart she was and how everybody liked her. It was incredible!

Sue kept drinking and drinking, figuring more has to make you feel even better, until finally, she was sick. The room was spinning and it was like the worst motion sickness she had ever had, but while the great feeling had lasted, Sue thought it was one of the most wonderful she'd ever had.

The next day she was still puking her guts out, had a terrible headache and was sweating like crazy. She felt like she had been poisoned. Thank goodness it was Saturday! Sue swore to herself that she'd never drink alcohol again...or maybe just not that much.

May and Joanie had filled out so many forms and talked to so many people in the government that May had finally memorized her social security number. Thankfully, their hard work was now paying off. May was approved for a housing supplemental program and a job-training program called ManPower. Getting the assistance they needed was fast tracked because Connie had been removed from the home for abuse, which had been documented.

They had found her an apartment in Johnson City and May and Sue were going to move out of Joanie's place and into their own. It was exciting and scary all at the same time. The move wasn't too difficult, as they didn't own very much stuff. Joanie helped a great deal and gave May many of her own household items so that Sue and May could at least set the table and make the beds. It was a small apartment, but it did have two bedrooms and best of all, it was their own.

Sue enrolled into another high school, making it three schools she'd been in for only one semester. Sue hated being the new girl in school again, but she was becoming a bit resigned to it. Sue had learned to step back and watch what other people were doing and see who was popular and who wasn't before she made any motions to make new friends. She was used to the guys checking her out and the girls being jealous. Drinking and stealing alcohol was a great way to fit in.

May was working at a sandwich-making factory. The sandwiches were sold in vending machines in cafeterias. She had gotten the job through ManPower, and it seemed like a good fit for a woman who had only been a housewife all her life. Unfortunately, May couldn't seem to get the hang of making the sandwiches fast enough and would hold up the line of sandwiches going into the wrapper, so after a couple of months they fired her. She was discouraged and embarrassed that she couldn't do the job right, but fortunately, the government agency put her in a training program with an upholstery factory to hopefully train her for full time employment. She was doing her best.

She was also going out every chance she could with different men. May was really enjoying being a desirable woman and the attention of desiring men. She loved to dance so most of the time, she would either go with a friend from work to a dancing place with live music or encourage her date to take her dancing. She just couldn't get enough of it after years of being cooped up in her stifling life.

Her sister Joanie was spending more time with Eugene; she still had children at home and was looking for more stability. Her dates with Eugene often included taking the children for a picnic and swim at Green Lake, instead of drinking and dancing as they had been at first.

Sue was slowly making friends and trying to catch up on the classes she gotten dropped into. It wasn't easy, but she was managing. One odd thing came out of all of the moving and changing. Sue's grandmother started writing her. Sue was surprised at first, because Grandma Johnson usually didn't want to have anything to do with her, but apparently, once Sue was out of her sight and any hope of her control, Grandma Johnson seemed to let go of her anger at Sue. Or was she just making sure she knew what was going on so she could continue to stir the pot? For whatever reason, Sue got letters from her grandmother nearly every week.

While May was training to be an upholstery worker, she met a man named Kip. Kip was really fun and really good-looking. He was in town visiting his brother. Kip and May seemed to be in love, as they went out almost every night and Kip started staying over some nights as well. Sue was grossed out, knowing her mother had sex with him. In the morning, May would cook him pancakes, and forever after, Sue hated the smell of pancakes and syrup. May said Kip was just such a fun and nice guy that it all made sense for all of them to move to North Carolina where he lived.

Kip worked on the military base named Camp Lejeune in North Carolina. After the long drive down, they all arrived at his apartment on base and combined the two families. Kip had a young teenage son, who loved bologna and catsup sandwiches and taking Sue's underwear out of her drawers. Sue didn't tell anyone about it, but found her undies in his room more than once.

They enrolled Sue in another school, making it now four schools she'd been in for the ninth grade. Sue thought it was so cool, because it was the first time she'd ever been in a school that had outside corridors. In New York, all the schools were enclosed buildings because of the cold and wet weather, and she hated being inside all day while at school. Now with the warmer weather, her new school had trailers and walkways that were outside, so going to and from class, Sue got to walk in the sunshine. She loved it, and it seemed very social. She made a new friend on her first day. The whole feeling of going to school was different.

Kip had this idea that May would stay at home and take care of the house and kids while he worked. He also seemed to think that he could go out on the town and out to bars every night like he was used to, but without May. Far too quickly it became obvious to all that this relationship wasn't going to work.

Two weeks after they'd moved to North Carolina, Kip was driving May and Sue back to upstate New York. It was a horrible drive back. Kip was done and wished he didn't have to see them again, let alone, drive with them for two days. May was feeling hurt and depressed and wished she could just get home. Sue was unhappy with both of them and with going back to her old life, her old school and now having to explain her nearly three week long absence.

Of course, the car broke down. Four people trapped in a car together who all want nothing better than to be away from each other, and the car broke down. It took most of one day to get it fixed, so instead of a horrible two-day trip, it became an even worse three-day trip. All four couldn't wait to get out of that car and home at last.

It seemed as if this event set the stage for things to go downhill from there. May began to feel insecure about herself again. She hadn't kept the sandwich-making job, and she couldn't keep Kip. Maybe she wasn't good enough. May was plagued with doubts about all aspects of herself. Luckily, her sister Joanie had convinced her to not let go of her apartment or ManPower before running off with Kip.

May was having a hard time at the upholstery factory when she returned. She tried to do what they said, but it didn't seem to work right for her most of the time. They kept saying that she was in training and she'd get the hang of it as she did it more, but she wasn't sure.

She wasn't sure about whether she was pretty enough anymore. She'd go out to the bars and it seemed to her that she wasn't being asked to dance as much as she was at first. One man she met wasn't as good-looking as she was used to, he had a bad complexion and seemed a bit rough around the edges, but she took him home anyway. He was an amazing artist, yet very eccentric in his ways. His name was Herb.

Sue didn't like Herb at all; he gave her the creeps. She was getting worried. She had hoped to be able to influence her mother's decisions, but that didn't seem to be happening. Men still had the power over her mom. When Herb finally left, Sue was very happy to see the last of him, or so she thought.

May was fired from the upholstery factory. Having the job was part of the ManPower's requirements, and someone had told them that May had gone to North Carolina while still collecting assistance. May had told the people where she worked that she was taking a medical leave, a suggestion her sister Joanie had come up with in case things did not work out with Kip. Joanie hadn't wanted May to lose what she had. It was against the rules to leave the state when you were living in a housing project and to keep the place too. Unfortunately, the government kicked May and Sue out of the housing project. Who had told the government about May leaving?

May was terrified. She didn't know where they were going to sleep that night. The terror must have shown on her face, as a kindly older woman approached her while she was still at the housing agency. Gently tapping her on the arm, she said, "Excuse me, but are you all right? I don't mean to pry, but you look very upset."

"Um, yes, I guess I'm all right. I just, ah, I don't know where my daughter and I are going to sleep tonight because we've been thrown out of our apartment," came May's shaky answer.

"Oh goodness! That's terrible! You poor dear! Come over here and sit and let's put our heads together and think about this. By the way, my name is Rhonda, what's yours?"

"My name is May, and this is my daughter Sue," May managed to say as Rhonda led her over to some chairs against the wall. Sue thought Rhonda seemed very genuine. However, she wasn't sure what to do in this situation as, up until now, they'd always at least had a place to stay.

The two women sat and talked for over an hour very intently. Rhonda could see that May was a sweet woman who didn't know how to take care of herself very well and having once been such a woman herself, her heart went out to May. May was grateful to be able to talk to an older, wiser woman who seemed to care about her and who wanted to help her. Oddly enough, it was decided between the two of them that May and Sue would come home with Rhonda and stay with her until May could get back on her feet.

Once the decision was made, Rhonda gathered the two younger women as a hen would her chicks and took them home with her. They were allowed to go back to the apartment the next day and get their things. May had thought about calling her sister, but Eugene was at her home most of the time, and she couldn't keep burdening Joanie by disrupting her life again.

May and Sue shared a small bedroom in Rhonda's house while May tried to figure out what to do with her life. Sue was enrolled again into a new school, making it five schools for ninth grade.

Living with Rhonda wasn't bad. She was a kind, large Italian woman and meant well, but for Sue, she just didn't know Rhonda and never felt fully comfortable around her. May was grateful for Rhonda's kindness and assistance, but didn't really know how to live in someone else's house that wasn't family, so it was uncomfortable for her too. However, Sue could eat Rhonda's wonderful cooking, especially her spaghetti, forever.

One thing about Sue, she had a strong conscience. While staying with Rhonda, she had some pot in her purse and was fearful of getting caught with it. As usual, she had a backup lie ready if she needed one; she'd tell them she was only holding it for someone else. However, her conscience was eating away at her so much that she just had to tell on herself. She broke down and told her mother and Rhonda that she had pot in her purse. The two older women didn't really know what to say or do about her confession other than to say she shouldn't smoke it and to flush it down the toilet.

Usually after supper, Sue would go off to her bedroom until her mother went to sleep, and then she would go out to visit her new drinking friends. Sue was still good at stealing and always had alcohol, which made her instantly popular, and she knew it.

It felt so good for all the bad things to just go away, which they did every time she drank. And when she overdid it, she would swear she'd never drink again, until, of course, the next time. Drinking made Sue feel free of all the worries, the doubts, the shame, the guilt, and all the not-good-enough things she felt about herself. Instead, she felt so beautiful, so special and so irresistible that it was nearly impossible for her to give up those feelings, and therefore, alcohol was like her best friend.

Finally, May was able to get subsidized housing again and food stamps, though not as much assistance money as before, so she would have to make do. May had tried to get alimony or help from Henry, but he said he would make her life a living hell if she tried to get his money after leaving him. The state did go after him for child support, though.

The Government housing apartments had a yearlong waiting list. After much searching to find a place they could afford, May moved Sue into a tiny apartment that was in the basement of a house. It was only one room with a bed in one corner, a tiny bathroom with a small shower, a sink, a toaster oven and an ice chest for cold food, but worst of all, the floor was dirt. The basement had never been finished. Sue was ashamed. This was living really low as far as she was concerned, lower than Sue ever wanted to go, and she didn't know what to do about it. This was the best May could do. While living there, Sue never felt clean; there was dust on everything, always, no matter how hard or how often they cleaned.

May got a part time job cleaning for a little extra money, which helped.

Grandma Johnson kept track of them with her weekly letters to Sue. She wrote and told Sue she was going to visit Connie and asked if Sue wanted to go too. Sue wrote back yes.

After Grandma Johnson took her to church the following Sunday, they went to visit Connie. May sent a letter with Sue to give to Connie, writing that she missed her and would like to take a bus to visit, if Connie wanted to see her. Henry stopped going to church after he was stripped of his deacon status, so Sue didn't see him that day. Sue prayed while in church, asking God to take care of her mother and thanked Him for all He was doing for her. Sue knew something wonderful was on its way.

When they arrived at Connie's foster home, Connie seemed different, as if she were on medication or something. She made them wait almost a half hour before she came downstairs to see them and she said she couldn't talk too long because she was in the middle of putting a puzzle together. Connie read May's letter without saying a word or showing any emotion. She acted as if she couldn't care less that her grandmother and sister had come to see her. It was hard to keep any conversation going.

Sue felt odd about seeing her sister living in someone else's house. It was strange to 'visit' her sister instead of live with her, and it was hard for Sue to realize how different a life Connie now had. It was almost as if they were on different planets.

Once again, Sue enrolled into another high school. This made the sixth school Sue had been in for the ninth grade. On her first day of school, after sitting in the administration office for over an hour, waiting for all the paperwork to be done and a schedule made for her, Sue was asked to go to the principal's office.

Wondering why, Sue followed the secretary. Mr. Stevenson smiled at her when she entered and asked her to sit down. Taking a folder on his desk, he looked through the pages and finally said, "I can see from your entry information that this is the sixth school you've been in this year, Sue, is that right?"

"Yes, Mr. Stevenson, my mom has been trying to find the right place and we've moved around a lot this year," Sue answered a little timidly, not knowing where he was going with his question.

"Well, Sue, that presents a big problem. Because you've moved several times and have been to so many schools, you haven't been able to get any grades anywhere. What this means is even if you were to get all A's for the rest of the school year, and there's not much left of the year now anyway; you still would flunk. You just don't have any records. It's as if you haven't even been in school this year. Do you understand?" asked Mr. Stevenson kindly.

"Yes, I guess I understand. But what am I going to do? Do you want me to be held back another grade?" Sue asked, not liking the possibility.

"We could hold you back a year and give you a chance to catch up, but before we do that, can you tell me if your living situation with your mother will be stable enough for you to stay in the same school for the whole time next year or not?" Mr. Stevenson asked.

Having never thought about this before, Sue thought hard about the answer. Her mother wasn't stable yet, and from the past year's experience, Sue couldn't honestly say she would be stable anytime soon. Sue understood her mother's inability to take care of herself and she had no expectations that her mother was ever going to be able to take care of her. Sue's mom might always need help or some man to take care of her. So, with a bit of surprise, Sue answered honestly, "No, Mr. Stevenson, I don't think my mother's situation will be stable soon."

"I see. Thank you, Sue, for answering so honestly. I know that must have been hard for you, but you can see that it puts your schooling situation in a difficult spot. It seems to me that there is no point in you going on to the tenth grade if you have no certainty that you'll be able to finish it. You also seem to be a very capable young lady. I have read about your many accomplishments in your earlier grades when you had a more stable home, which shows me you have strong capabilities and strengths. In your situation I feel it's best that you get a job, and later get your GED. With that you can go to college if you want to, down the road."

Again, this was a new concept to Sue, so she thought about it quickly, excited about all the possibilities. "Yes, Mr. Stevenson, I do think I could get a job. I'm a hard worker and once I set my mind to something, I do it. If I don't have to go to school, I'll go out and get a job and I'll be fine." Sue said with surprise.

"I'm sure you will, Sue, so I tell you what we're going to do. You are to finish the ninth grade as best you can, as there's only a month or so left. At the end of the school year, I will write you a letter stating that it is our opinion that you would be better off leaving school and getting a job. This will allow you to get your work permit earlier then what is normally required, so you can get a job sooner. If you have any trouble with the permit department, have them call me and I will tell them it was the school's idea for you to do this and that we think you're quite capable of working. So what do you think of that?" said Mr. Stevenson.

"I think that's great, Mr. Stevenson! Thank you so much!"

"All right then, Sue, that's our plan. Now let's get you a schedule so you can get to class!" Mr. Stevenson ushered Sue out of his office and into the hands of the school secretary.

All day, Sue was distracted in class. She kept thinking about what Mr. Stevenson said. Could she really quit school and go out and get a job? She knew somebody would hire her. She knew she could do anything that she set her mind to, so she wasn't worried about being able to do the job. She did look older than her fifteen years. If she could get a fake ID, she might have a better chance of getting a job, and she needed it to get into the bars anyway. In New York, you only had to be eighteen to drink. What kind of a job could she get? She couldn't work in an office because she didn't know how to type and she couldn't spell worth beans. Ever since her dad got so mad at her about that spelling word problem, it was if words just didn't come together right in her head anymore. It was now lunchtime, and Sue was embarrassed to stand in the free hot lunch line and be the new kid again. She'd gotten into the poor kids' line only because she was really hungry, so she endured the looks and whispers from the other kids. Yes, she knew without a doubt she was ready to work instead of going to school.

When she got home, she found her mother there already, which meant she didn't have a real job yet. Cleaning for a little cash helped, but she needed a full time job. Sue was really worried about how much worse things could get for her mother. They were living in a basement with a dirt floor. They barely had enough food. If Sue's mother didn't get another job soon, they may even be kicked out of this hole in the wall place and Sue couldn't bear the thought of how much worse a place they would get—if they could get a place—after this one. The reality of Sue's situation really sank in.

May didn't know what to do. She hadn't been really trained to get a job. She only knew housework and being a wife. This whole single life was, in many ways, much harder than she'd ever imagined. She had talked about it with Joanie months ago and thought she could do it. She'd tried to take care of herself and Sue, but she knew she was failing. It scared her, but she didn't know what else to do or how to do it. Her sister Joanie had a home and a car, plus some income from her deceased husband's estate. May had nothing but what little she qualified for from the Welfare programs.

May did finally get a real part time job. It wasn't a great job, but at least it was something. Sue continued going to school and thinking about all of her possibilities. The school helped her with her application for a work permit, and she had already started working nights and weekends at the local burger joint.

Sue had read an ad in the back of a magazine about buying fake IDs, which she thought would be a handy thing to have. She started looking at ads in the newspaper for full time jobs and places to live or share rooms or something in preparation for when she was done with the ninth grade. Most of the rents were too expensive for Sue to afford right now. Sue was always very practical, and would never take on anything unless she was sure she could afford it.

She knew she would always have ways of making money. Most of the jobs didn't pay very much, but if she could find a cheap place to rent and sell stuff she stole until she found a job that paid her for her selling abilities, she would be just fine. It was the nightmares and living all alone that was of the most concern to her.

She knew she could live on her own without her mother. It was her mother she worried about not making it on her own. That was the new worry that was running through Sue's head. What would happen to her mother if she moved out and left her? Sue felt responsible for her mother, especially because she had urged her mother to leave her dad. She knew May couldn't make it on her own, but maybe if Sue were out of the way, her mother would find it easier to get a man and stay with him. Even though Sue didn't want to believe it, she knew May would probably always need a man to take care of her.

For Sue, the truth was she could take better care of herself then her mother or father ever had. Sue wouldn't allow herself to sink so low as to live in a house with a dirt floor. She would work hard and when she was old enough, she would get her GED as Mr. Stevenson had recommended.

It was time that Sue moved out on her own at last. She was excited about all the possibilities and a little apprehensive, too.

Chapter Nine: Transitions

The alarm went off at seven-thirty a.m., as usual, and as usual, Sue was hung over. Dragging herself out of bed, Sue began to get ready to go to work. Popping some bread in the toaster oven, Sue buttered it when it was ready and continued her morning routine.

She had been living in the converted room in the garage of her grandmother's for about a month now. She had written her grandmother about looking for a place to rent for herself and was surprised when her grandmother wrote back that she could rent the little room in the garage. Her dad had put in a small bathroom with a toilet and a stand-up shower, as well as a sink, a small refrigerator and a hot plate for her kitchen area. There was a foldout couch for Sue to sleep on, and a small living area with windows. Sue loved the windows with a view of the garden, though she was a little concerned about someone getting in through them. It was affordable at forty dollars a month.

As soon as Sue was dressed and ready, she peeked outside to see if Grandma Johnson was anywhere around, or if she could see Sue from her house. Thanking heaven that her grandmother wasn't anywhere in sight, Sue took the car keys off the hook there in the garage, opened the garage door, got in and started the car. Backing out of the garage, Sue left the car running while she ran out and closed the garage. Hoping to escape quickly and quietly, Sue backed out of the driveway and onto the street. *Great! Another successful getaway*, thought Sue, illegally driving her grandmother's car to work, as she did almost daily.

She was nearly sixteen years old, but she didn't have a driver's license so it was always a kind of scary thing for her to not only 'borrow' her grandmother's car, but also to drive it anywhere. She was careful to drive within the speed limit, and not draw any attention to herself. Looking for the directions on signs and on the road took her total focus. Nevertheless, Sue was always happier to be able to take her grandmother's car than to hitchhike to work. But no matter what, Sue would find a way to get to work every Monday, Wednesday and Friday and to her GED classes on Tuesdays and Thursdays. She never missed a day.

Sue really loved working at the Head Start Program in Binghamton. It was great that the principal of her last school had helped her get her work permit and this job. She liked working with the kids and was very good at it. The teachers often told her she would be a great teacher, and encouraged Sue to go to college to become one. Sue seemed to be able to reach the really difficult children. She had a gift for it. In a way, it felt like nurturing the abandoned animals to Sue.

Arriving at work, Sue greeted the teachers and the kids as she came in the door. Mornings were always busy. Since many of the children hadn't had breakfast, one of the first things to do each day was to give them a snack. Sue would help the kids learn how to hold and operate knives, forks and spoons while they ate their snack. She also taught them their colors, how to print their own names and other simple tasks as part of her job.

One of Sue's jobs was to observe the children as they played and interacted with each other. She had been trained when she first started working there what behaviors to look for which would indicate when children have been abused or molested and then to report everything at the weekly meetings. She had a certain empathy and a radar that was much more accurate than the teachers for sensing problems with kids.

She'd been working with one little girl named Molly, who was doing surprisingly well with learning how to use a fork and spoon. The reason why it was so surprising was because Molly had the mannerisms of a developmentally delayed child as she waved her arms around and moved her body in that awkward way of the mentally challenged. Sue and the other employees were very puzzled by Molly's ease with learning new things, and it had been decided that Sue and one of the teachers, Mary, would go to Molly's house that day and do a home visit.

As part of the Head Start Program, a teacher would visit the home to see how the child acted in their own environment and to check on the child's parental care and home life. Sue took this very seriously, and it gave her a sense of importance. She knew that she was asked to come because of her uncanny ability to read with accuracy the home environments.

After the morning session was over and Molly had gone home, Sue and Mary drove to Molly's house for the home visit. Arriving at Molly's home, the two walked up the steps and rang the bell. Molly's mother, Mrs. Hemmings, answered the door and asked them inside. The small house was cluttered with toys and other stuff that children get into, but was a comfortable, though low income, home.

Mrs. Hemmings asked them to sit in the living room, and Molly came out of the bedroom to greet them. A few minutes later, two other young girls came out of the bedroom, standing a bit woodenly away from Mary and Sue and staring at them. Molly went over to them and tried to drag them closer to her teachers, but they resisted and their awkward physical movements gave them away as developmentally disabled.

Sue got up and approached them warmly. They responded by showing her their new shoes. Sue invited them to join her and told them she came to visit them too. They couldn't sit still, though they tried as best they could because they felt at ease with Sue. Their interruptions did not faze Sue in the least; she could stay focused on the home visit and interact with Molly's sisters too. Sue had made a genuine connection.

Mrs. Hemmings, Molly's mom, who didn't seem to be any more than average intelligence and maybe a little less herself, came over to the two girls and gently tried to push them back into the bedroom. Being kept in the bedroom was what the girls were used to.

She told Mary and Sue that these were her older daughters. They were too old for Head Start, so they didn't get to go to school like Molly did. All of a sudden, Sue realized what had been happening to Molly and she finally understood her behavior. Molly was copying her sisters' physical actions, but Molly herself wasn't delayed. Molly's mother might not even know that Molly wasn't like her other two daughters, since Mrs. Hemmings wasn't all that smart herself.

Now that Sue and Mary had a better idea of what was going on in Molly's life, they thanked Mrs. Hemmings and left to go back to the school.

Once they got in the car, Sue told Mary what she thought was really going on with Molly. Mary had come to the same conclusion about the situation herself, and Sue's explanation made perfect sense. The two were excited to be able to tell everyone back at the school about Molly, knowing they would be as surprised as they were. Sue also wanted to somehow brighten up the lives of Molly's whole family.

Sue worked until four p.m., when her workday ended. Saying goodbye to her co-workers, Sue drove her grandmother's car home. As soon as she parked the car safely in the garage, she immediately lay down on the couch and took a nice long nap. Sue had learned to get half of her sleep at night and the rest of her sleep during a nap, or she'd never be able to do all the things she did. After about two hours, Sue woke up, refreshed and ready to go out on the town.

Sue changed into her 'going out' clothes and re-did her makeup. She always dressed really sharp and stylish, as she stole the nicest things in town. She dressed in a blue silk collar blouse and tight fitting bell-bottom jeans. Putting on the final touch of lipgloss, hoop earrings, her fringed, suede leather coat with the heavy warm lining and grabbing her platform shoes, she was ready to party. She went out the door and walked a short way to one of the larger streets in town and stuck out her thumb. It usually didn't take her very long to get a ride. Sometimes the driver would be really nice and drive her right to her friend Heidi's door.

Arriving at Heidi's, the two girls would catch up on each other's day, check out what each of them were wearing and swap clothes or borrow some of Heidi's mother's clothes if they thought they would look better in them. Heidi's mother liked to go out to the bars herself, so she had lots of great clothes that the girls felt were cool enough for them to wear too. Really nice blouses with pressed jeans were in style.

Both girls wanted to look pretty and hip. They always listened to loud music while getting ready. Deciding they looked great, they went back out to the street and both of them stuck out their thumbs. With the two of them, it usually took less than five minutes before someone gave them a ride.

They went to their favorite bar to play some foosball and drink some beer. Sue's fake ID and her mature attitude got her into any bar in New York. The girls would hang out, challenge cute guys to a game of foosball and flirt. If there weren't any cute guys there, they'd go on to another bar until they found one that had some guys they were interested in. They were young, pretty and fun, so lots of guys were happy to accept their challenge at foosball.

They drank beer all night. When they got hungry, there was always a slice of New York pizza or a spiedie vendor just outside the bars on the street. On Saturday nights, they would find a place that had live music so they could dance. Both girls were popular with the guys and always got asked to dance. One time Sue got tired of saying no to some of the guys she didn't want to dance with, so she wrote, 'I'm not interested' on a napkin and would just hold it up when an unwanted guy kept asking her. It wasn't nice, but it was kind of fun.

When the bars closed at two a.m., Heidi and Sue would have lined someone up earlier at the bar to drive them home at closing. Most often it was someone they already knew from going out. Feeling safer together, the two girls would welcome the rides home and so far, they'd had no trouble. It was nearly three a.m. when Sue got home and crashed on the foldout couch. She was usually pretty drunk and fell almost instantly into a stupor, only to awaken at the screech of the alarm at seven-thirty the next morning. Sue was nearly sixteen years old, and this was her daily life.

After finishing, as best she could, the ninth grade, Sue had come to the decision that she could take better care of herself by herself, and once Sue made a decision, she acted on it. She decided the next thing to do was to find a place of her own.

Since she'd been in contact with her grandmother through letters and then with the visit to see Connie, when her grandmother suggested that she rent the room in the garage, it seemed a perfect solution for her. Sue knew her grandmother wasn't a trusting soul, as she wouldn't even walk down her driveway to the mailbox without taking her purse and locking her house up, but knew also that her grandmother would always welcome cash money whenever she could. Grandma Johnson was quite happy to have a family member rent that small room for forty dollars a month, so Sue moved in.

Her dad had fixed it up to be livable. It was perfect for Sue, who had very few household things and who was rarely home. Living in the garage made it easier for Sue to 'borrow' her grandmother's car without her knowing about it. Grandma Johnson only drove the car once a week to go to church, so she didn't miss it.

The principal at her last school had made good on his promise and helped Sue get her work permit and even a job. She was happily employed three days a week at the Head Start Program in Binghamton. She was also going to GED classes two days a week. And almost every night she was going out to the bars. It was a fulfilling life for a nearly sixteen-year old young girl.

Sue was a hard worker and a committed one. She loved working with the kids and the kids seemed to love her in return. She faithfully went to work those three days a week, hung over or not.

Growing up in a very white Baptist West Corners in upstate New York, Sue had never known any Black people. She knew of them from the National Geographic magazine, but before she started working at Head Start in Binghamton, she'd never had any contact with African Americans. Now that she was working at Head Start, she was meeting many people of color, and it was a new experience for her. Yet, since Head Start was created for low income people, and Sue certainly had been low income all of her life, she had no problem connecting with and understanding the people she was meeting.

And Sue was meeting lots of new people. She had met a nice guy at a bar whose name was Gregory. He owned the local car dealership, and was always buying her and other girls their drinks. He was an outgoing kind of a guy, friendly and generous.

After they'd met up at the bar several times and talked quite a bit, he happened to mention how messy his house was. Sue offered to clean it for him, thinking that an extra twenty dollars a month would be helpful towards rent.

He looked at her thoughtfully and said, "Well, Sue, my house is really messy because I party with my friends there a lot. Sometimes when we party, we smoke dope, drink beer and maybe do some other things too. I wouldn't want just anyone to come into my house. I mean, they might call the cops on me or something, you know what I mean?"

"Yeah, I know what you mean, but I wouldn't call the cops on you or anything, Gregory. We're friends, and I'm cool with drugs and stuff," answered Sue honestly.

He thought about it and realized he could trust Sue. She decided with that new information, forty dollars a month would be reasonable and would cover her whole rent, too.

Sue was as good as her word. She came twice a month for a few hours and cleaned his house. It looked like wild party animals had run through it with beer cans and bottles all over the house, along with trash, food and some leftover drugs. Sue helped herself to the dope and cocaine she found. She would eventually have a couple other select people she cleaned house for, and for exactly the same reasons. The drugs she found at these places she considered her 'tip', and she was making twice what a normal cleaning person would charge. With rent, food and bills all paid for with her cleaning jobs, her paycheck became her spending money.

It seemed that almost every night when Sue went out drinking with her friends that someone would bring up the topic of moving to California and out of the boondocks. As soon as California came up, everyone would all agree that California had to have the best pot, the best looking guys and gals and the easiest money to make in the world. All would agree that one of these days they were going to pack up and move to California, and then they'd turn back into their beer and play some more foosball. California was the dream place for everyone, but it seemed to be the alcohol talking for everyone as well.

When Sue wasn't working, going to school or partying, she was worrying about her mom. She didn't see her mother very often as she was so busy with her life, but she kept in touch. It was hard to leave her, but Sue knew that she had to get on with her life. May was working part time and struggling, but was still living in the basement apartment with the dirt floor. May seemed to be barely holding her own, and naturally Sue gave her money too.

So when Sue ran into Herb at a bar one night and he asked about May, Sue thought it was all right to give him May's address. Sue still thought he was creepy, but he was a creepy talented artist, and her mom had kind of liked him.

Grandma Johnson must have been worrying herself about her other granddaughter as she woke Sue up one Sunday morning and insisted that she was going to church with her and then the two of them would go visit Connie. Sue was hung over as usual, but managed to get herself up and dressed in time to go.

After church, Grandma Johnson drove to the foster home where Connie was staying, only to find that Connie had run away from there and was now in a much stricter foster home in Endicott. Grandma Johnson got the address and drove the two of them to the new foster home in the nearby city.

They arrived about one-thirty p.m. as they had gone to church first, then to the wrong foster home and now finally to another town altogether where Connie was living. Knocking on the door, Grandma Johnson introduced herself and Sue and asked to see Connie. They were ushered into the living room and told they had missed the visiting hour, which was between twelve and one p.m. on Sundays.

Connie finally came in carrying a mop, as she had been mopping the kitchen as part of her chores around the house. She didn't stay long or say much. She seemed very robotic and unemotional. This foster home had very strict rules, and Connie wasn't willing to break them and suffer the punishment just to chat with her grandmother and sister. Grandma Johnson promised they'd come back to see her another Sunday, and they'd come on time.

Connie barely nodded and went back to her mopping.

Grandma Johnson drove Sue home. Neither of them had much to say about the whole thing.

Connie's life had turned into a nightmare for her. She had gone into foster care hoping to escape her life at home and to be able to be with Linda, but then Linda stopped seeing her. She found herself left in a stranger's home, with no family or friends to help her or make her feel wanted. Wanting to get away from everything in her life, she ran away, only to be caught and then put into an even worse foster home.

Her new foster parents insisted she get counseling, and the counselor had put her on some kind of medication. The medication made things more bearable, but made her mind fuzzy and she had lapses in time. She still was very unhappy and felt completely lost, alone and afraid. Connie felt trapped in the foster care system and didn't know how she could get out before she was eighteen, another whole year away. Seeing her grandmother and sister, knowing that they couldn't help her, made her feel angry and frustrated with their visit.

The only bearable thing about her entire life was that Mike, her boyfriend from grammar school, had found her again. He'd done what Grandma Johnson had done, and gone to her first foster home and gotten the address of her second foster home from them. He actually came and visited her a couple of Sundays ago, and now was coming every week. Connie could only see him for an hour and they were chaperoned the whole time, but at least she got to see him. It was so wonderful to have someone who wanted her and cared about her.

May was feeling very much like her daughter Connie; lost, alone and frightened. She was managing her life and with Sue's help, had a little extra money, but was very alone. She still did not drive and took the bus everywhere.

So when Herb knocked on her door, she was very happy to see him. He came into her apartment and back into her life. He had carved out of wood the complete uncanny likeness of her from memory. May was won over.

Soon, he was practically living there and was creating some of his artistic pieces he made out of junk he found in the trash and on the streets. He did help a little with the rent and the bills by selling his wood art. Herb could whittle out of wood the most detailed replica of anything he saw. His presence was a comfort and great relief to May.

Herb was a big talker. May didn't realize this, as she believed everything he said. He was always going to just trip over that pot of gold at the end of the rainbow just around the next corner. So when he told May he'd been offered this job of being the assistant manager of a huge apartment complex in Vestal, she believed him. He said he needed to go and get things settled; then he'd come back and get May and they'd live there together. Fearful that she'd never see him again, May sadly let him go.

He did come back in two weeks as he said. Apparently, it wasn't quite the deal he thought it was and he didn't want to stay. What really happened was he was fired, but he wouldn't tell May that. He hadn't been back very long when a new scheme came his way. This time a friend said Herb could manage a brand new apartment complex in Livermore, California. This place was great, and had a pool and everything. It was just like Hollywood!

Herb wanted to go and wanted to take May with him. Within a couple of weeks, the two of them were off to the promised land of California. May barely had time to say goodbye to Sue and Joanie. Everything considered, it had to be better than staying in the place she was in now.

Love must have been in the air for Connie, too, as she was seeing Mike now every week and her foster parents had decided they trusted him. They would let Mike take Connie out for two hours on Sundays, from four o'clock to six o'clock, to go shopping or visiting. Mike had his own car now as he was nineteen years old and had been working at his family's business of making doors and windows for the past year or so. He had proven himself an upstanding young man to Connie's foster parents, and had earned the privilege of having Connie all to himself for two whole hours a week. Almost as soon as they got around the corner in his car, he found a quiet spot away from prying eyes and they had sex in the back seat.

It didn't take too many weeks of this behavior for Connie to get pregnant. When the morning sickness came and Connie had missed two periods, she knew.

She told Mike that Sunday, fearful of what they were going to do now. Mike really did care for Connie and he knew it was his child, so he suggested that she move in with him. She was seventeen now, and if she ran away to Mike's place, they probably either wouldn't come after her or would leave her alone if they found her.

The two decided they'd plan her escape for next week, so she could get her things ready. She stashed her clothes and things behind the garage nearby the next Sunday morning so all they had to do was pick them up before leaving for their approved two-hour visit.

They managed to escape safely, and Connie came to live with Mike in Endicott. They were like a young married couple as Connie got bigger with child and Mike went off five days a week to work. Connie thought she was happy for the first time in a long time, perhaps ever. Being pregnant was kind of scary, but being with Mike and out of the foster home was nearly heaven.

Of course, Grandma Johnson found out about it. She seemed to be able to find out about everything. She came over to Mike's place and found Connie there by herself and saw her condition. She didn't approve of children born out of wedlock and wasn't about to have a granddaughter who had one. She began insisting that Connie and Mike get married as soon as possible. It was bad enough that Grandma Johnson had to put up with the embarrassment of Henry no longer being a deacon in her church, but this, this was impossible. She would never live down the shame.

Henry had changed a great deal since May left him. At first, he was so depressed and bereft that he barely functioned well enough to go to work every day. He couldn't bear seeing happy families anywhere, not even on TV. When the church took away his deaconship, he quit going to church. He may have spent most of his life a devout Baptist, but if they condemned him for something he had no control over, then to hell with them.

For the first time in his life, he had no one telling him how he ought to act or how he ought to behave. He'd done what his mother told him and what the church had told him all his life, but now he wasn't listening to either of them anymore. He may have been out of safe waters, but he was his own man at last.

In time, he began to try new things and to do things just because he felt like doing them. He tried alcohol and found he liked it, so he started going out to bars. He tried smoking cigarettes and found he liked those too, so he took up smoking. He even tried dating, and was dating a lovely black woman named Tanya for a while, much to his family's surprise. Henry was a changed man.

After his mother had come home and told him all about the disaster that Connie had made of her life, Henry decided to contact his daughter to see if they could reconcile. He sent word through his mother that he'd like to see her and Mike again after all these years. Connie eventually said yes, and Henry visited the two of them. He was looking forward to being a grandfather.

Grandma Johnson did get her way, as she usually did. Connie and Mike did marry at the courthouse in Endicott before the baby was born, but not by much. It was a small civil ceremony, as neither the bride nor the groom's churches would have sanctioned their marriage, and no family members attended.

Sue too fell in love, but with a darling little black wirehaired terrier named Brutus. Her friend Heidi had brought it home as her own pet, but after a few too many 'accidents' on the rug, Heidi's mother insisted she get rid of it. Heidi gave Brutus to Sue, and it was a match made in heaven. Sue had a pet again, and she loved Brutus. He was at home waiting for her every day and she wasn't alone in her apartment anymore. Brutus weighed about four pounds. He was a fierce little dog and had the 'little dog syndrome'; he would attack bigger dogs whenever he could just because he was so small.

One day, Sue came home from work and her neighbor came over and sadly told her that his dog had killed Brutus. He felt terrible about it, but Brutus had attacked his dog and before he could stop it, the bigger dog had broken the little dog's neck. He showed Sue where Brutus was in the snow and she came and gathered up the broken body of her beloved dog and buried him. Then she cried and cried for days.

Sue went to work and to her GED classes and cleaned houses as usual. When she turned seventeen, she took her GED test, passing it easily. She now had her high school diploma of sorts and could go on to college or find better work or whatever she wanted. She just didn't know what she wanted.

It was another night, like any other night, and Sue and Heidi were out at the bars, drinking beer with their friends. Once again, the topic of the promised land arose, and everyone was saying the same old things they always said about how everything was better in California, and one day they were just going to pack up and move to California, and all the other BS young people go on and on about and never do.

Something inside of Sue snapped. That was it. She was going to go to California. That's where her mother was, where the cutest guys were, where the money was easy pickings and where the best pot was. It was the place where Sue wanted to be. Sue made up her mind she was moving to California and once Sue made up her mind, she did it.

Chapter Ten:
Who Am I?
Selling Herself 'Figuratively'

Sue was hanging out at the Livermore High School parking lot again because she had found out it was the place to be. From the first time she came and asked the high school kids, "Who parties around here?" she had gotten connected to all the coolest kids in the popular crowd, and all of them had their own cars and money to spare.

Maybe it was because she was new and pretty, but she'd been meeting all the football players and all the most popular kids at Livermore high. It was a really wonderful experience for Sue, because for the first time, she was in with the biggest cliques at high school and she didn't even go to school there. She loved being popular.

She had lots of guys interested in her, but she hadn't decided just yet which one she was going to go out with. She wanted to find the most popular guy first. She wanted only the one that everybody else wanted; that would be the one she'd go for. Her thinking was he had to be the best and then, and only then, would she be happy. That was just how her mind worked.

All the kids thought Sue was really cool because she was from New

York, she was out on her own, she had her GED, she had great clothes and she even had stolen a car without getting caught! Compared to all the other high school kids, she was definitely the coolest.

What Sue really liked about being with all these kids was that they didn't know anything about her except what she had told them. They didn't know her history. They didn't know how poor she'd been or about her sister or anything. That gave Sue a sense of freedom to be whoever and whatever she wanted to be. It was great.

She was thinking a lot about Terry Williams, who was the captain of the football team. As far as she could tell, he was the most popular boy at school. He was good looking in a healthy, wholesome kind of a way with brown hair and freckles. He was about five-ten, with a stocky build. It wasn't important to Sue to actually be physically attracted to him. The only thing she considered in making her decision was whether he was the one guy that all the other girls wished they could get; the prize. That's the one that Sue wanted, and was determined to have.

Sue was going out almost every night partying with the cool kids, and she loved it. What everyone back in New York said about California was true; the golden state did have the best marijuana, the cutest guys and everything was like a dream come true. Sue had never had it so good!

So far, California had been worth the long bus ride to get there. Sue had spent three days and three nights on a bus traveling to get to Livermore. Most of that trip, Sue had worried and stressed over whether she'd be able to find her mother or not and what she'd do if she couldn't find her. Sue had an address for her mother, but wasn't sure she would still be there, as her mother had already moved twice since moving to California.

Traveling a long distance alone by bus is rarely easy or pleasant, and Sue worried the whole way. It didn't help that she developed a strange lump behind her ear that didn't go away the entire time and was still there even a few days after she finally arrived.

She had brought plenty of money she had saved from her paychecks. While living in New York, she had paid for all of her living expenses and had lived quite well on the money she'd made doing her special cleaning jobs. By the time she arrived at Livermore, she was exhausted and desperately wanted a shower.

Arriving at the bus station, Sue looked at maps and asked around until she found what bus would take her closest to the address she had for her mother. Getting on the bus one more time, Sue rode for the last leg of her long journey west. Following the directions she'd been given at the bus station, she carried her suitcase the three blocks to the apartment complex where hopefully her mother was living.

Knocking on the apartment door, Sue felt the most amazing sense of relief when her mother answered the door. Nearly falling into her arms, Sue was so glad to see her mother again.

"Mom! You're here! I'm so glad I found you!" exclaimed Sue.

"Sue! Oh my gosh! How did you get here? When did you leave? I got your letter saying you were coming, but I didn't know how or when. It's so good to see you!" May happily hugged her daughter.

"I took the bus. It was an awful three-day trip, but I'm so glad you're here!" Sue said again with relief.

"Of course, I'm here. Where else would I be?" May asked, puzzled by Sue's concern.

"I was scared that you would have moved again since I last wrote you, and then I'd never be able to find you. I worried the whole trip here that you'd be gone when I got here."

"Oh, I see. Well, no, we're pretty settled here now. As best we can be, considering that Herb still isn't actually hired on here," May explained with a bit of worry in her voice.

"Herb still isn't hired on yet? I thought the job was a done deal? What happened?" Sue asked with surprise.

"Well, the owners still haven't gotten the permits for the whole second floor, so they can't rent any of the units. And if they can't rent the units, they don't need two managers. But as soon as they get the permits, then they'll hire Herb and everything will be just fine. Just you wait and see," May said.

"I'm sure it'll all work out okay, Mom. Why don't you show me around the place?" Sue suggested.

"Of course! Bring your bag into the second bedroom here, and I'll show you around." May took Sue by the hand.

The apartment complex was fantastic. It was brand new, never been lived in, and really nice. The nicest place Sue had ever lived. Sue loved the smell of 'brand new'. Everything was wonderful.

Because Herb didn't actually have a job at the complex, he and May had been squatting there, rent free, for a couple of months. The electricity was on in the main areas for the maintenance guy, Frank, but not in the units. The water was on too. Herb had figured out to plug in an extension cord in the hallway and was running all the lights and appliances off the one cord. Naturally, it was important that no one find out they were living there. Other than that, it was a great place.

There was a pool and a recreation room downstairs they could use anytime they wanted. The rec room had a bumper ball table and the pool was open to everyone that rented there. Sue had never lived in such a rich-looking place and though she really liked it, she was also kind of scared because they weren't supposed to be there.

The real manager, Frank, lived across the hall and been living there for quite a while with his girlfriend, Shelly. He had been hired to be the maintenance guy for the complex and to keep the place up until all the building permits were in, and then to stay on after. They had been there for quite a while and were very settled in. Frank was the one who had contacted Herb through a cousin and invited him to come out. Frank thought he would need an assistant for the five hundred unit apartment complex when the permits finally did come through. He didn't see any harm in Herb and May moving in while they waited. It was rare that anyone from the property management company came by, so no one would find out.

May and Herb didn't have a car, so they would go to one of the local car dealerships every once in a while and test-drive a car. While they had the car, they would go grocery shopping and then drop everything off at the apartment before returning the car. Often Frank and Shelly, who did have a car, took Herb and May with them when they went shopping.

The two couples would have dinners together sometimes, and they all seemed to get along quite well. Sue liked them and thought they were really nice. May had signed up for food stamps when she first got to California, but they gave her only twenty-five dollars' worth a month temporarily. So even though there were some concerns about how everything was all going to work out, Sue was really happy she moved to California. She was thinking about getting a job pretty soon, but was really enjoying being able to spend time with all of her new friends. She felt free and accepted at last.

May was pregnant. After all these years, she was pregnant again. She and Herb hadn't been using anything for birth control because they didn't have much money and they'd been safe for so long. Not anymore. Now May was pregnant, and everything had changed.

She was thirty-five years old, squatting in an unfinished apartment, over two thousand miles from the town she was born in, not married to the man she was living with and pregnant by, and those were the certainties of her present life. Her uncertainties were too many to name and too terrifying to look at. May just hoped and prayed that Herb would be able to take care of her and the new baby that was coming. She didn't know what else to do.

Sue had been trying to get a job, but kept running into the problem that she had no experience, so no one wanted to hire her. *How can a person get experience if no one will hire them*, Sue wondered. She had some money, but she wanted to pitch in more to help out. She needed to get a job.

Finally, she got a part time job at a burger joint nearby. It gave her a take-home pay of only fifteen dollars a week, but at least it was something. It turned out to be a really good thing when they were kicked out of the apartment a week later.

Fortunately, Herb was able to get a job at a Motel 6, where he would do all the maintenance for a free room. He moved May and Sue in immediately and they settled in as best they could. It was only one room with a bathroom, and it had only one bed. Sue slept on the floor. They had a hot plate and a small refrigerator in the room, which helped. They had a roof over their heads but no money except what Sue made, so Sue bought food for them on what little she had. She would usually buy a loaf of bread and bologna for the week from her paycheck, and maybe some milk too. Whatever money she had left over, she spent on partying for herself. Sue felt strange that she was the only one with any money, and she wasn't sure how much she was supposed to contribute for May and Herb. But she was worried about her pregnant mother not having enough to eat, so she had to do something.

Herb had always been rather odd, but Sue hadn't realized that he was odd in 'that way'. Maybe it was because he had too much time on his hands or May was pregnant or who knows what but soon after they got kicked out of the apartment, Herb was arrested for peeping into the windows at the Motel 6. He went to jail and was convicted, and Sue and May never saw him again. Now it was just Sue and a pregnant May and no place to live.

As quick as she could, Sue found a shared rental place for the two of them. Sue and May shared a bedroom in a house. Sue was scared. Now she had to take care of her pregnant mother all by herself. She decided she had to get another job, and a full time one at that.

Because she'd at least had some experience working at the burger joint, Sue was able to get hired at a sandwich place that wasn't far from where they were living. It was a good place to work because the cook let her know her first day that since it was only the two of them working there, her job included pocketing half of whatever money she got from the customers and splitting it with the cook. Sue was happy to have the extra income.

Working at the sandwich place, Sue had made a friend of a customer who came in often and, over time; they'd talked and gotten to know each other. Chrissy was eighteen, nearly a year older than Sue, but the two young women got along like a house afire. Chrissy still lived at home while she worked as a waitress at the House of Pies.

Thank heavens for Medical and other government assistance, as they paid for the hospital and all the medical bills for Peggy's birth. Fortunately, May had no complications, and was able to bring baby Peggy home within two days after giving birth. This also meant May would get welfare. What a relief!

Sue was helping out, too. She decided she needed to find some kind of job that would pay even more than the sandwich place did, as she now wanted to get a car. Naturally, she worried about how she was going to do it all, but she was determined to do it. Sue was always very loyal and devoted to the ones she loved and would do whatever it took to take care of them.

Her friend Chrissy suggested that Sue try to get a job at House of Pies. The business had recently been sold to new owners, and Chrissy said Sue could apply for the job and tell the new owners that she was a former employee of the old owners and that would give her the needed experience to get the job. Chrissy made drawings of where everything was and where everything was kept so that Sue could appear like she had worked there before. It was an excellent plan and it worked. Sue got the job.

Finally, Sue was working full time, getting a decent paycheck and good tips. Being a waitress gave Sue the opportunity to practice her salesmanship skills and she really mastered them while waiting on customers. Sue learned that everything is selling and it's all about your presentation. Sue made better tips than anyone there.

The house where Sue and May were living had other borders there, and May had gotten to know many of them as friends. They were all women, so a new baby was actually a welcome addition and was given much attention by all. May had help while Sue was gone every day from the other women in the house. After Peggy began to sleep through the night, May felt comfortable leaving her with one of the other women in the house and going out socializing again. She was tired of being cooped up in the house all the time, and she was tired of being alone.

Sue went out almost every night partying. She had started seeing Terry, who would pick her up in his car and take her out to different parties and places. Sue really liked having the most popular boy in the whole high school hot after her. It made her feel special. But she wasn't so crazy about how Terry kept pressuring her to have sex.

Sue was still a virgin at eighteen years old. She and Terry had done a lot of kissing and touching, but they hadn't really had sex yet. Sue had been putting Terry off by saying they had no place to do it, and she didn't want her first time to be in the back seat of a car. Both of their living situations didn't offer any privacy because no matter what, someone was always around. Sue thought she had put Terry on hold indefinitely, but she had underestimated him.

Terry picked Sue up with an air of suppressed excitement. Sue noticed something different about him, but didn't know what. She did notice when Terry didn't drive her to the party she thought they were going to, but drove into a motel parking lot. Leaving her in the car, Terry got out and went into the motel office to register. Coming back out, he got into the car and holding the key, gave Sue a big smile.

"What are we doing here?" Sue asked, really surprised.

"We're going to spend our first night together here! I planned it all out so we could finally be alone together without anybody bothering us so we can finally do it," said Terry with an excited smile.

"Now? You want us to do it now?" Sue asked incredulously.

"Yeah, now. I mean we've been putting it off for so long because we didn't have any privacy, well, now we have privacy!" explained Terry.

"But I'm not really ready. I didn't know we were going to do it so soon," Sue said, trying to make him slow down.

"What do you mean so soon? We've been waiting for two months!" Terry said with frustration.

"Why does it have to be tonight?" asked Sue.

"Why not tonight?" came back Terry.

"Well, I just hadn't expected it, that's all. I was surprised," Sue tried to explain.

"I wanted to surprise you. I've been saving up the money so I could pay for a room for us so we could finally be alone, and I thought you'd be happy that I did all this for you," Terry said with a bit of a whine. "I bought us some beer too."

"Well, yeah, it is nice of you to rent a room and everything, and I guess we can do it tonight. I mean, we might as well, since you've already got the room and everything," Sue finally said with some resignation.

"Great! Let's go inside and see how it looks!" said Terry with renewed excitement.

Terry had had sex with his last few girlfriends, but he was more nervous with Sue. He loved her and respected her for waiting for the right guy, unlike his other girlfriends, so he wanted her first time to be special.

The two teenagers went inside the motel room and looked all around. They bounced on the bed. They checked out the bathroom and the free soap. Then they drank some beer. When there was nothing else to do but to do what they came there to do, they did it.

Even though they'd been 'practicing' with each other for a couple months, the first time is usually a bit awkward and uncomfortable at best. The embarrassment of being in a motel room just to have sex was making both of them very self-conscious and distracted from any natural sexual attraction they may have had. Terry, being a young male, didn't stay distracted for long, but for Sue, the sexual desire wasn't really there in the first place and was even less so under these circumstances.

Finally, it was done. Sue wanted a shower while Terry felt on top of the world. Sue was embarrassed about the blood on the sheets and wanted to wash it out before they left. Terry wanted to do it again while they still had the room, but Sue didn't, so they didn't. Their relationship did change after that night, for both of them.

Terry wanted to do it all the time. He'd write notes to Sue telling her how badly he wanted her, how he thought about her all the time and then suggested places they could meet to do it. Sue wasn't as enthusiastic, but would comply with his desires when she had no other way out of it.

Her connection with Terry wasn't particularly sexual as much as it was mental, because, to her, he was the prize that she'd won, and she wanted to keep it, so that no other girl could have him. When a couple of his girlfriends from the past started calling him, Sue's need to keep him made her want to have sex with him. It was part of selling herself; she knew how to close the deal, which was easier to do since he was in love with her.

Then there was the guilt. Having finally lost her virginity, Sue felt guilty that she'd had sex before marriage. Her upbringing in the Baptist church nagged at her all the time about being a sinner. In time, her guilt actually kept her in the relationship with Terry far longer than she wanted to, because he was the first man she had sex with and she felt she had to stay with him.

May, on the other hand, had met Mr. Wonderful. One night, she'd gone out to a bar and met a wonderful man named Ken. He was kind and gentle and loving and thought she was the best thing since sliced bread. They started dating.

She brought him home to meet her baby daughter Peggy and her grown daughter Sue. He passed all the tests. Both daughters liked him right away. He was a good man with a big heart and May was finally in love, this time for keeps. It wasn't very long before Ken asked May to move in with him and eventually marry him. He raised Peggy as if she were his own. He was a good husband and father and he made May very happy at last.

With May happily living with Ken, Sue was finally free to just take care of herself. She moved into an apartment that had a wonderful landlady named Mrs. B. Mrs. B took Sue under her wing and helped her get settled in. She even gave Sue some furniture she had and didn't need any longer. A few of the pieces were very nice antiques, and Mrs. B explained to Sue a bit about antique furniture and how to care for it. Mrs. B was always happy to have Sue visit and the two would paint pottery together, which they both loved doing.

Sue was making good money working at the House of Pies and was burning the candle at both ends. She had the stamina of youth, which enabled her to party most of the night, grab a few hours of sleep, work an eight-hour job, and then turn around and do it again. She was smoking pot and drinking, which didn't seem to make any difference in her ability to do her job and to do it well. She made the best tips of all the waitresses. She knew how to sell.

Sue finally got her driver's license and started looking at cars. She found a lime green Ford Pinto, but because she had no credit, she was told she needed a cosigner. It cost $1,395. She had three hundred dollars to put down on it, and a friend cosigned with her. The car started having problems right away. It only ran for two months. It was not worth fixing and it started getting tickets because it was parked on the street and didn't run. Sue couldn't get it towed to a junkyard because she didn't have the title. The interest rate was twenty-one percent, and she had a two-year loan. She was really stuck with a lemon she couldn't even get rid of.

Sue was becoming close friends with Chrissy. They worked together and partied together nearly every night. They talked a lot about what they wanted to do with their lives and about their dreams. Sue loved having dinner over at Chrissy's because her mother treated Sue as if she was one of the family. Sue loved her. The two girls talked often about traveling and seeing the world. They both had a lot of confidence in themselves and they wanted to strike out on their own somehow.

Sue had been living in California for over a year now. She was nearly nineteen years old. She'd been with Terry for most of that year, and she'd stayed with him because of guilt more than any other reason. Her mother and baby sister were happily living with Ken and were safe and secure at last. Her dad wrote and said Connie was having another child, and that Grandma Johnson was going to church with Connie's family every Sunday. Connie and her family were now involved in all of the church functions. Everyone in her family seemed to be settling down while Sue felt a sense of wanderlust, a desire for change, a need to explore and to be free. She was ready to go onward to something else.

After many more talks with Chrissy and some planning, the two young women decided they would go off together and see the world. The first thing they did was to get Chrissy's old Toyota completely fixed up and squared away so they would have a safe vehicle to drive wherever they were going to go.

Next, they decided to sell everything they owned. They wanted to make sure they had money for the trip and to leave money with Chrissy's mother, so she could pay Chrissy's monthly Macy's card bill and continue making the payment on Sue's car loan too. They had discussed their plans for the trip and their desires and expectations of what they wanted to do and to experience.

Together, they had come to the decision that they wanted to get rid of all their possessions and not wear any makeup and go out in the world and see how they were received and how they were perceived without any outward trappings or masks. Sue had not ever felt any real love connections. She knew she could get or do whatever she wanted because of how savvy she was, but it didn't feel real to her. She felt confident she could sell herself and get whatever prize she wanted, but she wanted to feel loved for who she really was.

With all of this in mind, the girls held an 'Everything is $4.99 Sale' at Sue's apartment. They sold all of the furniture, including the antiques, the household goods and everything else except the bare essentials they were going to take with them. They went to Sears and bought themselves a tent so they had the option of camping out instead of paying for a motel or sleeping in the car.

Finally, mapping out a simple route of where they wanted to go first, the two teenagers left the golden state of California and headed east. Their first stop was Winnemucca, Nevada. Their second stop was in Wyoming, where they spent the night at the home of one of Chrissy's mother's friends.

Sue noticed that the family where they were staying seemed very stiff and uncomfortable around Chrissy and her. The mother seemed fearful of the girls, mainly because her son was showing too much interest in them. After dinner, Sue and Chrissy offered to do the dishes as a courtesy and a thank you for allowing them to stay. Much to their surprise, the mother not only had them wash the dishes, but also brought all of the kitchen appliances and took them apart so Sue and Chrissy could wash those too. The waffle iron and beaters looked like they had not been washed in a long time. Chrissy and Sue couldn't help but laugh to themselves about it.

The girls had brought about five hundred dollars between them, and had intended to find work whenever they needed more money and then to continue traveling once they had a stash again. However, Wyoming wasn't the place for them as the air was so dry and altitude was so high that Sue was getting constant nosebleeds. However, both girls did really like the drive-up windows that sold liquor!

Driving on, the next stop was in Colorado Springs, the Garden of the Gods, and then on to Missouri, where they camped out for the night. When they finally arrived in Chicago, they were grateful to be able to spend some time at the home of another one of Chrissy's mother's friends. This was one of Chrissy's mother's best friends from her childhood and they had remained close over all the years.

Unlike their stay in Wyoming, where the mother wasn't happy to have them and was distrustful of them, this friend of Chrissy's mother was really hip and wanted the two young women to have lots and lots of fun while they were there. She introduced them to two young men who were her neighbor's sons and were record producers.

These two guys were from a rich family. Their parents owned a cigarette vending machine business that was doing very, very well. They serviced all the private clubs in Chicago. These guys called themselves record producers, but really they were rich kids on the loose. The first thing they did was to put the girls up in an expensive hotel downtown. Once they got into the rooms, the guys took one of the mirrored closet doors off and laid it across the bed so they could do lines of coke on it. Sue thought that was very impressive.

Sue had never been in such a fancy hotel room before. It had big fluffy towels and a Jacuzzi tub! All the soaps and shampoos were really nice ones, not the cheap junky kind. There were even little bottles of alcohol in the small refrigerator.

That night, the guys took Chrissy and Sue to one of the private clubs for dinner, drinks and dancing. On the ride there, one of the guys was showing Sue the pistol he kept in the glove compartment when it went off and shot a hole in the car. What an adrenaline rush! Sue did wonder if these rich guys' parents might have been connected to the mob, but she wasn't about to say anything about it. When they were in Wyoming, they'd been warned about the mob in Chicago. One thing for sure, the girls' stay in Chicago was certainly memorable.

Driving on to New York, their next stop was at Grandma Johnson's, where the girls stayed in a pop-up camper Henry had in the driveway. Henry had changed a lot since Sue had seen him last. He had settled down and wasn't depressed anymore. He was still dating, though most of his dates were for fishing and camping now. He had mellowed with age and was glad to see his daughter after all this time.

Sue and Chrissy did what they'd come east to do, which was to party. Now they were on Sue's turf, and she knew all the right people and places to go for parties. Sue enjoyed coming back to New York and telling all her old friends of her success stories about California and how she was now traveling around even more. During their travels in the upstate New York area, they went to the border city of Champlain.

Champlain was a small, inbred kind of town, where the barber was also the mortician and there was only one hotel-bar. At that bar, Sue and Chrissy met a woman named Patsy, who had recently bought the place. She hadn't bought it as a hotel business, but for the antique furnishings that were in the hotel. She knew how valuable the antique solid maple beds and desks and chairs were, and exactly how much money they were worth on the market. The furnishings were far more valuable than what she'd paid for the hotel. After talking with Sue and Chrissy, Patsy offered them a job selling her antiques with her at a big antique sale in a couple of weeks in West Virginia. Both Sue and Chrissy decided to take the job, as they needed the money and it sounded like fun. They agreed to meet Patsy in West Virginia in a couple of weeks.

After staying another week in New York, the girls continued their journey with stops in New Jersey and Massachusetts before making their way down to West Virginia to meet Patsy. The antique sale was a new experience for the two girls and both of them learned a lot about antiques, what to look for and how valuable they were. They didn't make a bunch of money, but enough to keep them going for a while longer. Once again, Sue witnessed firsthand how valuable her selling talent was. There were people from everywhere selling and buying antiques. The sellers camped there for the ten days, and many had their dogs with them. Sue and Chrissy felt right at home camping with them.

By the time they reached North Carolina, they were about out of money. Sue announced to Chrissy that she wasn't going to eat another peanut butter and jelly sandwich, so it was time to get a job.

Shortly after Sue's announcement, they happened to see a carnival just ahead on the road. The two girls looked at each other and with excitement said, "Let's see if we can get a job at the carnival!"

Turning into the road where the carnival was being set up, the girls got out and wandered around until they found someone they could ask. "Excuse me, but we were wondering if there were any job openings here?" asked Sue.

"Well, there might be some openings here, but you'd better not call them jobs, or they'll know you're not a carny and will turn you away. What you need to ask for is if they have any 'holes'. That's what carny people call jobs," the man said.

"Thanks a lot!" Sue said as she moved on to find someone else they could ask about getting a 'hole'.

Not surprisingly, there were a couple of 'holes' for the girls, and why not? They were young and very attractive and would certainly draw customers to the booths. After being sized up by the carnival manager, Sue was given her own hole, which was the duck pond booth. Chrissy worked with someone else making, as prizes, heated Pepsi bottles that were stretched and filled with colored water.

Sue was given an apron to wear at her booth and always inside the apron pocket was the one and only duck that had the number twenty-five on the bottom. That was the winning duck that would allow the person who picked it to choose any prize in the booth they wanted, including the television set! All the other ducks had numbers less than twenty-five and would win lesser prizes. A customer would pay twenty-five cents for the chance to pick one duck out of the duck pond as the ducks moved around in a circle. If the duck they chose has a number between one and fifteen, they got the cheap prize shelf. If they got one between sixteen and twenty-four, they got a prize from the second shelf of better prizes.

None of the prizes, which included back scratchers and a cloth snake that when laid on someone's arm and rubbed would look like it was crawling, were worth more than five cents, so no matter what prize anyone chose, the carnival always made money. Sue would take the customer's money and put it in her apron pocket. She was not allowed to look at it or count it. Her boss would come by every hour or so and reach in and take it. He was always pleased with her intake of cash.

One time, an off-duty cop came up to the booth when Sue was working and asked if he could buy all the ducks. She nearly panicked, as she had the only number twenty-five duck in her apron pocket and was told if she saw a cop to put it in the water. Sometimes they would check to make sure the Duck Pond game wasn't a scam, and she was told that in some states, this game wasn't allowed.

Sue's face and neck had turned red and she felt hot, so she told the cop she would have to ask her boss and went off to do just that. Fortunately, her boss told her to tell the cop he could buy all the ducks, but when he picked up a duck, he would have to put it back in the moving water before picking again. Naturally, the cop decided not to do it. He had thought he could show the game was a scam, or pay less than ten dollars to get the winning duck. Sue was really happy to see him go.

Working with the carnival was a new and different experience for Sue and Chrissy. The carnies would rent out one motel room for every twenty people, which meant just about everybody slept on the floor where they could find space. It was a different experience for the young girls, as life on the road with the carnival was an odd and isolated lifestyle.

It was easy to only talk to carnie people because after a couple of days, they'd be in a new town among strangers again. Also, sleeping so many people in one room made everybody comfortable with everybody. The girls made pretty good money; often they made three to four hundred dollars for only three days of work! Sue used her talents for selling and they both did very well for themselves. They always put their money together.

One day, Chrissy burned her arm, quite painfully, heating up the Pepsi bottles. She cried and decided right then and there that she was done working that job. They had been working fifteen-hour days, which certainly added weight to the decision. So the two girls left the carnival and again struck out on their own.

They decided to head down to Daytona Beach, because it was summer and they'd heard they could find a cheap place to live during the off-season. They'd never lived near the beach before, so they were excited to be in Florida and by the ocean. They found a cheap place for the two of them and started looking for work.

Sue found a job selling at Florsheim Shoes. Finally, Sue was doing what she did best—selling! Right away, Sue did well. She sold more shoes than anyone. This was an opportunity for Sue to shine and she just glowed. She made twice as much in commissions as just about everybody there. Many of her co-workers were jealous, but there wasn't anything they could do about it because they didn't have the talent that Sue had. At nineteen years old, she was the best salesperson in the place.

Maybe it was the jealousy or maybe it was homesickness or maybe it was just time to move on, but when Sue learned there was a job opening in the Florsheim store in Concord, California for an Assistant Manager, Sue decided to transfer, and Chrissy was ready to go home too.

Chapter Eleven:
Real Men May Not Eat Quiche, But Real Women Do Sell Cars!

Sue really could sell cars. She sold a car her first day on the job. She averaged a car a day in 1982 for the amount of days that she worked. She had found the perfect career.

It all started when she was the assistant manager at Florshiem Shoes in Concord, California. The local car salesmen would come in to Florshiem and buy their shoes for work, and since there were lots of dealerships around, there were lots of salesmen buying shoes. Sue would not only sell them a pair of shoes for work, but she would upsell them socks, boots and shoe polish too! She was, of course, the best salesperson there, and making the most money in commissions.

She had been working at Florshiem for a few months when Ron, one of the closers at the local Pontiac/Honda dealership, came in and after buying several things more than he came in to buy, again, he looked up at Sue and said, "You should be selling cars. If you sold cars, you would be making three times the money you're making selling shoes, you could have your own brand new demo car to use after a ninety-day trial and the dealership's car insurance covers all the demos. What do you think of that?" Ron said, looking intently at Sue while he spoke.

"Really? A new car? A great job and a car too?"

"Yeah, I think you could really sell cars. You should try it. Seriously, you should try it. If you decide to go for it, here's my card," he said, handing Sue his business card, "and I'll put in a good word for you. You certainly have always sold me more than I intended to buy."

"Okay! Thanks, Ron. I'll think about it," Sue said excitedly.

Sue still didn't have a car, so she often got rides from co-workers or others after work. That day, Ron offered to drive her home and when she gratefully accepted the ride home, he made sure to drive by the Pontiac/Honda dealership on the way, so she'd know exactly where it was and do a little selling of the dealership to Sue.

The idea of selling cars was one Sue had never thought of before, but now that she had, she couldn't get it out of her head. She thought about it and thought about it and thought about it. Then she made a decision and, as usual, she acted on it immediately. Sue went to the Pontiac/Honda dealership.

With Ron's recommendation, as well as a good word from several of the other salesmen who had bought shoes from Sue, Sue was hired and she was on Ron's team. She gave Florsheim her two-week notice and began her new career selling cars the day after she stopped working for Florsheim.

She sold a car on her first day and almost every day the first month she was hired, and she made salesperson of the month. She never slacked off, she never let up. Sometimes she sold as many as three cars in one day. She was given her own demo car only two weeks after she started selling, instead of the usual ninety-day waiting period.

Sue was really happy to have her own car at last. Her last car, the lemon, was finally turned over to the court, which had ordered Beneficial Finance to give the title on her Pinto to the junkyard, just to get it off the street. Sue knew she picked out that car and it was not the lender's fault it was a piece of junk. She had continued to make her payments on it until it was paid in full.

At her new job, management loved her. They took this sweet young thing out to expensive dinners and nice bars every week. It was the '80's, and one of the perks of the job was cocaine from co-workers, and Sue was certainly given her share. Management loved the money she was making for them and the attention she got.

Unfortunately, some of her co-workers weren't so generous. The red-faced salesMEN grumbled that she must have been sleeping with the customers or in some way giving sexual favors to make so many sales. They didn't want to accept that it might be her talent and their lack. They were jealous and unhappy with her, but there wasn't anything they could do about it.

One day one of the guys said, "You can't wear corduroys to work here!"

Sue said, "There are three guys here that wear it almost daily, one standing right there. If you were not looking at my ass, you wouldn't have even noticed." She stood her ground, but the fact that the management really spoiled their top talent made for tense days on the front line.

The women who worked in the office at the dealership were very jealous too, as they really resented giving this nineteen-year-old high school dropout a paycheck that was three times their salaries. Sue was aware and uncomfortable with their jealousy. She asked her boss, "What do I do about the hate coming out of the business office?"

He said, "Sue, do you want them to like you?"

"Yes," said Sue.

"Okay, if you want them to like you, just be an average sales person. If you want them to LOVE you, be below average."

Sue got it. They always shoot at the one on top.

Sue was a 'liner' salesperson. Her job was to line the customer up to buy. So she would greet the new customer, talk to them and make them feel at ease, and find out what they drove now and what their needs in a car were. She would show them different cars, talking and sensing what car was the best fit, and finally take them on a test drive. Once the customer had decided on which car they wanted, Sue would talk to them about the down payment, help them to fill out the credit application and tell them what their payments would be. Her job was to line them up to maximize the profit and set up the finance department with extra payment. It was called 'legs' in the deal.

Then her team closer, Ron, would come in. After the customer had been nicely set up to be struggling with the high payment price, he would negotiate with the customer and close the deal. It was a tried and true system that had worked for many years in all forms of sales. The closer looked like a hero getting the sales manager, behind the closed door, to agree to the deal the customer could live with. Sue knew that when negotiating a deal to put the offer out there and then shut up. The first person to talk always gives something up.

At that time, Hondas were the hottest cars on the market with a waiting list of customers. Selling Hondas was pretty easy. Naturally, the Pontiac/Honda dealership insisted that the salespeople sell all the cars, including, not only the Pontiacs, but the used cars as well. Sue did. Sue never let 'no' bother her. She never took it personally and she worked constantly for the 'yes' that was the win; then she felt on top of the world. That's all she was focused on—the 'yes', which was one of the many reasons she was such a good salesperson.

Selling made Sue feel great about herself. She felt so successful and so creative at the same time. She was always looking for ways to make the deal work and thinking of new ways to bring in more business and more sales. She found marketing fascinating. Just like Darin Stevens from the Bewitched show so long ago, she felt excited and driven to find new and inventive ways to sell and to market. The recognition she got from doing so well at this job was exhilarating.

After work, Sue would go out for drinks with the managers and the head of marketing at the nicest bars in town. Sue loved schmoozing with the bosses and talking about marketing. Sometimes, she'd do a line of coke in the bathroom before having several drinks at the bar. She lived for basically two things: getting high and being the number one salesperson at the dealership. She was living her dream as a nineteen-year old top salesperson with money to blow. Nothing could stop her now!

She was driving a new Honda Prelude, and knew that when it hit five thousand miles she would get to pick out something else. She had had a Pontiac Grand Prix before this and had been racing in it. With only fifteen miles on it, the lifters got stuck or something, and she gave it back. Sue loved knowing that she could have her pick of new cars at the dealership pretty much whenever she wanted!

After she had been selling cars for about three years, the newspaper ran an article about her with the title—Real Men May Not Eat Quiche, But Real Women Do Sell Cars! —the title itself appeared on the front page of the newspaper, making her front-page news. This really made her coworkers seethe with jealousy.

One time Sue was giving a test drive for a used 450, five-speed Pontiac Trans Am and had the customer in the passenger's seat beside her as she drove off the lot. That particular type of Trans Am wasn't legal to sell new in California, because it was so fast. Sue put the car in reverse and gave it some gas. The Trans Am flew backwards and smashed a new car into another new car. Sue thought, *Better to sell the Trans Am and have smashed those cars than not to sell the Trans Am,* so she continued on with her test drive.

When she got back to the dealership, she fell apart, went into the bathroom and was afraid to come out. Another salesperson finished her deal, and they ended up splitting the commission.

One of the women in the office was asked to go into the woman's bathroom and get her. The kindly woman told Sue, "You're not going to get in trouble, the dealership has insurance for accidents," which made Sue feel okay enough to come out of the bathroom and face her coworkers.

Once again, Sue was burning the candle at both ends. She worked all day selling cars and partied half the night. Getting high made all the doubts, the worries and the fears go away and left her with a feeling of being all-powerful and all-wonderful. The party lifestyle was all around her, and she felt she deserved to celebrate often, especially when she sold a car.

Fortunately, her partying didn't seem to affect her ability to do her job. She continued to be remarkably successful. In fact, by the time she was twenty-two, she was making really good money. Sue hated paying rent, seeing it as a waste of money, so she decided to buy a house. Houses in Concord were very expensive, too high for even Sue to afford at that time.

With that in mind, Sue began looking at the areas around her where housing was cheaper. She decided on the Fairfield/Vacaville area, which is east of San Francisco on the way to Sacramento. Driving up to Fairfield, Sue found a Honda dealership there and went in to talk to the manager.

"Hi. My name is Sue Johnson, and I'd like to work for you selling cars. I've been selling cars in Concord for the past three years, and I've been the top salesperson every year I've worked there," Sue said with a winning smile.

"My name is Barney, and I'm the manager here. Were you a liner or a closer?"

"A liner."

"We don't believe in that system. You have to be able to close your own deals here. We're pretty busy right now. How about you go out and bring back the lunch order for the guys?" suggested Barney.

So Sue went and brought their lunch back and just kept hanging around.

It was a Saturday, and very busy.

"You see those people over there? No one has been able to talk to them yet, so why don't you go over there and say hi, let them know someone will be with them as soon as there is a free salesman," Barney said with a sly smile.

"I'd sure hate to sell them a car if I don't work here," Sue said with confidence, a challenge in her voice.

"Let's see how it goes," said Barney, answering her challenge with one of his own.

Sue made the sale and got the job. Again, she averaged a car almost every day in sales and was top salesperson of the year.

At twenty-three years old, Sue bought her first home, a condo in Vacaville. She moved in and went to work at Fairfield Honda.

But Sue also loved to do marketing. She loved thinking up new ways to bring in more customers and make more sales. She came up with the idea of holding an after-hours Women's Clinic on how to buy a used car without having to bring someone with you that knew the basics about cars. She had an announcement placed in the local newspaper about the clinic and was pleased to see a number of women come to hear her presentation.

She talked about mostly basic stuff, such as what to look for under the hood, check for leaks, check the color of the oil and to see how the tires were wearing. Most of all, she ended up getting women customers who wanted to buy a car from Sue, and only Sue. They trusted her.

Eventually, Sue wanted to move up the chain and get into the financing end of car sales. She asked Barney if he would give her a job in financing, but he kept turning her down because she was doing so well on the floor selling. He would tell her it was because she didn't have any experience in financing, but, really, it was because he didn't want to lose his cash cow.

Barney did concede to appease Sue by giving her the advertising responsibilities for the dealership. Sue was happy to be in charge of advertising, as it gave her a creative outlet for her drive to sell. One of the advertising ideas Sue had developed for her own sales was to create a personal flyer urging people to come buy a car from Sue that she would leave in the local laundromats and markets.

One day, she had left her personal flyer on her desk at the dealership and was out to lunch when the local newspaper's advertising gofer came to pick up the ads for the week. Without her knowledge, he picked up her flyer off of her desk with the other ads by mistake and a full-page ad of Sue was put in the weekend newspaper that week.

Boy, were the other salespeople mad! Her boss was hot about it too. Not only was Sue doing better than the other salespeople were, but now she had a full-page ad urging people to come buy a car from her. Fortunately, on Monday, the young gofer from the newspaper admitted to taking the flyer without being told to, so Sue was forgiven for his error. The other salespeople still weren't happy about it.

All seemed to be going well for Sue, except her condo. It turned out to be a homeowner's nightmare. Her unit was on the corner of the building and it got severe water damage from water that was seeping up through the ground. Several times she had to have her carpeting taken up and big industrial fans brought in to dry out the floors. The parquet wood floor in the kitchen had buckled and swollen. The water had so warped the floors and foundation that the doors upstairs wouldn't close. Water came in through the roof too.

At one point, the condo was considered uninhabitable by the city, and Sue had to move out. When she sold it five years after she bought it, she made sixty-nine dollars over what she paid for it.

While she lived in the condo, she bought herself a wonderful bird, an African Grey, and was given a double yellow napped parrot named Paco. Paco spoke three languages, English, Spanish and Portuguese. He was an incredible mimic. Sue loved her birds as she always loved all animals and creatures, and was happy to have them in her home. However, her neighbors weren't as happy as she was. The whole condo association said no pets, but birds and fish were allowed.

Paco could mimic just about anything and apparently, he began mimicking the sounds of a newborn baby next door. All day long, while Sue was at work, this bird would make sounds like a newborn baby crying, until finally someone called the police. Sue had to let the police in to make sure that she wasn't some horribly neglectful mother who had left her new baby alone in her condo every day.

Maybe it was the sound of the baby crying or just loneliness, but Sue decided one day that she wanted a boyfriend. With her usual determination, Sue went to the Fairfield mall to find herself one. She had decided she wanted more of a businessman this time; someone who wore a suit and tie and who would come by and take her to lunch wearing his suit.

Walking into the mall on a mission and eventually into the Florshiem Shoe store, Sue saw a good-looking guy in a suit and tie who looked exactly like what she was looking for. Wasting no time, Sue approached him and while talking about shoes, gave him the full blast 'Sue treatment'. He didn't stand a chance. He was struck with her beauty, her style, her confidence and that she obviously wanted him. His name was Paul, and they went out for the first time that evening after he got off work. He was a district manager for Florsheim shoes.

Paul was a very nice man, very settled and stable in his ways and in his life. So much so, that he had been with the same girl three years and engaged for nearly a year and was planning on getting married that summer to his fiancée, who was from a prominent family in Sacramento. Then he met Sue, and his whole world changed. He was smitten. He'd never met anyone like Sue, and he didn't know what to do about it. They saw each other whenever they could and within a month from meeting each other, he broke off his engagement and moved in with Sue.

Sue, on the other hand, wasn't in love, and fell out of infatuation with Paul after living with him for only one month. She was done.

He was completely blindsided. He couldn't believe that after he had given up everything in his life for the love of Sue, that she now didn't want him at all and wanted him to move out. He was actually in shock. He simply couldn't comprehend what had happened to him.

Sue felt very badly about it, but was also very clear in her feelings. She knew he didn't have the money right then to move out and into his own place, because he had spent so much moving in with her. So she offered to loan him the money if he would sign a contract and leave several prints and his stereo as collateral. That seemed reasonable to Sue.

Paul reluctantly took her up on her offer, once he could finally comprehend that she really wanted him to move out of her place and out of her life. He never returned for his things.

Perhaps it was the drinking and partying, perhaps it was the shock on Paul's face, perhaps it was time in Sue's life, but Sue realized she had a drinking problem and needed help to face it. Like all things in Sue's life, once she made a decision, she acted on it immediately. Sue went to AA.

One of the feelings Sue had during her first AA meeting was relief. She realized for the first time she had a choice. She did not have to drink. If she didn't take the first drink, she would be fine. The fact that God was in charge again, not Sue, was of great comfort to her and she started going back to church too. She was one of the youngest people in the meetings and some of the old timers said things like, "I have spilled more then you could have possibly drunk."

The people in AA talked about drinking and said that it made things worse, not better. It was a temporary fix for a short while, but when you sober up, you'll find you not only haven't improved anything, you may have made it worse by saying or doing something you regret. They also said when you take away the drinking, you have to work on yourself or you will hate being sober.

Sue was so relieved to feel that she didn't have to drink anymore. She stayed sober for over four years. She went to meetings and did not drink in between.

Sue was what they call a two-stepper in AA. She always had to be the leader and in control. Her two steps were that she admitted she had a drinking problem and then she went right to helping other people. She never was a sponsee, only a sponsor. She did not work all the twelve steps, but helped others work them and felt like that was just as good as doing them herself with a sponsor.

This was a very good and healthy time for Sue. Sue treated her sponsees like she did all the other people she took care of and worried about in her life. When they told her their secrets, she understood they were just like her in many ways and she was very comfortable with them. These were her real friends and she cared for and protected them just like she did her mother May and her many animals. They looked up to her because of her outer success. Many of them had been in debt, had been in jail, had car accidents, all of the troubles AA talks about that happen to people who don't stay sober, work the steps and work with others.

Sue was twenty-three years old, she owned her own home, such as it was, and was making really good money. But it wasn't enough. She wanted more in her life, she wanted a challenge, and she wanted to be more creative and even more successful. She wanted to be the Finance Manager.

Working with Barney at Fairfield Honda, Sue came to the realization that she wasn't going to be allowed to move up to financing. She also knew she needed to get some experience if she was ever going to be hired anywhere, so when she heard there might be a financing job coming up at the

Volkswagen dealership in Santa Rosa, Sue decided to make some changes.

She got hired as a salesperson at the dealership in Santa Rosa with the intention of getting into finance. They told her she had to get some finance experience, and if she did get some, they would give her a shot.

Sue bought a condo in Santa Rosa and rented out her place in Vacaville. Then she found a Chevy dealership in Tracy, a two and a half-hour drive from Santa Rosa, that was willing to take her on and train her as a finance manager, just based on her interview and past history in the auto industry. Lastly, she rented a room in the house of a kind woman named Diane in Tracy and got to work.

She stayed in Tracy all week until she had two days off in a row and then would go back to Santa Rosa, where she owned a brand new townhouse. She worked in Tracy four months until she knew all she needed to know about financing. Now she was ready to move up and live in Santa Rosa.

Sue got a job working in the finance department at Volkswagen, working for commissions only. The man who had been working in finance there before her had been averaging about three hundred dollars a customer in financing, and he was paid a salary.

The dealership thought he did a fairly good job, but because Sue was new in the financing end of things, they offered her a straight commission of fifteen percent of all the sales she made, figuring that they would end up paying her less than the man before her. Of course, they underestimated Sue.

Right from the get-go, Sue shocked the dealership with her rate of sales. The guy before averaged around three hundred dollars per car, while Sue averaged about one thousand dollars per car from the very first sale! Naturally, she did consistently well, selling extended warranties, paint protection, alarm systems and maxing the rate, if she could. Not surprisingly, she also made some errors; forgetting the down payment, putting the wrong names on the contract or wrong VIN numbers, but she sold the customers and she sold the banks on approving customers that other dealerships had passed on.

At first, they thought perhaps the other guy was just a bad salesman and that anybody could do better than he did, hence, Sue's success. When they talked to Sue about it, they said, "This is only a sixty thousand dollar a year job. We are going to lower your commission structure."

Sue simply told them that they already paid a lower percentage than the normal finance departments did and if they wanted someone that only made sixty thousand dollars a year, it was not her. She stated she was more talented than that. Sue knew she was at least a hundred thousand dollars a year person, and she naturally would make better sales and better money for the company and herself. She had the track record to prove it. They finally got her point.

Feeling pleased with herself, Sue bought a used Porche Targa 911. She already had a brand new demo car too. So now she had two cars and two homes; a new town house in Santa Rosa and a rental property in Vacaville.

When her mother came to her because she and Ken wanted to buy a VCR, but their credit wasn't considered good enough to get one, Sue co-signed for them and they were able to get it. Sue was now very successful. She had a Porsche, and she was considered one of the best finance people around. But Sue wanted more.

More came to her in the form of a blind date.

Sue had been working in finance for a while and had gotten to know many people from various companies whom she needed to work with in order to complete the financing process. She knew people at credit companies, at banks and at insurance companies. Over time, she became friends with a woman named Mary, who worked at Farmer's Insurance Company. Mary began nagging Sue about meeting her boyfriend's brother, Kevin. Mary was just sure Sue would like him. They'd be great together. Finally, Sue gave in and went out on a blind date with Mary, her boyfriend, his brother Kevin and Fred, another friend of Mary's.

Fred knew the whole thing was a blind date setup to get Kevin and Sue together, but he simply couldn't resist asking Sue out himself and sending her a bunch of balloons the next day. She impressed him.

She also impressed Kevin. It turned out that Kevin was from a prominent family in Healdsburg and had been the star quarterback on the football team at his high school. Sue was sticking to her preferred type, the Big Man On Campus jock who was the most popular guy in school. Kevin was six feet tall with a lean athletic build, black wavy hair, olive skin and a winning smile. He told her he lived on a horse ranch just outside of Windsor. So Sue told him where she lived, which was quite nearby, and Sue said, with a laugh, that she had smelled him before she met him. It seemed to be a match made in heaven, but was it?

Chapter Twelve:
A 'Normal' Family

Sue went to work at the Volkswagen dealership five days a week. She was now the Finance Manager and was making really good money. She really liked her job, really loved the art of selling and really loved being successful. She felt proud of herself for accomplishing so much at such a young age. As usual, she came to work early, and she looked great. She had always dressed well and now that she could afford really nice clothes, she had lots of them. She kept herself up well. She had her hair and nails done, she kept her slim and curvaceous figure, and she always looked professional and well put together.

Life was good.

Just last week, she had met Kevin on a blind date. Tall, dark and handsome with a winning smile, he'd even come over the next day just to hang out with her and she'd enjoyed their time together. Last weekend he'd taken her to a party, and he was the most popular guy there. Everybody hung around him, and it made Sue feel special that she was his date. She could see that the other women there were a bit jealous that she was with Kevin, and that made her like him even more.

She really liked that he was so well known in the area and that he was so well connected. Sue didn't have many friends and, often, the people she worked with would be jealous of her, which was a compliment in its own way, but not necessarily friendly.

At the job, Sue gave her full attention to working out the financial arrangements for every car deal and upselling all the aftermarket products she could. It was always kind of exciting for Sue to see how much she could sell each customer. Most days she went home with a well-satisfied smile of success.

Sue loved owning her own home and having a rental home too. The feeling of responsibility was comforting to her.

The only thing lacking was the right man for her. Kevin was starting to look like a good candidate to fill that spot. He was good-looking, black hair, tall, in great shape, had a nice smile, lots of friends, a big family and all the girls wanted him. In Sue's mind, he had all the right requirements. Sue thought she'd just let things go on and see how they went. She wasn't in any hurry. Her life was going along just great right now, and Kevin might just be the icing on the cake.

They were going out to another party tonight. He seemed to go to one party or another almost every night of the week, but since Sue liked to party as well, she was happy to go. It was making it a bit difficult to stay clean and sober, but Sue was managing it. She'd been clean and sober for seven years, so she was pretty good at it by now.

After she got off work, Sue went home and changed into something really nice for a night out. She could tell he liked it that she looked so stylish and that he could show her off to his friends. Taking one last look in the mirror, she was ready. Sue was older than Kevin, and his friends commented on how sophisticated Sue was and how stylishly she dressed.

Kevin arrived and they went out and got into his car. Kevin loved his car. It was a BMW. Most of the money that Kevin made as a contractor went for his car payment alone. He loved driving it and impressing all his friends.

They arrived at the party, which was already in full swing. There was some loud rock and roll music in the background, though no one was dancing. Everybody was milling around and talking in small groups. When Kevin arrived, half the party seemed to converge on him.

Parking Sue by the refreshment table, Kevin moved around the party from group to group and then came back to Sue. He offered her a line of cocaine, but she turned him down. He then did one for himself.

Afterwards, he became very lively, but stayed with Sue and paid her much more attention.

He introduced her to his friends. He took her around to several of the groups and they stood and talked with his friends for a while. There was a lot of pot and alcohol being passed around, but Sue stuck with her Coca-Cola. Through it all, Kevin did remain attentive to Sue and didn't even glance at all the other women who were trying to get his attention. This really impressed Sue. She wanted the man that all the other women wanted, and Kevin seemed to be it.

After the party, Kevin drove her home and let her go with only a few kisses good night. Sue was a different kind of girl than most of the other girls Kevin had been with, and he didn't want to push her for sex just yet. Sue was happy to get home without having to invite him in or to fight him off.

Getting ready for bed, Sue was very happy with the way things were going with Kevin. She was pretty happy with her life in general.

The truth was, Sue wasn't sure how attracted to Kevin she really was, but felt a love for him, she'd never been really attracted to any of the guys she dated. What attracted Sue was whether the guy was 'the best', 'the prize', the one guy that everybody else wanted or thought was above all the rest. What she felt was love at the level she was emotionally capable of.

Kevin was voted the most popular guy at his high school. He had a large extended family and lots of money. He had been the quarterback for the football team in high school and could get any girl he wanted. He was very social with tons of friends. He had all the things that Sue never had: a normal family, prestige, social connections and was considered the most desirable by others. Sue had found 'the one'.

Kevin found Sue to be very attractive. She was pretty, shapely, older, had a professional job, owned two houses, had great credit and owned a Porche 911. She was everything he wasn't.

It was comfortable and easy between them and they both slid into a relationship together. They would go out to parties and Sue was always impressed with how many people knew Kevin and how popular he was. Lots of women gave him 'the look', but he didn't look back. Anytime women wanted the man Sue was with, made Sue more attracted to her guy.

Sue was working as the finance manager at Volkswagen and making a lot of money. She had found a great place to make a great living doing what she did best—selling. She was twenty-seven years old and had it all.

The partying was making it difficult for Sue to stay clean and sober. She went to some of her meetings at AA, but not as consistently as she should. Kevin liked to drink and party. He always seemed to have coke with him.

Sue's life continued with her usual burning the candle at both ends by working five days a week and going out several nights a week with Kevin. Their relationship was progressing nicely. After a sufficient length of time, they finally had sex; which naturally changed their relationship from casual to boyfriend-girlfriend.

Neither of them had made any real commitment to each other, but they were still considered a couple. Maybe they weren't in love, but neither of them really knew what being in love was. This was the closet either of them had come to love so far, even if it was born out of a need for each other. Kevin wanted the structure Sue offered and was attracted to her earned success and discipline. Sue wanted to feel worthy in the world, and Kevin's status gave her that.

After seeing Kevin for nearly nine months, Sue found out she was pregnant. Thank heavens she'd been clean and sober the whole time! Sue was happy to be pregnant, and looked forward to having this child. She wasn't worried about whether she could take care of her baby; she knew they'd be fine. She could handle it, no matter what.

Kevin wasn't so sure. He didn't know whether he was ready to be a father, and he sure didn't know about being a husband either. He knew he would do his best for his child, but he was scared too. His family began pressuring him to marry Sue, as they not only wanted him to legitimize his future child, but they really felt Sue was a great catch for him. They wanted Sue and the baby to be a stabilizing influence on Kevin, hoping the two together would help Kevin to finally grow up.

He compromised by moving in with Sue when she was about seven months pregnant. After moving in, there were some adjustments to be made by both of them. Sue was very used to living her life the way she liked, and so was Kevin. Unfortunately, they lived very different lives. Sue liked extreme cleanliness, order and keeping a beautiful home. Her furniture and carpets were white. She asked everyone to remove their shoes, and Kevin's friends made snide comments about it. Kevin started greeting them in the garage. Kevin liked doing whatever he liked when he liked doing it and not having to answer to anyone. The two adjusted to each other, but they also had no idea of what being truly intimate was really all about. They didn't talk about their internal lives, only the day-to-day necessities of living together.

Kevin came from a very large family that thrived on the next family milestone. Every week there was a birthday, a christening, a wedding, a funeral or some other event that Kevin, and now Sue, would be invited to and expected to come. There were dinners and parties and events, which kept the two of them busy.

Sue had never experienced anything like this before. She had never written a thank you note, nor did she know what was appropriate to wear or to say at a wedding or a funeral. Suddenly, she had to know how to do all of these social niceties. Sue only knew what she learned from watching TV and from the media-fed programming of what 'normal' life looked like. She'd never learned etiquette or proper behavior. Naturally, she felt a bit uncomfortable and in her uncertainty, she withdrew.

Unfortunately, Kevin's family saw her withdrawal as aloofness and consequently, some of them didn't like her very much. Some tried to control her at every chance they got, but they weren't very friendly with her. Sue really had a hard time being close to anyone. Being great at sales and her loving animals were the only things that made her feel validated.

Sue thought all of this was normal, and since she didn't know what normal was, she didn't question the attitudes and actions of Kevin's family. She just tried to do the best she could whenever she was with them. Sue had figured out that she could work two days a week and still make a good living. She figured if she was really 'on' for two days a week and hustled, she could make great money and get a free car, insurance and gas from the dealership too.

With Kevin now living with her, Sue quickly came to realize that Kevin wouldn't be providing much in the way of financial support. What money he made doing construction mostly went for his car payment and going out. He did pay for some of the bills, but Sue ended up paying more of the living expenses in the initial years.

Sue thought that she could be the woman that would inspire Kevin to change. She hoped she would shine as such a superior and special woman that Kevin would want to become worthy of her; which would show the world around her how special Sue really was. It was the usual unfortunate fantasy of many women—to be the cause of some man changing himself and his life. In real life, it rarely happens. In Sue's life, it wasn't happening either.

In all the adjustments of living together and getting used to Kevin's family obligations, Sue finally gave birth. She was in labor for only three hours and forty-five minutes and gave birth to a healthy, adorable baby boy. They named him Payton. Because he came so quickly, they couldn't give Sue any painkillers before delivery, but afterwards, Sue desperately demanded they give her something for the pain. They gave her Vicodin and sent her home with a prescription. After the pain of childbirth, it felt so great to be back in that numb feeling that drugs and alcohol always gave Sue. Her clean and sober days were over for now.

Sue had already figured out how she was going to work and still be a mom. She was only going to work two days a week, she didn't breast feed, so formula-feeding would do and her mother May and husband Ken moved up to Healdsburg just to help take care of Payton. Sue was really happy to have her mother close by to help her raise her son. Sue also loved her baby sister Peggy and her stepfather Ken. It was a truly wonderful gift for Sue to have them near her and to be so supportive.

Life quickly became a routine of working and childrearing. Sue was completely wrapped up in taking care of Payton, making lots of money and being with her family. The rest of the time, she spent with Kevin and his family. Everybody was happy to have a new baby in the family and for May, it was the first grandchild that she got to really take care of. Now that Payton was born, Kevin was getting more and more pressure to marry Sue and make it legal. Sue had been struggling with her Baptist church upbringing all along, but felt okay about the way things were. They probably could have gone on as they were for a lot longer if it weren't for the 1989 earthquake in San Francisco.

Healdsburg is about sixty miles north of San Francisco and though it was affected by the earthquake, it was relatively minor compared to San Francisco itself. But living in the Bay Area, everyone is affected by the knowledge that one day the 'big one' might happen and the 1989 quake was close enough to the big one to make lots of people scared.

Kevin was one of those people. The day after the quake, Kevin came home and said, "Sue, let's go to Tahoe this weekend and get married."

"What? Get married? This weekend?" asked Sue. She was happy about the idea. She wanted to be his wife, but didn't want it to be for any reason except that he loved her and wanted to marry her, then she would feel truly loved.

"We can drive up to Tahoe, get married in one of those chapels, spend the night and then drive back Sunday. Payton is old enough to stay at your folks for the weekend. It'll just be the two of us and a couple friends as the witnesses!" Kevin said excitedly.

"Okay. Yeah, that's a great idea," said Sue, "But what about a dress? I don't have a wedding dress!"

"We'll buy one on the way." He had already given her a ring, but just not talked about marriage. "It's no big deal, we can just stop and buy one on the way and then have the weekend to celebrate. Come on, Sue, it'll be fun," Kevin insisted.

Sue was excited. Now she knew she would be happy. This was a real family: husband and wife, a son and a dog. "Let me call my mom."

And that's how Kevin and Sue finally got married.

They drove to Tahoe early Saturday morning. They found a Macy's along the way and bought the dress. Sue had figured out that she would only wear the dress for an hour or less and would take really good care of it, so she could return it on the way back home the next day. With that in mind, she bought the very best dress Macy's bridal department had; expense was no object.

They found a little chapel in Tahoe that seemed pretty nice. They bought the whole wedding package with video and wedding pictures taken of the two of them. They decided to not do any partying before the wedding so it would be a 'real' experience, and then they could celebrate afterwards.

They returned the dress to Macy's on the ride home. Sue took it in and sadly told them she didn't get to wear it. They refunded her money, with no questions asked; they felt so sorry for her.

Now they had the picture perfect life. Kevin and Sue were finally married, making his family happy. Payton was eight months old, happily taken care of by his mom and his grandparents. Sue was working only two days a week and still making really good money. Kevin was still partying and often Sue would go with him. Sue had fallen off the AA wagon and was drinking with Kevin.

The two of them would go to a party or an event together. They'd party and feel great and have a wonderful time. They shared their party times and the mundane times too, but had no real intimacy. Sue didn't know what 'real' felt like and neither did Kevin, so they didn't know what they were missing. During those years, Kevin and Sue spent a great deal of their time involved with Kevin's family. There were various parties and milestones that had to be attended. The events were always perfect. The table was set perfectly, the food was perfect and the house was perfectly clean. Sue was always the outsider. One of Sue's sister-in-laws, Joan, was the only one who was truly friendly with Sue. Sue would try to hang out with Joan whenever she could.

Even after Sue had her second child, Trey, three years after Payton, he couldn't fill the empty space inside of Sue that she felt every time she was around Kevin's family. Sue felt shunned because it was a ritual that all the sister-in-laws gave a baby shower for an expecting sister-in-law. They did not give her one for Trey or Payton. She had thought at first the reason was because she was not married when she was pregnant with Payton, but when they didn't give her a baby shower for Trey, she could no longer believe that excuse.

At least Sue felt proud of herself because she had quit drinking three months before she got pregnant with Trey and didn't drink or do anything during her pregnancies that was unhealthy for her or the baby, not even coffee.

It was hard for Sue to always feel as if she was looking in on Kevin's family from the outside. His family looked so big and so involved in each other's lives. There was favoritism, gossip and fights, but there was great love and devotion too. Yet, Sue felt left out, excluded and not quite good enough, no matter what she did. She wanted to somehow show them, prove to them that she was valuable and special, but she didn't know how. She felt as if she'd done all the right things, but somehow didn't get the validation that she deserved. The only thing that made her feel better was alcohol, because then she felt numb.

Sometimes, when Sue was with Kevin's family, she felt as if they knew something that she didn't. Sue would wonder if Kevin was cheating on her, but could never catch him at it. She tried to talk to his brothers and sister-in-laws in a subtle kind of way about it, but they always said she was insecure behind her back and brushed her off. It became just one more reason why she didn't fit in with Kevin's family.

Who knows how much longer the two of them could have gone on like this, expecting nothing different, knowing nothing better, if fate hadn't stepped in. Sue was reading Smokey Robinson's autobiography one day when she read the passage about how Smokey and his dad were at a baseball game. Smokey said, "We need a hit."

His dad, thinking he was talking about the game, said, "Yes, we do."

But Smokey heard it as if he was saying, "We need a hit record." Smokey then opened up his spirit to the Universe to creating a hit record, and he did it.

The light bulb went off in Sue's head. She'd loved inventing things all her life and after the inspiration from Smokey, she asked the Universe to give her an idea. She opened herself up to it, knowing that if you can believe it, you can conceive it and you can achieve it. Out of the blue came this amazing concept for a sunless tanning product. Sue had her idea!

Chapter Thirteen:
The Big Success to Fix Everything, or Delusions of Grandeur

Sue was fixing breakfast for the kids after having woken them up and made sure they were in the shower and getting ready for school. As soon as she got their breakfast ready, she started making their lunches. She always made them breakfast and lunch, even on the two days a week that she worked at Nissan in the finance department. She was always there for her kids.

When Payton and Trey came down, looking clean and nicely dressed for school, they sat down at the table and dug into their breakfasts. Both boys chatted with their mother, teased each other in the usual brotherly way and brought their plates to the sink when they were finished, as they'd been taught. They were nice looking, well-behaved boys any mother would be proud of. Sue walked them to school and then headed back to the house to begin her workday.

When she wasn't working at Nissan, Sue was working on her computer, researching all she could for her sunless tanning invention. Sue knew that there had to be a way to create a sunless tanning formula without the added dyes and makeup. She herself didn't have time to lie in the sun, but liked a tan. She thought other busy moms must want a better way of getting a sunless tan, too. She also was aware that young people were still using tanning beds even knowing they caused cancer. Sue had bought clear sunless tanning products that you couldn't see while applying them and ended up with streaks. She had also bought the sunless products with dyes and bronzers that showed where she was applying them, but were messy and the dyes stained her sheets and clothes. Sue knew there was a market out there for sunless tanning products and had seen for herself the flaws in what was presently available, which made her determined to create a sunless tanning product that was flawless.

She spent hours and hours on the computer learning about different ingredients, different light responsive compounds and how to get her idea patented. She had gotten her idea while at Disneyland. When entering the park, they stamped her hand and the hands of her young children. Right there, Sue had a light bulb moment. She thought why not take the ingredient in all sunless tanning products, dihydroxyacetone, that is invisible when applying it and add a light responsive ingredient that shows up under a special light. You could then see where you were applying your sunless product under the handheld light. If you missed a spot, you could fix it. No need for any added messy dyes or bronzers.

Two days a week, Sue volunteered in each of her sons' classrooms. She insisted upon being involved in her children's education, to show her support and was willing to help out wherever she could. She was a devoted mother and after her Head Start experience, she wanted to help as many kids as she could. In between working for Nissan, volunteering in the classroom and researching her invention, Sue kept the house spotless, did all the shopping and cooked all the meals. She worked out at the Club and brought her boys with her. They played baseball, basketball and did Karate. Payton took lessons to learn the guitar and Trey learned the drums.

As always, Sue found comfort and joy in her animals. These days she had two inside animals, Lucy the Red Heeler that she'd given Kevin for a Valentine's Day gift and Toni, the feral kitten her son Trey had found. Toni was now a good-sized cat that was no longer feral, but an independent and much loved household pet.

However, the poor cat had only been with them four weeks when one night Kevin accidentally stepped on her as he was coming down the stairs. They rushed her to the vet and were told she was going to need serious surgery that cost over a thousand dollars. Kevin had been debating in his mind whether to just put the kitten down when Payton asked, with tears in his eyes, if they were going to do all they could, no matter what it cost, to save poor Toni.

Looking down into her son's face, Sue realized right then and there what the true value of money was—it's only paper, what we spend it on gives it its value. It felt good to have the money to take care of Toni. When Sue was growing up, this kitten would have been taken out back and shot, to put the poor thing out of its misery.

Sue had gotten used to having the house to herself for much of the day and to being alone. In truth, she'd come to like it. She was a strong, resourceful, assertive woman and had found that she didn't really need anyone as she took pride in doing whatever needed to be done by herself. A quote by Rudyard Kipling stuck in her head, "He travels the fastest who travels alone," and it became her motto.

Kevin wanted her to go to another family event this evening, but Sue was already figuring out an excuse not to go. In the beginning of their marriage, Sue felt obligated to go to all of the family events and try and make closer connections, but these days, she found more and more excuses to get out of going.

It was always the same old thing. Most of Kevin's family would only talk about how great their kids were or would gossip. Kevin always invited a few of his buddies so he spent most of the time with them and Sue would spend most of the time alone.

Sue would often hear whispers that would stop as soon as she'd enter a room. There seemed to be a well-kept secret that Sue was not in on. She felt no real connection to this family, though she did love Kevin's mom and step-dad. In truth the well-known secret is why no true connections could be made. There was always alcohol at every event, even children's birthday parties, so at least she got to drink, which helped a lot.

When the boys came home, Sue would oversee their homework and help them where she could. They had a special study area with all the supplies. Sue would fix dinner and they'd sit down together like any normal family, except most of the time it was just the three of them. Kevin had a very active social life, and it was seldom that all four of them ate together. After dinner, if the boys had done their homework, they could go out and play if it was still daylight. They weren't really into television, except The Simpsons, especially because of Bart. As usual for most evenings, Sue cleaned up the kitchen and had a glass of wine as she relaxed after dinner.

Finally, it was bedtime for the boys and Sue would tuck them in. As soon as they were down for the night, Sue would go back to the computer and her research. She often brought the bottle of wine in with her and would polish it off before passing out.

This night, as had happened a couple of times before, Kevin came into to the computer room and hung around for a while. He didn't really talk or even want to talk. He just seemed to watch what Sue was doing and kept looking over her shoulder at the computer. It didn't make sense to Sue why he kept doing that. Finally, she turned to him and said, "What's going on?"

"Nothing. I just wanted to see what you're doing on the computer all the time. You're on that thing practically twenty-four hours a day. What could you possibly be doing that could take up so much of your time?" asked Kevin accusingly.

"I told you, I'm doing research for my patent. It takes a lot of time to find out all that I need to know before I can submit it," Sue explained again.

"Yeah, that's what you keep saying, but I think there is more to it than that. You're just glued to that thing every time I see you!" Kevin said.

"I'm doing everything I can to find out about UV lights and sunless tanning lotions and light responsive ingredients. What do you think I'm doing, talking to men?" Sue asked. Sue had a sense that Kevin was hoping she did have someone else. *This would let him off the hook,* she thought. She had a nagging feeling Kevin was involved with other women.

"When I'm rich and famous from my sunless tanning product, you're going to know why it's so important for me to be working on this all the time. Now get out of here so I can get my work done!" Sue turned back to her computer again.

Kevin stood for a few more minutes looking at Sue's back before giving up and leaving the room. Sue spent a few minutes fantasizing again about Kevin's family wanting to ask her questions about her enormous success, and even bragging about her too. Outer success was a cause of envy and a driving force in Kevin's family. Some part of Sue chose this family to, again, create a situation where she had to prove her worth.

Finally, around eleven p.m., Sue finished her bottle of wine and shutting off her computer, got up and made her way up the stairs to her bedroom. Sue was a maintenance drinker. No matter how much she drank or how often, she never missed a day of work nor volunteering with the kids. She tried not to let the kids see her when she'd had too much to drink.

Someday it would all be worth it. Sue often thought about how great it would feel when she was rich and famous from her very own invention. She thought about how all of Kevin's family would be sorry they hadn't been nicer to her and now they would want her at all their intimate gatherings. Sue always felt like an outsider and knew they had a secret that kept any real connections from happening. She could practically see their faces when they realized how smart she really was, how stupid they were for not seeing it and how lucky Kevin was to be married to her. Sue would finally have her big 'YES!' validation she'd always wanted.

Sue would fantasize about that wonderful day when a limo would pull up with a VIP from Revlon, asking her to go for a ride and offering her an exclusive licensing deal with a ton of money up front. That's what she lived for, that day. That's what she worked so hard for, the recognition of her true value and to be seen at last.

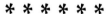

Sue's schedule was a busy one. She worked hard for two days a week at Nissan, making almost as much money in those two days as she'd make working five days. She volunteered two days a week at her children's school. She kept the house, did the cooking, supervised the boy's homework, went to their athletic events and even managed to go to a family event or two and church every Sunday. All of the rest of her time she was on the computer, researching her sunless tanning product.

She had finally learned so much that she was ready to test her formula, so she made up a batch in her own kitchen to try it out. As to be expected, it wasn't a complete success, so she went back to the computer and researched some more. She would actually try many more batches before she created one that was truly flawless.

She also needed an organic chemist to uncover and include all the categories of light responsive ingredients. Sue was concerned that another company would use a similar light responsive ingredient that could then replicate her innovative idea of being allowed to see the product as one was applying it. Sue decided to include all of the possible ingredients in her patent to protect her invention.

Finally, she'd figured out how to make a mistake-proof sunless tanning system. She tried it out, and it really worked. Sue was so excited. She really was an inventor! It was amazing to realize that it all started out as only a thought.

Sue called her friends Jenné and Laurie and shared with them the good news. She didn't really tell Kevin about it, or at least not with any excitement. She knew he didn't really care so she only mentioned something in passing to him about how she now was ready to move forward with her invention. He just shrugged and went back to reading the sports page.

Sue had become more of a loner these days. She was always 'on' at work in order to make as much as she could in the finance department, so that when she was home, she was much quieter and not really interested in going out or seeing a lot of people. She was very focused on her boys and her invention, and that was about it.

Kevin didn't seem to mind. He was used to Sue not going to any of his family events, and he was just as happy to go without her. He had other interests himself. Sue didn't have any real connections with his friends or family, and only went when she had to.

Sue was devoted to her sons. She wanted to be the best parent to them she could be and to do all the things she thought parents should do, even though she hadn't been parented very well herself. She didn't want them to feel alone as she had for most of her childhood and she wanted them to know they could always tell her everything, no matter what. After the trauma of her own childhood, Sue was determined to be connected to her children so that nothing secret could happen to them. Her world was pretty small.

Sue's desire to take care of her children was a big part of why she worked so hard on her invention. She wanted to financially provide for her sons and to show them that a person could do anything if they put their mind to it. She considered herself to be a living example for them so they could see how hard work and determination would pay off, and that a person didn't have to go about it in the same way that everyone else did in order to succeed.

Now that Sue had successfully mixed a few formulations, she became consumed with researching for her patent application and trademarks. During this process, she realized that what she had really invented was a product that was a solution for all the sunless tanning mishaps.

After doing tons of research, Sue applied for her patent and her trademark. It took several years of hard work and persistence, but she finally got her first patent. Now she turned her considerable attention and determination toward the thing she did best—marketing!

Sue switched from spending all of her time on the computer to now spending all of her time on the phone. She entered a contest in a national magazine for new ideas and was a first place winner. Over the course of one year, Sue would get over one million dollars worth of free publicity for her sunless tanning product. She contacted beauty editors and newsrooms. She called TV stations and radio stations all over the country. She spoke to one magazine editor after another and all of them thought she had a fantastic solution for sunless tanners. As a salesperson, Sue had learned long ago that every 'no' brought you closer to the 'yes', and she only focused on the 'yes'. Sue got articles about her product in Fitness, Allure, Elle, Spa and Health magazines and as well as several others.

Her friend Jenné began talking about opening up her own spa and the two of them spent hours on the phone talking about what kind of spa she was going to have and what services she would offer her clientele. Sue was excited for her friend, and was looking forward to helping her succeed.

The next logical thing to do, as far as Sue was concerned, was to go to Las Vegas. Sue and her friend Laurie flew to Las Vegas to get Sue's product in some of the spas and resorts there. After landing and then checking into their hotel, the two women got dressed up and went to the Canyon Ranch at the Venetian. Upon arriving, Sue asked to see the spa director. They were ushered into the director's office. "Hello! My name is Sue Botticelli and I have created the perfect sunless tanning product," Sue said with a big smile and her hand outstretched.

"Glad to meet you, Sue. My name is Gwen Smith," she said, shaking hands with Sue. "Unfortunately, we no longer offer sunless tanning products here at Canyon Ranch because we found they just had too many problems for our clients."

"That's exactly why I created the product that I have. I'm just a mom and I actually mixed this up originally in my kitchen, but what I created was a product that addresses all of the mistakes of the other products and fixes them!" exclaimed Sue.

"Well, I'm willing to listen to what you have to say, but I make no promises of whether we'll buy your product. We have been very displeased with all the other products of this kind before. They just didn't work well for our clients," replied Gwen with obvious doubt and skepticism in her voice.

"I know exactly what you mean, but my product was created so that, first of all, it could be applied in dim light. No more blinding light necessary to put it on! Also, you can easily see how thick or thin you're applying it and if you've missed any areas, so no more streaking or white spots. No one will ever know that your tan didn't come from the sun! Finally, it doesn't rub off onto clothes or bed sheets! Believe me, this is really a mistake-proof product!" Sue said with excited authority.

"Can we test your product? Are you willing to let us try it and see if it lives up to your claims?" questioned Gwen.

"Please do! That's why I came and why I brought my product to you. I have no doubts it will stand up to any test you can give it!" Sue said assuredly.

"All right, Sue, I'm willing to test it. We'll let you know in a couple of days if we like it or not," said Gwen seriously.

"Thank you so much, Gwen! I really appreciate your willingness to try it! I look forward to talking with you again and hopefully doing business with you!" Sue and Laurie got up, shook hands again with Gwen and left her office.

Sue and Laurie were really excited. They had gotten their foot in the door, and that was all the start they needed. The two of them then went on to the MGM Grand and several other world class spas in Las Vegas and pitched Sue's product to all of them.

Gwen got back to Sue in two days, and was so impressed with Sue's product that Canyon Ranch spa actually reinstated sunless tanning products, but only Sue's. The MGM Grand and many of the other spas also began selling Sue's product. Sue had come to Vegas, and conquered it.

One of the best things Sue did was to pitch to the newsrooms in several areas around the country. She got short news stories on ABC, NBC, CBS and FOX news from many different cities. She pitched the whole thing as a news story because she had created a product that solved all of the sunless tanning problems, which was already being sold in world-class spas and resorts and she was not even a chemist. The news people ate it up.

Every time someone said it couldn't be done, Sue would do it. Sue wanted to sell her product on QVC, but was told that QVC wouldn't talk to anyone but a sales representative offering more than one product. This didn't stop Sue. She just started calling all the QVC numbers she could find until she found a real live person whom she could talk to and she gave them her elevator pitch. From that phone call, she was brought in for a meeting and after pitching her product to the product buyer for sunless tanning; she was put on QVC.

Sue excitedly shared her success stories with her friend Jenné. She was happy to hear that Jenné had already started construction on her new spa and had a rough date for the grand opening! Sue was really looking forward to being there for the event.

Sue was also really looking forward to the next family event because they must know by now about all the TV coverage she'd been getting. She'd been gone a lot, not only to Las Vegas, but also to other spas around the country. Not that she'd been very available when she was home before her traveling as she'd been on the phone most of the time setting everything up.

Kevin didn't seem to mind. He even was kind of proud she had her own product. He liked being the guy that had it all. Everything was outer appearances. May and Ken took care of the boys while Sue was gone. Kevin was out most evenings on his own. It was upsetting to Sue to call home to check on the boys and find that Kevin was never home.

Their marriage, which had originally been based on partying together and not much else, had settled into an isolated existence of separate lives. They didn't talk, they didn't share and they rarely saw each other these days. As far as the two of them were concerned, what they had was a normal marriage—two people living in the same house together, sharing the same bed and raising children. Whatever either of them may have felt or hoped or dreamed about, they didn't share it. It was hard to believe they'd been married seventeen years.

Sue had shared her successes and failures along the way with her mother. It was such a blessing to have May, Ken and Peggy living so close by all these years. May was so happy in her second marriage and Ken treated her like gold. Their marriage was so different than what she'd had with Henry that it felt like a different life to May. Even the way she raised Peggy was so unlike how she'd been with Connie and Sue.

May had lived most of her youth in a self-induced haze. She didn't actually live her life, she mainly accepted whatever happened to her and kept her own internal fantasy world to herself. Somehow all of that changed with Ken.

Ken was so kind, caring and considerate. He wanted to know what May thought and he cared about what she felt. In time, May began to open up and share with Ken her hopes and dreams, which he always respected and he appreciated her honesty. After years of love and being treated well, May was a different person. She was a happy, much loved woman, and it showed.

One of the things Ken wanted was to share his love of bowling with May, so he asked her to join his bowling team. May said, "But Ken, I will feel so bad when someone loses." Ken knew what a soft heart May had, but he helped her to get over it and she ended up playing on the bowling team for years.

May was very proud of Sue. Sue had, in her own way, always amazed May. May moved whatever way the wind blew without a thought that she might have any choice or option in her own life. But Sue, she had gone her own way, even as a small child. Sue would decide she was going to do something and then simply do it. It never occurred to Sue to let anything stop her. May thought the world of her daughter. Naturally, May and Peggy used Sue's wonderful invention on themselves. They were living billboards for Sue's sunless tanning product and didn't hesitate to tell anyone and everyone about it. They were completely supportive of Sue.

After a whirlwind year of calling, setting up meetings and interviews and traveling all over the country, Sue could truly say she was a success! She had not only single handedly gotten herself on countless TV news programs, in national magazines, placed her product in world famous spas, but she'd actually gotten onto QVC when they said it couldn't be done. Sue was thrilled. She'd done it!

There was a Botticelli family event going on that evening. Sue was definitely going. She couldn't wait to be asked the standard "How are you?" She really looked forward to seeing their faces as they realized how smart she was, how successful she'd become and how lucky Kevin was to be married to her. Finally her dreams were going to come true and she would be acknowledged and honored for who she really was! Sue needed a drink as she practiced what she would say. It had to sound like her amazing success was only normal life in Sue's spectacular world.

Arriving at Kevin's parent's huge home, there were already overflows of cars parked in the driveway and on the street. Sue was really glad she'd dressed up glam this evening, because she really wanted to shine.

They went into the house and began saying hello to all the family members around the entrance. They gravitated to the bar and both got a drink.

Finally, the two of them found a small group of people and sat down to chat. Sue waited somewhat impatiently for an opportunity to tell them about her news. At last her chance to talk came when she got the "How are you," she needed, and Sue jumped in.

"I don't know whether Kevin has told you, but I've been working on a sunless tanning invention for several years now, and it really took off this year. I've been traveling all over the country doing different TV interviews telling them about my product. Someone called just this morning and said they saw my sunless product on The Today Show," said Sue with great expectations.

"Oh, that's great, Sue. I've been using this other sunless tanning product for a month and I absolutely love it, and it smells really good too!" exclaimed one of Sue's sisters-in-law.

Sue said, "Have you tried mine?"

Her sister-in-law said, "No, but maybe I will."

"I'm sure you'll do fine with it, though there are an awful lot of sunless tanning products out there already. I'm sure the market must be a hard one to break into and actually, you know, succeed at. I guess you'll just have to wait and see if you really do make any money," said one of Sue's brothers-in-law with a certain amount of doubt in his voice.

No one was excited for Sue. No one suddenly saw her in a different and better way. She was still the same old Sue they'd always known.

Sue was shocked. She was stunned that all her hard work and success didn't seem to mean anything to them. She had worked so hard to be seen and accepted by Kevin's family, and the world in general, that she couldn't really take it in that she didn't matter to them. No matter what she did, she didn't matter to them at all.

Sue got up and got herself another drink, and this time she had them make it a double.

She couldn't wait to leave. She had so anticipated this evening to be her triumph, and had found it to be her moment of truth instead. Between the alcohol, her hurt feelings and her final disappointment that her fantasy of acceptance had been shattered, Sue was barely able to maintain herself. It seemed forever before Kevin was ready to go home.

Sue was depressed for one day. She felt so let down, so lost and unsure of herself. She didn't know what to do with herself and her life. She knew she'd go on, but her driving purpose was suddenly pulled out from under her. One of the few things that helped was thinking about the upcoming grand opening of Jenné's new spa. Sue began to feel that maybe she didn't have the support of Kevin's rich family but she did have the support of her family and friends and that would be enough to validate her worth.

On the evening of Jenné's grand opening, Sue again got all dressed up. She wanted to look good for her friend and to look good as the inventor of the new sunless tanning product her friend would be featuring at her new world class spa. Sue felt this may not have been the big fantasized event showcasing her success, but it would be vindication for being so invisible to Kevin's family.

The drive to the spa didn't take long, and Kevin parked the car not too far away so there was only a short walk to the spa. For a local event, they had a good turnout with many familiar faces Sue knew as friends and family of Jenné's. Sue and Kevin greeted everyone they knew and then joined Jenné and her husband in the front of the spa.

Jenné got everyone's attention and gave a nice speech about how grateful she was for everyone for coming and how excited and happy she was to open her new spa. Taking a big pair of scissors, she ceremoniously cut the ribbon and threw open the door to the spa, where there were food and drinks inside. People began milling in, helping themselves to the refreshments and exploring the spa.

Sue got a glass of wine and as soon as she could, she went over to the shelves of products the spa had to offer. Looking around for her product, she was surprised that she didn't see it. She looked again, this time slowly and thoroughly. No, she still couldn't find it. Puzzled, she went to find Jenné. Sue took her aside and asked, "Jenné, I looked all over the shelves and I can't find my product anywhere. Do you have it someplace special or in the rooms or what?"

"Your product? Um, no, Sue, I don't carry your product. I got a really good deal on another product and everybody knows that brand already and they don't know yours, so I had to go with the other product. Sue! I am so sorry! I didn't think about it. I just did what was best for my spa. I hope this doesn't hurt your feelings!" said Jenné, quite startled and concerned.

Sue was stunned. She almost didn't know what to say to her friend, but managed to say something to cover her hurt and disappointment in the moment. Luckily for Sue, someone interrupted them, needing to talk to Jenné, and Sue was able to slip away without having to say anything else to her. Again, Sue couldn't wait until they could leave. Since Kevin wasn't particularly interested in the spa and it wasn't his family or friends, he was quite willing to drop her off and go out with his friends.

The two events were a real blow to Sue. She had thought that all of her hard work and effort would show her family, Kevin's family, her friends and the whole world how valuable and how smart she was. Instead, no one saw her and no one cared, outside of her mother and sister. It all seemed to be for nothing.

Chapter Fourteen:
Everything Takes Water to Grow,
Even if it's With Tears

Sue hated waiting. Sitting in the waiting room with May waiting for the doctor to show up for their appointment was making Sue anxious. May was her usual patient self. She only made this appointment because Sue insisted.

Finally, they were ushered into the doctor's office and were again sitting in the chairs in front of his desk. After the usual polite questions, Sue cut right to the chase. "So, Dr. Ruben, why doesn't my mother feel any better? When is she going to be well again?"

Casting a questioning glance at May, Dr. Ruben turned to Sue with a serious look and said, "It's not good."

"I just want to know what the bottom line is here, Dr. Ruben. It's been a few months now, and she still feels the same," Sue said.

Dr. Ruben didn't say anything for a moment or two, as he looked first at May and then at Sue before responding. Then he took a deep sigh and looking directly at May, he quietly asked, "May, is there anything you want to do or is there anyone you want to see? Because if you do, then you ought to do it now," he pronounced solemnly.

The room was silent for a very long minute.

"What?" Sue asked at last.

"There's nothing we can do for her. There are no treatments that have worked for adrenal gland carcinoma. We can do Chemo to slow it down. Towards the end, we can make her more comfortable, but that's about it," Dr. Ruben said sadly.

Again, silence filled the room.

May was in shock and silent. Sue felt numb.

"There's nothing you can do?" Sue couldn't help but ask.

"No. I'm sorry. This kind of cancer just doesn't respond to chemo or radiation. There's nothing we can do. Chemo will slow it down, and we will keep checking her. She could have several more months or a year where she will be comfortable enough to be active. I strongly suggest," looking directly at May, he continued, "that you do whatever you want to do during that time."

Ken had just gone to the pharmacy to handle the past bill at the hospital, thinking this was a routine visit. May had been not feeling herself for about a year and they had made several trips to the doctor. May even had had a tumor removed and been given a clean bill of health, but she just never felt herself again.

The doctor looked down at his desk as if to gather his courage before facing them again. "Here is a pamphlet. Fill it out and put it on your refrigerator. This way if an ambulance has to come, the doctors will know what May's wishes are."

Wow, this was shocking. Sue expected that the doctor would just order more tests and finally get to the bottom of this. Sue was thinking of Ken, who had been to every doctor's visit with May, and now they were getting this news without him. Sue would have to tell him.

"May, you can decide if you want chemo to slow it down or not. Think about it, talk it over with your family and then let me know what you want to do," Dr. Ruben said with an air of finality.

"Okay, then. Come on, Mom, let's go find Ken." Sue stood, reaching for May's arm to help her out of the chair.

As if coming out of a trance, May stood up awkwardly and then turning to the doctor and returning to the kindness and politeness that was the essence of who she always was, May thanked him for his time and all his help, even though he had no help to give her.

Ken was just walking back towards the hospital when he met them in the parking lot. Before he could ask any questions, Sue said, "It's not good." Ken cried, soft tears that he just couldn't stop even though crying is not what he wanted to do in front of May. He had to stay optimistic.

The drive to May's home was more silent than talkative. A million thoughts were running through Sue's head. How was she going to live without her mother? What was this going to do to her sons? How would Peggy handle it? What were any of them going to do? Was there anything of any kind that anybody could do to help May? Was there some kind of cure somewhere else, maybe not regular medicine, but something?

May sat quietly, still too stunned to really talk about any of it and afraid to think of what the doctor had said and what it really meant. She seemed to be in a daze and it was difficult for her to focus on anything Sue was saying, so Sue stopped saying anything.

When they got to May's house, Ken came around and helped May out of the car and walked arm and arm with her up the steps to their home. Setting her down in the living room, Sue asked May if she wanted anything. May was still a bit dazed, but finally agreed to having a cup of tea. Sue went into the kitchen to fix it.

When Sue came back with the tea, May was sitting just as she'd left her with the same look of dazed amazement on her face. Finally May spoke and said she was going to be that one percent the doctor talked about that beat this cancer.

Ken, desperately maintaining his optimism for May said, "Let's plan a trip. We could go see your whole family back east."

Sue put her arms around her mother and said, "That'll be fun, and give you something to look forward to."

They spent most of the afternoon talking in bits and pieces about all the crazy thoughts they had going through their heads. Often there were silences until one of them had another random thought connected with the practicalities of May's remaining life and May's repeatedly saying she was going to beat this.

When it was time for Sue to go home to fix a snack for the boys after they came home from school, May said she'd like to lie down for a bit and get a little rest before everybody else came over. Sue thought that was a good idea.

Driving home to see her sons, Sue tried frantically to think of what to tell them and how. She decided that she would have the three of them go for a walk in the hills behind their house so she would be in nature, God's country, when she told them. She hoped it would somehow make it easier to tell them their beloved grandmother, who greatly helped raise both of them, had cancer.

The boys sensed right away that something was wrong with Sue as soon as she walked in the door. They tried to ask her what was the matter, but Sue just said there was something she wanted to talk to them about, but it would have to wait until they got a bite to eat. After they each got an apple, the three of them headed out the back door for the hills. Naturally, the family dog came too.

"Payton, Trey, there's no easy way for me to tell you this, but I just found out today that your grandmother has a rare form of cancer. We saw the doctor and he told us there's nothing they can do for Grandma's cancer and that she has a few more months, maybe a year, left to live," Sue softly began.

"No! Mom! No! I thought Grandma was getting better! I thought she was cured! How did this happen? No, I don't believe it!" came the chorus of denial from the two boys.

"I know. I thought she was going to get better too, but she's not. As terrible as it is, we're going to help her and research the internet for options. You know she loves the two of you more than anything and you'll always have that, no matter what," said Sue, trying to reassure her sons.

"This is going to be hard on all of us. Think of poor Grandpa Ken and Aunt Peggy. All of us are going to miss Grandma so much. But let's try to spend as much time as we can with her and help her as much as we can. Anytime either of you want to talk about this or just need to be sad or whatever, you know you can come to me. Let's just all try to be there for each other and together, we'll get through it," offered Sue, the best motherly and helpful thing she could do in such a still unreal situation.

Holding her arms out to both boys, they each hugged a side of Sue and of each other as they gently cried and held on to each other standing there in the woods.

When all three of them had cried as much as they could for the moment, they began to walk back to the house. They got in the car and drove to Kevin's office to let him know. He too loved May, and was greatly saddened by the news.

Driving back home, Sue decided to leave the boys to do their homework, knowing that Kevin would be home soon. Then Sue drove to where her sister Peggy worked, knowing she would be getting off work soon, and faced the final hardship of the day; to tell her baby sister that their mother was dying. With shock and denial, Peggy tried to dispute the words Sue said, but finally broke down and the two of them just held onto each other for a while. With tears and promises to pray for a miracle, both sisters went to their cars to drive over to May and Ken's home.

May was up and had started dinner in the kitchen when Sue arrived. Sue gave her a hug and offered to help. The two women worked quietly in the kitchen together, doing the mundane things one does to prepare dinner.

Ken came into the house with his usual cheeriness, greeted his wife in the kitchen with a hug and a kiss, and said confidently, "We'll get through this."

Turning and seeing Sue, Ken said, "Oh hello, Sue! I didn't see you standing there. You didn't have to come all the way back here today. Are the boys here too?"

"Hi, Ken. No, I'm not staying for dinner. I left the boys at home and Kevin will be home soon, so I'll have to leave in just a bit. I just wanted to be here for Mom and you."

Still holding May loosely in his arms, Ken asked, "May, have you thought about our trip?"

Looking at May, Sue said, "Yes, that sounds fun for you Mom."

Waiting for a minute or two, Sue then felt she could bring up the subject again, "Mom, I told Peggy and Kevin. Peggy said they've come a long way with cancer cures." Looking now at Ken, Sue continued, with more hope than conviction, "Mom will be fine."

Ken nearly collapsed. Sue watched as all the joy drained out of him. He clutched May to him tightly and held her as if to never let her go. But he couldn't speak. Not yet. All the news from earlier that day was starting to sink in.

Just then, Peggy arrived for dinner. Walking into the kitchen and sensing the tension in the room, she looked back and forth from May and Ken to Sue and said with intensity, "Mom is going to beat this. I just know she will."

"I feel better than I have in days," May put in to corroborate her daughters.

Peggy rushed to her mother and put her arms around her. Crying softly, she said over and over, "We will beat this, Mom. We will." Crying seemed to be the only sane thing to do. There comes a moment when everyone realizes that they can't stay frozen in time anymore and they must somehow, someway, move.

May went to the bathroom to clean up. Ken went with her. Peggy came and hugged Sue and then left to put her things away that she brought in with her for her mom.

When everyone gathered back in the kitchen, there was an air of sadness but a sense of trying to figure out how to go on with everything. May continued to fix dinner, Peggy joined her and Ken stood around watching them all. Sue realized this was a good time for her to leave and go take care of her own family. Saying she had to go, Sue hugged each of the three of them and with their shared grief, sadly left the house and drove home.

Arriving home, she found Kevin in the kitchen. He had ordered a pizza for them.

"Are you okay? How's your mom? Is there anything I can do?" kindly asked Kevin.

"Yeah, I'm okay, or as okay as I can be under the circumstances. How are the boys?" Sue said tiredly. She felt emotionally quite drained.

"They're cleaning their rooms, and they're pretty bummed out about this. This is going to be hard on them you know, because May took care of them so much even as babies. She's practically their second mother."

"I know. I talked to them the best I could, but this is just the beginning. It's going to get worse and I don't know what to do when she dies. I don't know how I'm going to make it myself without her, and I'm scared what it will do to the boys too."

"Yeah. Well, we'll figure it out as we go. It's part of life."

"Yeah, I guess we will. We'll have to." Sue opened the refrigerator and took out a bottle of wine. She really needed a drink.

Kevin went back to getting pizza on the table. Sue poured herself a large glass of wine and sat at the kitchen table with it while she tried to make some kind of sense of her life.

Thinking about it, Sue was pretty sure this had been the worst day of her life so far.

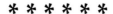

"Mom, um, Trey and I wanted to talk to you about something but we were scared to tell you," began Payton.

Sue, immediately feeling alarmed because of her own childhood experiences with secrets, turned and looked at both of her sons, as if by looking she could see if they were really okay or not. "What are you scared to tell me? You know you can tell me anything. I've always said that secrets are worse than the truth, no matter how bad the truth may be."

"Yeah, we know, which is why we decided we had to talk to you about it," Payton continued. Then, looking at his brother to make sure they both really wanted to say this and getting his non-verbal agreement, Payton began again. "We think Dad is doing something with Carrie that works for him. Something bad."

"What? Where did that idea come from? Why would you think that?" Sue asked.

"Well, we've both heard him talking to her on the phone. He seems to be trying to hide it from everybody. I mean, one time, he was in the hall closet talking to her, and another time he abruptly hung up as soon as I came into the room. When you're gone, he goes out in the evening and he doesn't come home until really, really late."

"Your father leaves you alone in the house?" They were both teens now.

"Yeah, sometimes, but only when he thinks we're asleep."

"He acts funny around her too, Mom, like what someone does when they're afraid to get caught," added Trey.

"But you've never actually seen him doing anything with her?

"Well, no, but that's because he's being really careful," defended Payton.

"Okay, listen, Payton, Trey, neither of you know for sure that your dad is doing anything he shouldn't be doing with Carrie. I really understand that you think he is, and I'm grateful that you trusted me enough to tell me, but until I know for sure that he's doing something like that, I'm not going to accuse him or act any differently. And I don't want you two boys to act any differently either. He's your father, and you have to show him respect and that's all I'm going to say about this now." Sue turned back and went into the kitchen.

The two brothers gave each a look of understanding and then shrugged, accepting that their mother didn't want to know the truth, but they'd done all they could do. Then they both turned and went back upstairs to their rooms.

Sue had her suspicions too, and having her boys bring it up was like getting kicked in the stomach. But Sue's worries about her mother were the only thing she could focus on, so she set her suspicions aside.

Two days later, Sue and Kevin were in their bedroom getting ready for bed. Kevin asked how May was doing again.

"She's still in shock, I think. I did as the doctor suggested and asked her if there was anything she wanted to do before she, well, you know, and I was really surprised that she said yes. She wants to go to New York and Florida to see her siblings before she... before she's not feeling up to it. She hasn't seen any of them since she moved to California," Sue explained.

"Listen, Sue, I'll pay for the trips for your mother. I mean, I've got the money and I'd be happy to pay for everything for her. It's the least I can do. She's always been there for you and the boys and you know I think the world of her. I'd like to give her and Ken this time together, if that's okay with you," gently offered Kevin.

"Oh, Kevin! That would be wonderful! Wow! Thank you! I know my mother will really appreciate it, and it's really generous of you to offer. I know Ken can't really afford it, but he'd do it anyway and this way, he won't use up all his savings for them to go. Thank you! I'll tell her tomorrow." I felt a deep gratitude and love for Kevin.

"She should go sooner rather than later, so, well, you might as well tell her sooner," said Kevin.

"Okay, I will. Thank you, Kevin," Sue said, coming over and giving him a hug.

Kevin said, "You're welcome," and the two broke apart.

They both moved away and went about their usual preparations for bed. Finally, they got into bed, turned out the lights and each went to sleep on their own side of the bed as usual.

The next day, as good as her word, Sue told May about Kevin's generous offer. May was thrilled. She really wanted to see her brothers and sisters, but didn't know how they could afford the trip without putting Ken into debt. May deeply appreciated Kevin's kind gift.

Sue and May immediately began planning the trips and started calling the airlines and May's siblings to set up dates. The two of them spent the next few days getting everything planned out and arranged. May was really going to have this last great wish of hers after all.

Fortunately, May's trip was over two weeks away because the next day, Kevin's stepfather, Grandpa B as his grandchildren called him, died suddenly of a heart attack.

Immediately, the entire Botticelli clan descended en masse on Kevin's parent's home. The Botticellis had a very large family with many extensions all over the country, so the funeral was a massive event. Everyone wanted to be a part of it and wanted to help, and everyone was grieving and reacting. There were many, many tears; many, many emotions; and many, many people.

Kevin was devastated. His stepfather was a man that everyone had expected would live many more years. The two men were close and involved in each other's lives. Kevin felt an immense sense of loss and emptiness. He retreated within himself and quietly grieved.

Payton and Trey were also devastated. They adored their Grandpa B, having grown up going to the big house for countless family gatherings and events. Their grandfather had played with them, teased them and lovingly took pride in them, so both boys were in shock and grief as well. They also had never experienced death at such a close level before and were still young enough to feel the unreality of someone one loves suddenly being gone, never to return. It was a very difficult time for everyone. Sue was shocked and saddened too. She loved her father-in-law and appreciated him, especially as a grandfather to her sons. She'd never been real close to him, as he was close to his family. He was kind and friendly with Sue.

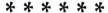

The funeral itself was a big event. In a family known for having many family events as part of its normal lifestyle, this funeral was even more elaborate and expansive. They had to rent a large hall to hold the reception and, of course, it was catered. They ordered nearly a fleet of limos to take everyone to and from. There were flowers and food and wine everywhere. There were many, many tears and lots of speeches praising the beloved patriarch. As with all things, this too came to an end, and everyone finally went home to grieve privately in their own way.

Kevin was quieter after the funeral. Payton and Trey were also quieter and seemed to cling to both of their parents a bit more than one would expect for teenaged boys. Sue was grateful she had the support of her mother, but also realized that somehow she was going to have to live without her mother's support far sooner than she'd ever thought she would. Sue's father-in-law's death made May's imminent death all the more real to Sue.

May was grateful that she was still home when all of this happened, so she could help Sue and the boys get through the funeral. She did the best she could for her daughter, grandsons and even her son-in-law, Kevin, knowing that sometimes the only thing you can do is just to be with them while they go through the grieving process.

Yet, the time finally came for May to take her longed for trip back east to see her siblings. She somehow knew this was her last chance to find what peace she could with her old life. Oddly, having lived a lifetime of avoiding painful realities, May found the courage to face her past and to finally let it go.

When she came home after weeks away in the east, she had an inner sense of peace that she'd never had before. Now all she had to do was face her own sickness and to help her loved ones understand she was going to be the lucky one that beat this. Surprisingly, she felt up to the task.

Every family has its history, its patterns and its cultural framework that interweaves into all of the lives of the members. Sue's family history of poverty and ignorance contributed to Sue's personality, development and expectations. It also caused a longing in Sue for something more, something better and so Sue spent all of her life trying to create a 'normal' life. And now she had exactly that. She had a husband, two sons, a big house, rentals, RV, expensive cars, a limo, a boat, nice clothes, good jewelry, gardener, housekeeper. She had all the things that signified success and the American dream. Sue had it all. She was living what everyone would agree was the perfect life. She never stopped and asked herself if she was happy or not, this is what she believed was normal. It was expected that all of those things must make a person happy, so Sue must be happy.

Kevin's family history had a different cultural framework than Sue's. His family had come to this country and retained much of their native culture and attitudes. Over time, they brought more and more family members over from the old country until they had a huge family in the new country, and other than speaking English and being much richer than they were in the old country, they were still the same. They valued family unity, even if that meant ignoring infidelity or unhappiness or troubles. They overlooked alcoholism and illegal activities, as long as the authorities weren't involved.

Family was family, and they all stuck together, no matter what, and everything else, they shoved under the rug.

So when Kevin's brother Tom went into a thirty-day rehab program for alcohol abuse, no one came to see him. His family was pretending that he was on vacation and no one talked about what was really going on with him. It was a courageous thing for Tom to do, knowing how his family would react to it, but after his stepfather's death, Tom faced some of his own problems for the first time, and this was one of the results.

Sue was the only one who came to visit him in rehab. Sue was still going to AA at times and she always valued the AA program, so she knew Tom could use all the support he could get, and she was happy to give it to him. They talked about his drinking problem and how he was handling it. Sue was very accepting, and her support meant a lot to him. He deeply appreciated her kindness in coming.

Sue was glad she went to see Tom. She understood the need for support, particularly now as May was in the final stages of her life. Sue was spending as much time as she could with her mother. It was getting very close to the end, and May was in a great deal of discomfort. She was being given very heavy pain meds and was often incoherent. It was only a matter of days for May, and everyone knew it.

And then, she was gone. Quietly, softly, she simply slipped away. As she had lived most of her life, so in her death, May died without any fanfare or drama. Ken was with her when she breathed her last. Sue was glad that she and the boys weren't there, as she feared they would somehow be damaged if they were there at the end. It was hard enough for Ken to see the light suddenly go out of his beloved wife and know it would never return. Sue had had a difficult time visiting her mother and allowing herself to feel the grief and pain, as she had lived most of her life separate from her raw feelings.

One of the few solaces Sue had was taking long walks in the hills behind her house. She would walk in the beautiful woods and see the forest animals; many of the deer knew her from all her walks in the past. They would help her feel at peace and gave her the sense that fundamentally all is well. She would often talk to God during these walks too. One day, feeling confused and uncertain about all that was going on in her life, Sue asked God to show her the truth, whatever it may be. She just wanted to know what was really true about herself and her life so she could figure out how to go on and face reality.

Mostly, Sue was a zombie. She was functioning on automatic pilot, going through the motions of living her life and getting things done. Somehow she had to plan the funeral for her mother, help her sons grieve, still go to work, still fix dinner and still manage to put one foot in front of another. It all seemed too much and yet she was still managing to get it all done, until she got a phone call from Tom.

Sue was at work, trying to make funeral arrangements in between making calls to banks for customers at the Nissan dealership when Tom called. At first, Sue was almost too distracted to talk to him, but the intensity of his voice made her pay attention.

"Sue, I have to tell you something. I can't live with myself another day without telling you. I realized you are a real friend when you came to visit me in rehab, and it made me feel even more guilty for not telling you and letting it go on for so long. I've got to let you know that Kevin's been having an affair with his secretary, Carrie. We all knew about it, but no one wanted to tell you. He's our brother, so we didn't want to interfere. But I just can't do it anymore. When we all went to Mexico last time and Kevin brought Carrie, well, that was too much for me to tolerate. I just can't look you in the eyes anymore and let you go on not knowing the truth, and I can't lie to you anymore."

Tom had bluntly told Sue what he had been holding back for years and it all rushed out, without stopping so he could get it said and done. He didn't give Sue any chance to interrupt or ask questions until he said all he had to say.

Finally, Sue spoke. "Thanks, Tom, for telling me. I don't know what to say right now, but I am grateful you told me," Sue said, even though she felt as if all the blood had rushed out of her body and that she was going to faint. She was shaking. Amazingly, she also felt strong and for the first time, wanted to confront Kevin right now.

"Okay, Sue. Sorry about everything. Maybe we'll talk more later. Goodbye."

Sue was stunned. Her whole world had finally, completely and absolutely fallen apart. After a lifetime of separating herself from her feelings, Sue had no defense against all of this. It was too much. It was more than she could bear. Here she was planning her mother's funeral, still working, still taking care of everything when her entire life jumped off the cliff. This was finally it. She'd had enough.

Sue hung up the phone and stepped into the only frame of mind she could do and still survive; she went into 'fuck it' mode. There just wasn't any other way she could survive all of this except to say "fuck it" to everything. For the first time in her life, Sue did only what she needed to do for herself. She called Kevin, but he didn't answer.

Sue was full of energy. She wanted to confront this now. She walked into the office of the owner of the dealership she had worked at for several years and said, "As you know, my mom just died, and now I just found out Kevin has been seeing his secretary for years. I am quitting. I have to figure my life out and be there for my boys." By the look in his eyes, Sue could tell her boss had known too, as he had gone to sporting events, bachelor parties and other places with Kevin over the years.

Without another word, Sue left the office and drove home. She was anxious for the boys to get home. As soon as they came through the door, Sue sat them down to let them know what was going on.

"Boys, I want you to know that you were right when you talked to me about your dad all those months ago. I just found out today that your father has been having an affair, as you suspected."

Then Sue turned and looked directly at the boys, wanting to impress upon them that what she had to say was very important and they needed to pay attention. "I'm not telling you this so you'll be mad at your father or even to blame or judge him. I am telling you this because I want you both to know that you can trust your instincts. You can trust that inner sense you have that tells you the truth about something. It's important for you to be able to trust that inner voice inside you, because sometimes it can save your life and I don't want you to ever distrust that inner knowing again, okay? Listen to what you know is true inside and don't ever stop, no matter what anyone tells you, not even me, okay?"

The boys, bewildered, frightened and shocked, nodded. Sue saw that they understood her.

"I also want you both to know that your father and I love you. You two are the most important people in our lives. Don't ever forget that," Sue said with such intensity that both boys could only nod their agreement. Realizing the talk was over, they both looked at each other and one motioned with his head suggesting that they leave, and they did.

When Kevin came home, he first noticed that Sue wasn't in the kitchen making dinner. In fact, there was no dinner ready at all. Surprised, he walked around the house calling Sue's name. She didn't answer, but he finally found her in their bedroom. She was very angry.

"Sue? What the hell is going on here? What are you doing? Where is dinner?"

"You are moving out tonight," Sue answered as if that explained everything. "Your brother Tom finally told me the truth today about you and your 'secretary.' I've had the feeling for years that you'd been cheating on me, but no one would ever tell me the truth. Now that I know, I'm done with you. I'm divorcing you, and you're leaving this house tonight." Sue spoke with that kind of scary calm voice that brooks no argument.

"My brother told you? How could he betray me like that? He had no right to tell you! I'll get that bastard for talking behind my back!" Kevin ranted.

Sue was shocked. Right there, she saw that Kevin thought cheating was an acceptable thing to do and wondered if his family had been covering for him for all of their marriage, figuring they probably had.

"Man! When I get hold of him!" Kevin continued ranting.

"I can't believe that you are more upset that your brother told me than you are about the fact that our family is broken now. All I can say is that this just proves what kind of a marriage we have. Our marriage has been a lie for so many years, I don't know when the lies started. But what I can tell you is this. I'm done with lies. I'm done with living my life pretending everything is fine and normal," Sue asserted angrily.

"Wait a minute, Sue. Just because I've been having an affair doesn't have to mean our marriage is over. I am confused. We just need to sort some things out."

"No Kevin, we're done. We're beyond working things out, because we don't have anything between us to work out. I want you to move out tonight. Pack a bag and go stay at your girlfriend's, but you're not staying the night here. We'll talk more about this in a day or so when both of us have had some time to think things over, but for now, you've got to go."

Sue couldn't help adding, "I should have believed your other brother years ago when he told me you were messing around. I asked you and you swore it wasn't true, that it was just your brother trying to get a shot at being with me. Well, we're over, Kevin. You have to go now," Sue said with absolute finality.

Kevin really looked at Sue. When she made up her mind, there was no changing it. Then he nodded, as if to silently agree to all that she had said, and then turned around and went into the closet to get a big gym bag. Without saying another word, he began to pack his bag. Leaving their bedroom, Sue went downstairs and poured herself a glass of wine. Sue couldn't help but think about all the rumors she'd heard over the years, especially that his older brother had had a thing for her, which was why she had believed Kevin's explanation when she shouldn't have.

When Kevin came down, bag in hand, he turned to Sue and quietly said, "Let's think things over and then talk in a couple of days. Tell the boys I'm staying in the RV at the ranch and that I love them."

Sue nodded. "Okay, I'll tell the boys and we'll talk in a few days."

"Goodbye, Sue."

"Goodbye, Kevin."

Though the two simple words they each spoke sounded normal and mundane; they both knew that what they were really saying was goodbye to eighteen years of marriage. It was over.

Sue spent much of the night coming to grips with her life. In a very short time, she had lost everything. She lost her mother, father-in-law, her husband, her marriage, her job and all the things she thought life was supposed to be about, such as having a normal family. She realized that she and Kevin had been going through the motions, not really living or sharing their lives together as a married unit. They'd both been living separate lives for so many years she couldn't remember when it began, or if they'd ever had any 'realness' between them in the first place. She always said they were the flip side of the same coin.

What was becoming very clear to Sue was that she wanted to live a 'real' life and be a 'real' person, and to hell with normal. All of her life she'd tried to fit herself into some kind of 'normal' mold so that she could finally look like and be like everybody else. Now she knew it wasn't worth the price. She'd never really been herself and she'd lost touch with her true feelings. Sue was ready to begin to live a real life, no matter how difficult it might be. At least it would be real. She would be real.

That night, Sue cried for her boys, her mother and the end of her marriage. She cried for who she had been and for all of her past. The grief she felt was very painful, but for the first time in her life, she allowed herself to feel it. She wasn't going to separate herself from her feelings anymore. She did not want to drink. Then, being Sue, after a few weeks, she dried her tears and faced her future.

Yes, she'd spent her life trying to create a 'normal' life, but now she was going to spend the rest of her life living a real life. She was going to be true to herself in every way she could. She knew things were changing. She had never felt so clear or so certain about anything in her life before as she was about knowing the importance and necessity of being authentic and living an authentic life. For the first time, she didn't care what anyone thought. What *she* thought and felt was her new gauge.

After this epiphany, Sue felt as if the air was cleaner, the colors were brighter and life was different than it had ever been before. She knew whatever she had to face, she could do it, and she was ready for anything.

Unfortunately, what she wasn't quite ready for was her sons' reactions to everything.

For Payton and Trey, their lives too were all about loss. Their beloved Grandpa B and Grandma May, two people who had significantly been a part of their childhoods and lives, had both passed away within months of each other. Now their parents were getting a divorce and their dad had moved out. Their mother had even quit her job after years of working for Nissan. Their entire lives had been thrown up in the air like a deck of cards, landing in a huge mess and with the joker face up.

Payton was seventeen and a senior in high school. He had always been a 'good kid'. He said no to drugs and alcohol, he had gotten good grades, was a sponsored skateboarder and, for the most part, had never given his parents a day of worry.

Trey was the more adventuresome and the more peaceful of the two boys. He played guitar and was very good at art. Trey had been very close to his Grandma May, and the loss of her affected him the most. She had been his second mother all of his life and her passing cut very deeply into him. With the breakup of his parent's marriage, Trey was turning his grief into anger.

Both of the brothers seemed to have caught the 'fuck it' disease that Sue had. Their lives had suddenly held so much loss they just said "fuck it" to everything. Payton not only came home stoned, but was caught with both pot and alcohol at school. Since alcohol was easier to get a hold of, Payton began drinking whenever he could. Since Trey had already tried both alcohol and pot, his 'fuck it' answer was anger. He started writing angry, violent rap lyrics that expressed his rage and frightened his mother.

Worrisome and frightening things were happening with both boys. Once, Payton was out driving in his truck when he looked in his rear view mirror and saw a vision of his Grandma May in the back seat. She leaned forward and told him to be careful with his driving; that she was worried about him. He reassured her that he would be fine because he had his seatbelt on. Shortly after that 'conversation', he rolled and totaled his truck, and only his seatbelt saved his life.

It was a hard time for Sue and her sons. There had been so much loss and so many changes that everyone felt insecure about what tomorrow would bring. Sue did her best to help her sons through it, but there was only so much she could do.

Their concern for their sons enabled Sue and Kevin to get together and calmly discuss how they were going to handle the divorce. They both accepted the marriage was over and that they both loved their sons and wanted what was best for the boys. They agreed there was no need to speak badly of the other especially in front of the boys and that everything was to be divided up evenly between them. They didn't need mediation to resolve their money issues, they just sat down and split up everything and had a legal assistant write it up and file it. No lawyers were even involved.

Kevin finally admitted to Sue that he was worn out by all the lying and hiding he'd had to do. He felt like he'd been living on a merry-go-round, and he was glad to get off. Though they both were sad to end their marriage, they were still glad that they hadn't stayed together just because of inertia. They continued to be close friends to each other and to always work out any problems amiably.

She was perfect for him and he for her until they weren't, and despite their issues, they had loved each other with all they were capable of at the time. Many people never knew any other type of love than the one they had together, because of their limits to love. She had truly loved him; theirs was a connection that wouldn't ever be broken.

Sue began to look at her life in a new way. It reminded her of getting a new purse. Once you get a new purse, you have to empty out the old one and decide what to put into the new one, and what to throw away. That was how Sue was changing her life. Now she was deciding what to put in and what to throw away. Her new purse would definitely be lighter than the old one.

Chapter Fifteen:
New Beginnings

Sue awoke at her usual early hour, around five-thirty a.m., and getting out of bed, she quietly got into her red sweat pants, specially fitted sports shoes and her favorite white Juicy Couture coat with a cute terrier on the arm to go take her morning walk. She always wore the same outfit, so that the animals would recognize her and not be afraid.

Sue would start out from her back door just as the slightest streaks of light were starting the day. She would go through the gate, going from her backyard to the woods and the gentle hill that lay behind her house. As she'd been doing now for so many years, she started her day with her walk, quietly, in nature, among the animals she'd loved all of her life, gently communing with God, the whole world and her own inner self. Her morning walk was one of the things that had kept her sane through her many difficulties and grief, and she always found time for it, except sometimes when she was on the road for sunless tanning business.

The deer would raise their heads as she walked, alerted by the noise she made, but seeing her and knowing she wouldn't harm them, they would simply put their heads back down to graze again.

Sue knew all the names of the dogs in her neighborhood. Unfortunately, she often didn't know the names of the dogs' owners, but she knew all the dogs and they knew her. Sometimes she'd see them on a leash being walked on the street and the dogs would strain to greet her, their friend,

Sue.

Mornings were her alone time, her quiet time. When she and Kevin had first moved into this home, which bordered the woods, she'd asked him if he wanted to accompany her, but he never did. Walking with Sue in the woods wasn't something Kevin enjoyed doing. It wasn't a sport or some kind of body building exercise, so he wasn't interested. Sue got used to going on her walks by herself and enjoying her solitude.

This morning, Sue was thinking about all that had happened over the past year and how her life had changed. She was still mourning the passing of her mother and still seeing how the two deaths of her boys' grandfather and grandmother were yet affecting her sons as well. Things were better. Time heals as it changes things, and her sons were becoming more accustomed to the divorce, the deaths and to growing up. Yet, they were different, not as innocent, not as optimistic, not as secure in their world.

Sue wasn't as secure in her world either, but for different reasons. Somewhere in all the changes, her old self slipped away like the shedding of a skin. Sue was still getting used to her new way of thinking and of her freedom. She was happier too.

After a lifetime of trying to be 'normal', Sue no longer cared what anyone thought or whether she was like everyone else. Sue only wanted to do and be what was really true for her, who she truly was, and to live her life with integrity and truth. Her own truth, whatever that may be, and Sue was still in the process of finding out what that truth was.

So much of her past had been a false front, such as living in a lavish home with expensive furnishings, signed sports memorabilia, limousines and luxury box seats at all the home football games. Sue still didn't know how a football game was played, but she'd been to many of the home games and had hung around as Kevin watched every game for years. It seemed absurd to her now. Why would she spend so much of her time and effort doing something she didn't enjoy and actually knew nothing about? Yet that's how she'd lived her life.

She'd spent eighteen years of her life doing what her husband wanted her to do, being what she thought he wanted her to be, and never asking herself whether she liked it or wanted it or not. She had been in such a pursuit of a 'normal life' that she didn't realize she had no life at all

After the whole thing fell apart, Sue decided to throw everything out the window and start over with herself, her life, her likes, her goals and even her thinking. Sue wanted to only be what was really and truly Sue, whatever that might be.

Sue found that she didn't want to eat meat anymore. She loved animals, had always loved animals, in fact, animals had been her main solace throughout all of the really difficult parts of her life and it seemed crazy to her now that she would eat them! So she stopped. Just like that.

Sue loved the arts and music and creativity and really didn't like sports at all, so she got rid of all the sports memorabilia in her home and never went to any kind of game again. She started going to concerts and art galleries and musical or artistic events, and soon, the new people she was meeting were inviting her to go to lots more events now with them. She was making new friends that better reflected her true self.

These new friends liked her for who she was. They appreciated her sarcastic humor and thought she was funny. They saw her as a leader. They were enchanted by her drive, passion and success. Sue, on the other hand, wanted what they had—patience without an agenda and a willingness to just be.

One thing Sue really got from her breakdown, the loss of her mother and the ending of her marriage is that she now knew what was real in her life: her feelings. Knowing this, she became very clear about what she chose to be and chose to have in her life, and being real was the most important part.

Naturally, when a person goes through such a huge change internally, their external world changes too. Sue began to draw creative, real people into her life and to draw to her the things and the work that matched her new way of being.

One day, out of the blue, an old colleague, Christopher, contacted her and asked her to come work for him. They'd worked together before and he knew how talented and powerful she was. He wanted her to do special projects for him. He was starting up a new business called No Gas Motors, an electric car company, and he wanted Sue to do her magic.

Sue was interested and offered to do a trade show for him in Detroit for free, just to see if she liked it. Once in the thick of the event, Sue found she not only liked it, she loved it! She decided to take the job, but only if it was part time. She had too many dreams of her own that she wanted time to work on manifesting.

Sue did decide that if she was going to work for someone else, she wanted to do so only to help someone else fulfill their dream. She didn't want to just work for the sake of the money or just to have something to do. She wanted to manifest her own or other people's dreams because that was what was important to her now.

Sue enjoyed the three and a half days a week that she worked with Christopher. It was a perfect job for her as her main role was to jump in and create attention, marketing or exposure for No Gas Motors in whatever inventive way she could come up with. Sue was really an inventor at heart. She loved to create new marketing ideas and plans. She loved thinking up new ways of doing old things and she loved putting them into action.

Every day brought new ideas and new directions and much happiness for Sue. She was finding herself and finding her way in this new world she had created. Life was good—because Sue had made it so.

No Gas Motors was a company on the cutting edge. Christopher Bernstein was a man who was driven to succeed at whatever endeavor he aimed at and he had found his niche, electric cars. He knew it was only a matter of time before electric cars were the mainstream and he knew how to draw powerful people and money to his projects. Everyone who ever met Christopher knew he was going places. Christopher knew it too.

When he saw Sue again after all the years in between, he knew it was meant to be for him to run into her and hire her. He'd seen her sell cars and work with people, and he knew she was a dynamo. He'd seen how her passion and her determination made things happen and he wanted to catch her magic in a bottle and shake it over his own business. He was glad she chose to work for him and was willing to work out whatever arrangements she wanted. Christopher was a smart businessman. He knew one of the ways a person succeeded was to hire great people to do what they did best.

Sue loved having the freedom to create and invent new ways of doing things, especially marketing. Innovative successful marketing ideas are a true art form and Sue was an artist. Sue also was the kind of person who always gave her all, so she passionately pursued everything she could do to make Christopher's business a success.

Sue loved going to work. She would research events that were going to take place around the country and see if any of them could be an opportunity for her to bring attention and sales for No Gas Motors. Once she found one that could provide a unique opening for No Gas Motors, she would begin creating a campaign of what she would do at the event.

Over the years, Sue had developed many friendships/acquaintances with famous people and the people who worked behind the scenes of famous people. She often would find ways to promote No Gas Motors while being a part of an event that included several celebrities she knew. It was a win/win situation. The world wanted 'green' products, and electric cars were the best green product out there. Everyone, celebrities alike, wanted to be on the green wagon.

For her own dreams, Sue was still promoting her sunless tanning product in every way she could think of as well. Again, her celebrity friends were often a big help. Sue was able to get her product in the celebrity giveaway bag of goodies for the Emmy Awards several years in a row, which was quite a feat!

Another change in Sue's life was that she began dating after eighteen years of being married. Sue was still petite, thin, yet curvaceous, and quite lovely, with a passionate intensity and subtle strength that many men found attractive. Unlike her youth, where Sue was very picky about what kind of men she would go out with because she was seeking the one man all the women wanted, Sue decided to go out with whomever asked her. She wanted to see, first of all, what kind of a man would ask her out, and then to see what kind of a man she was attracted to. It sounds so simple, but she'd never asked herself before what kind of a man she actually wanted; she just had always wanted the things other women wanted for status.

The first man Sue went out with looked just like her ex-husband, the black-haired, handsome, Italian- looking type. He took her out to dinner and to a basketball game. He was a really nice guy, but was very much into sports as her ex had been and simply reminded her too much of what she had had before. He was a good test to see if she really no longer wanted the man everyone said was the one she should want. She didn't. Just sitting at that basketball game, she again began feeling this heavy loathing. There was so much focus on the whole win or lose mentality, and the pressure to see who was the best and the worst.

She had witnessed, over the years, parents push their children to play sports. She had seen how the children had felt so awful, as if they'd let everyone down, because they weren't chosen for the team. She'd listened to too many fathers that only talked of their children's sports accomplishments. She'd gone to too many parties where acquaintances asked, "What sports do your sons play?" and when Sue answered skateboarding and guitar, her acquaintances were at a loss for words. Sue had empathy for those children that didn't get to play enough to please their parents when they did make a team and saw how sports could actually erode the confidence of a child, if it was not their true desire to play. Sports became a symbol for Sue of the cruelty of trying to fit in.

Her first date's sports interest didn't turn Sue off of dating entirely. She dated a few other men, usually for only one date, as after the first date, she knew she wasn't really interested in them. They were all nice, but just weren't what she was looking for. She was open and had no agenda as far as guys went. She was told how hard it was to be single at her age, and found that was not at all true for her.

She began to see that she liked men who were artistic or musicians, men who were talented and intelligent and appreciated nature. She dated a charming Argentinean man who had two degrees, one in engineering and the other in music, who was very talented. They had many things going for them and Sue cared for him quite a bit as a friend. He was a real eye opener for her, as he was so different in many ways, yet the two of them enjoyed each other very much.

However, he was torn between staying in Northern California, which he liked, and Los Angeles, where he could better pursue his career. His career finally won, and since Sue didn't ask him to stay with her, he moved to Los Angeles. Dating him was a move in the right direction for Sue, as he was a thoughtful and artistic person, who had depth and realness to him, which is what Sue was finding that she really liked and wanted in her life.

Her sons weren't crazy about their mother dating at first, as all children usually aren't. In their heart of hearts, they still wanted their parents to get back together, but since both parents were dating other people, they soon came to the realization that their parents' remarriage was unlikely. Sue had never introduced her sons to any of her dates.

They had their own lives, too. Payton was working for his dad at the ranch. He had a head for business and wanted to either start his own or make the family business a more successful one. He seemed to have inherited some of both of his parents' drive.

Trey was wrapped up in the world of music, playing in several bands and writing his own music and lyrics. As happens with young and artistic people, they often flounder at first, so Sue would help Trey out financially when he needed it, but he seldom asked. They were good sons and good young men. Sue was proud of them.

Like Sue and their father Kevin, both sons were very much into animals and each had a dog. Sue would often babysit her sons' dogs when they went out of town, which was no hardship for Sue, since she loved them too. Sue had a very independent shelter kitty that she got when he was already six years old, but surprisingly, he fit right in.

One of the many trips Sue had to take was an annual participation in the Detroit Auto Show, the biggest car show of the year. Sue loved it. She loved doing all the work creating the booth, the media blitz and bringing as much attention as she could to No Gas Motors. The convention itself would be a madhouse for ten days, but Sue was up for it. She was ready to sell, and ready to capture any and all opportunities.

As the fates would have it, on the Friday night of the convention weekend, Sue decided to step out of her hotel room in her adorable PJs, pop into the snack room and get some ice. As she was approaching the snack room, she couldn't help but overhear two men talking. It seemed they were making a film about electric cars, probably a documentary as they were talking about finding someone who really had and drove an electric car, who lived an electric car kind of a life. They said there are many here selling them, but they needed more people that actually owned them.

When Sue heard that, she couldn't help herself from interrupting them and saying, simply: "I only have and drive a one hundred percent electric auto."

The two men looked at her as if she'd just dropped in from Mars and was speaking another language, so she said it again. They looked at her with disbelief, as if she was a groupie, saying whatever just to be part of the movie.

"Really, I live that life. I gave up my S Class Mercedes and drive only my electric car. I totally believe in the electric car for our future, and for the future of the world."

Now that got their attention. They all introduced themselves and eventually sat down and talked for several hours about the future of electric cars and Sue.

The two men, Tom Schneider and Frank Goodman, were indeed making a documentary about electric cars. They had come to the Detroit Car Show looking for electric car businesses that could be useful for their film. What they found in Sue was a lovely face they could use to humanize and make real to the public what electric cars were, and what they could mean to the world. They were thrilled with Sue.

The next two days of the convention, the two filmmakers spent much of their time with Sue; talking to her, filming her and getting her ideas, excitement and passion about the future of electric cars. They promised they would keep in touch with her about the progress of the film and if they succeeded as well as they hoped, they wanted to include her in the publicity and promotion of the film as well. Sue was thrilled too.

Sue could feel that her life had turned over a wonderful new leaf. She experienced each day differently than she ever had before. Everyday colors seemed brighter to her, the air was fresher, she felt as if her life had a purpose and she was right on point.

Life still had its ups and downs, good days and bad, but on the whole, Sue felt good about herself and her life. It made such a difference in the quality of her life and her self-esteem to be living her life doing what she felt was right and allowing herself to fully feel and be her authentic self, whatever that may be in the moment.

So when she saw the most handsome man ever, who was tall, had long black hair, a huge smile that radiated kindness and a guitar hanging off of him at the annual Health and Harmony festival, Sue immediately thought, *I'll take him!* Being more confident and sure of herself than she had been in years, Sue did what any guy would do under the circumstances; she walked right up to him and gave him her card, saying simply that she could help him with his career. He looked her right in the eyes and seemed to get who she was in that long stare. He said he would call her back within thirty-two hours. And he did.

That auspicious meeting was the chance encounter of a lifetime for Sue. By this time, Sue had dated for over two years since her divorce and she had learned just what kind of a man she wanted in her life, and as the fates would have it, Ricardo had all of the qualities she sought and more.

Ricardo Hernandez was nearly ten years younger than Sue, but he was an old soul. Some people seem to be born knowing what is true in life and what is important to know and to do, and Ricardo seemed to be one of them. He grew up in a small village in Mexico, within a loving and large extended family that cherished music and God. It was natural to him to follow his heart as it had never occurred to him to live any other way.

Ricardo was a very talented musician and songwriter. He played several instruments including the piano and recorded his own CDs, which he sold at the gigs where he performed. He was a leader for Praise and Worship at a church in Los Angeles for many years. He had strong commitments to his family in Mexico and made himself available to help out there when he was needed, resulting in his taking several trips a year back and forth to Mexico.

Sue and Ricardo began seeing each other so naturally and effortlessly that they simply eased into a relationship together. Both were committed to being completely honest with each other and to being true to themselves, so the match was perfect. Because they both respected themselves, they naturally treated each other with respect, understanding they were two full-grown adults who had their own lives to live.

Ricardo had the quality of being fully present with whomever he was with, so he would listen intently to what people said and would answer with complete honesty. There was a gentleness about him, regardless of his outward manliness, that everyone always seemed to intuitively get and value about him.

Sue was in love and blown away by the contrast of this relationship when compared to all of the other relationships in her past.

In ways, they seemed an odd match. Sue's greatest creativity was coming up with amazing marketing ideas. She loved the hustle and bustle of the sale, of the business world and of money and commerce. Ricardo lived in a world filled with music, which he viewed as the expression of God through sound. Sue traveled to various shows and events and was passionately focused on creating media attention. Ricardo was focused on following his heart, whether it led him to play for peanuts for a charity event or to go help build a church in some tiny town in Mexico.

Yet, both of them traveled a great deal, which meant happy reunions at home. Both truly were following their hearts even though their hearts were led in seemingly incongruent directions. Ricardo seemed to be a softer, gentler kind of person than Sue, but Sue was also quite devoted to her family and understood that to selflessly give what your loved ones need is simply part of how family works.

One of the first times Ricardo stayed over, when Sue got up at her usual five-thirty a.m., he asked where she was going. When she told him she was going on her daily walk, he asked if he could go with her. She said yes.

After being married for eighteen years to Kevin, who never wanted to and never did take that walk with Sue, she was amazed that this man would instantly recognize the importance of her daily walk and want to share it with her. This was what Sue had been missing in her life, someone who wanted to share life with her.

And they had so much to share. They both enjoyed movies and reading books aloud and being in nature. Of course, Ricardo loved animals. In no time at all, they had created a sanctuary outside in the backyard, just at the edge of the yard where the woods began. They put a hammock out there, hooked up speakers to the overhanging tree and watched movies or YouTube on their laptop. Now they could spend lovely evenings outside, listening to music as they watched the stars or laughing at movies under the moonlight. The dogs and cats would join them on the hammock too.

Sue was very grateful that Ricardo felt the same way she did about the infinity of God. Sue and Ricardo had gone from the fire and brimstone angry God they had learned of from their early church life, to God being energy/thought, and, finally, that allowing God inside was a lifestyle they lived every day. She and Ricardo spoke often about their relationship with God and each of them recognized the importance of developing that relationship on a daily basis.

Easily, naturally, Sue and Ricardo's relationship developed and in no time at all, they moved in together. Since Sue owned her lovely home right next to the wonderful woods and the delightful hill of her morning walk, Ricardo moved in with Sue. Of course, he brought all of his instruments. Sue had seen her house change from having sports memorabilia all over from her husband Kevin, then to having the art that she loved replacing the memorabilia, and now she was adding the music that Ricardo loved.

Ricardo moved his two pianos, several guitars and all of his recording and sound equipment into Sue's house. Fortunately, it was a big house.

Sue loved that Ricardo would often play the piano while she made breakfast. Music became a daily part of her life. Sue often thought that Ricardo lived what most people actually strive to become: selfless and completely loving.

Of course there were some conflicts, though honestly, not many. Sue had to remind herself to make time for Ricardo, because she could so easily become a complete workaholic. Every time he was gone on one of his trips,

Sue would fall back into being fiercely independent, so when he returned, she had to learn to share her life again. Ricardo had to remember to stay in communication with Sue when he was traveling, especially in Mexico. This made the transition back together easier.

Thankfully, Sue's sons liked and respected Ricardo from the start. They could see what a genuine guy he was and how well he treated their mother. It didn't hurt that he was an amazing musician and that Trey was a musician as well. They often played together while Sue listened. He even got Payton into playing the guitar again.

Life was good, and it was going to get better.

The following year, Tom and Frank, the two documentary filmmakers, contacted Sue. They asked for proof that her insurance and electric bills were cheaper. They wanted film footage of her daily use of her plug-in, one hundred percent electric auto. Sue, of course, sent tons of proof, YouTube links and lots of film footage that Ricardo had taken of her driving to work every day.

Finally, they had finished the film and were ready to introduce it to the world. As the fates would have it, Sue was actually in a significant part of the film. She had been so passionate and so photogenic that the editing department used a lot of the footage they shot of her for the film. Tom and Frank wanted Sue to be a part of the 'green carpet' event they were planning in Los Angeles. Sue, of course, jumped at the chance.

No Gas Motors was thrilled to have Sue be so prominently featured in the film and to be a part of the green carpet event, which, of course, would be great media for the company, so they pulled out all the stops. Sue spent weeks contacting celebrities she knew, as well as other media people to help promote the event. She was really excited to be a part of this whole thing and loved promoting it.

Sue arranged for Ricardo and both of her sons to go with her to Los Angeles for the event. She wanted as many of her loved ones as possible to take part of this momentous occasion in her life. They were all happy to go.

The green carpet event was to take place at the famous Grauman's Chinese Theatre in Hollywood, where the Academy Awards used to be held. Sue and her loved ones arrived early the Friday before so they could go out on the town in Hollywood and really enjoy the weekend. Sue was still contacting celebrities and making sure all arrangements were taken care of so that the event would go off smoothly. She had ordered her classy black dress from the newest Ralph Lauren collection a couple weeks prior and brought along her favorite pearls. She also hired a top makeup artist to get her ready in her hotel room. She had sent her sons with Ricardo to get some new clothes for the event too.

Finally, it was the big day. Sue was dressed impeccably and looked fantastic. Sue spent most of the evening talking with the media, being photographed by Ricardo with different celebrities and being the star of the show. Naturally, she included Payton and Trey wherever she could, so many of the celebrities were also photographed with Sue's loved ones. Thankfully, Ricardo had been going to events and working as a photographer for Sue since the beginning of their relationship. In fact, going to events was another fun thing Sue and Ricardo did together. As usual, No Gas Motors paid Ricardo's expenses, because he always came back with hundreds of great photos.

It was exciting. It was wonderful. It was finally over. Sue and her family spent Sunday seeing the sights of Los Angeles and then flying home to Vacaville. It was an amazing event, and the ripple effects would last for years.

Sue knew she was helping her friend Christopher make his dream come true. She had made her dreams come true too. She had come quite a long way from the backwoods, upstate New York girl of little formal education and lots of hardships. After a lifetime spent trying to find herself and her way, Sue had truly found both. She was very successful. She had accomplished her dream and helped others to accomplish their dreams as well. She had two loving sons and a man in her life that she cherished and who cherished her right back. She lived in a home that was in the city yet right next to the woods so she was always near the busy life she loved and the nature she needed. She had her animals around her. She had herself. Life was good.

Lately, she'd been thinking about writing a book of her life story. Not because she wanted everyone to know about her, but because she thought there were people out there who might have had similar kinds of troubles she'd had as a child and the same kind of need to be accepted, to find a 'normal' life as she had.

Lately, the nightly news had been talking about children committing suicide because they weren't accepted. Maybe Sue could help others come to understand that normal was really whatever you were used to having.

Normal is relative. Nobody would really want a 'normal' life, if they knew what the dictionary defines normal as—average. Sue jokingly always says, "The only place the word 'normal' belongs is on the washing machine!" Everybody can create their own life, exactly the way they want it to be, if they are willing to do the work and let go of other's fantasies of what they think they're supposed to have.

A funny thing started happening to Sue. Past acquaintances and friends have been contacting her on Facebook and saying how amazed they were at how far she had come, given her lack of formal education and extreme poverty growing up in the backwoods in upstate New York. Having long ago let go of any resentment that could have stifled her inner growth, Sue graciously encouraged them and helped them to realize their potential and to start creating their best life.

Seeing how helpful her encouragement was to her old friends made Sue think more about writing that book. And the more she thought about it, the more she liked the idea, and knowing Sue, if she made up her mind to do it, she'd do it.

Ginny Scales-Medeiros

Born and raised in rural upstate New York, Ms. Scales-Medeiros now resides in the San Francisco North Bay Area. , Finishing only the ninth grade and getting her GED, Ms. Scales-Medeiros has many accomplishments including being an entrepreneur, a real-estate investor, an inventor with multiple patents and trademarks and an animal lover and advocate for animal rights.

With her first invention, she won first place in a national contest for the best new idea/product . A master marketer, she was a record-breaking salesperson in the auto industry and created over a million dollars of free publicity for her sunless tanning invention, including being an on air guest on QVC. In recent times, she has been a speaker for 100% electric transportation, on the board of Directors for ZAP a PR/Marketing Consultant and can be seen in the 2011 movie, "What is the Electric Car?"

Presently, she is focusing on speaking engagements and promotions about her upcoming book, "What is Normal?" and was the on-air interview guest on The Stevie Mack Show, The Personal Best Show in Chicago, upcoming ABC morning show, will be on the Dr. Mommy show and Gap tooth Diva promoting her new book. This is Ms. Scales-Medeiros first novel.

Anne Mackenzie

Anne has worked, throughout her life, as a server, teacher, small publisher, writer, poet, office worker, hypno-therapist, healer, medical intuitive and spiritual counselor. It has been her pleasure and honor to help Ginny's story be told.

100% TOTAL SATISFACTION GUARANTEE:

If for ANY reason you are not 100% satisfied with the book, audio CD, or DVD you purchased, just send the product back along with receipt (or proof of payment). We will gladly refund 100% of your money, no questions asked!

Nemours Marketing, Inc.
7531 Azurebrook Court
Winter Park, FL 32792
info@NemoursMarketing.com
Tel: (407) 738 - 1608

CPSIA information can be obtained
at www.ICGtesting.com
Printed in the USA
FSOW02n2009240516
20778FS